MW00669270

BECOMING TANIA

BECOMING TANIA

A Novel of Love, Revolution, and Betrayal

IAN ADAMS

Toronto and London

Copyright © Ian Adams, 1990

All rights reserved. The use of any part of this publication
reproduced, transmitted in any form or by any means, electronic,
mechanical, photocopying, recording, or otherwise, or stored in a
retrieval system, without the prior written consent of the
publisher – or, in the case of photocopying or other reprographic
copying, a licence from Canadian Reprography Collective – is an
infringement of the copyright law

Canadian Cataloguing in Publication Data

Adams, Ian.
Becoming Tania

ISBN 0-7710-0656-X

I. Title.

PS8551.D32B42 1990   C813'.54   C90-094526-5
PR9199.3.A32B42 1990

Every attempt has been made to attribute copyright material in
this novel. The Publisher welcomes any information regarding
errors.

Distributed in the United Kingdom by Sinclair-Stevenson Ltd.

Printed and bound in Canada
The paper used in this book is acid free

McClelland & Stewart Inc.
The Canadian Publishers
481 University Avenue
Toronto, Ontario
M5G 2E9

To my sons, Shane and Riley

Author's Note

All but two characters who speak in this novel are either dead or fictitious. The two characters still alive, Pombo and Urbano, along with a third man, Benigno, were the sole survivors of Ché Guevara's guerrilla force in Bolivia. The few words I have put in the mouths of Pombo and Urbano are paraphrases drawn from the famous Bolivian diaries kept by El Ché and his guerrillas. These three survivors, whom I call by their *noms de guerre* (their real names were made known long ago by the Cuban government), escaped death by walking–pursued much of the time – an astonishing eight hundred kilometres through the Andes to Chile; a journey that took them four months through some of the most difficult terrain in South America.

Acknowledgements

Many thanks to my colleague and friend, Aníbal Vitón, whose contributions were generous and many. And thanks to Mary Jane Gomes; to Bryan Everitt and Adam Litzinger for their encouragement; to John Montagna for showing me another way; and to my editor, Dinah Forbes, who, in this enterprise, was the Ace of Wands.

I have drawn upon Joseph Campbell's ideas about the myth of the hero. And in a few places my characters paraphrase these thoughts.

... the heroes of all time have gone before us. The labyrinth is thoroughly known. We have only to follow the thread of the hero path, and where we thought to find an abomination, we shall find a god. And where we thought to slay another, we shall slay ourselves. Where we had thought to travel outward, we shall come to the centre of our own existence. And where we had thought to be alone, we will be with all the world.

Joseph Campbell

The night Nicolás met Tania began strangely. Nicolás first saw the three men as he walked along Avenida del Libertador, near the heavily guarded U.S. Embassy. An unusual evening ground mist, thick and poisonous with traffic fumes, hung heavy above the slick pavement. In search of clean air, Nicolás crossed Avenida del Libertador at the Monumento a Los Españoles. He dodged through the fast-moving traffic and slipped into El Rosedal. In the dusk of this warm spring night the flower garden was full of young lovers. They strolled hand in hand along the paths. Other couples crowded the benches; lips and bodies glued together, male and female hands restlessly stroked and sought each other's flesh.

Disconcerted to be alone in the midst of this collective lust, Nicolás paused to look at a flower bed and was astonished to read in a subtly arranged and growing design of red, white, and pink roses the subversive message, *Viva El Ché!*

Nicolás imagined the gardener had already been arrested. He felt sad. After having encountered the gardener's spirit, he would like to meet him. But then he realized the roses were undisturbed. No one in authority had yet noticed the subversive floral message. So then the gardener must still be free. *Ché lives!* Nicolás smiled. To the right of the flower garden, Nicolás could see the lights of the cars massed in Villa Cariño. More lovers! He escaped El Rosedal along one of the paths that led under the overhead train tracks.

Again, the three men were ahead of him. As he drew closer, his first reaction was that there was something inhuman about the three figures. Their bodies were thick, heavy with menace. They shambled slowly through the ground mist, not as men relaxed in companionship but, as they moved along the path a few feet apart from each other, more like marauders in a skirmishing line.

To avoid catching up with them, Nicolás took the path that forked to the right, the one that led to the footbridge across the small lake and on to Avenida Infanta Isabel. He picked up his pace just west of the little lake. A man in a boat, obscured by the mist that moved over the surface of the water, yelled an unintelligible warning to him. Then, as he passed through the wooded copse, the three men were suddenly in front of him again. It didn't make sense, the men couldn't have got there without racing through the woods.

Nicolás felt alarmed, but mysteriously impelled to go on. It was too late to turn back, he told himself. And unable to shake his nervousness he broke into a jog, the quicker to get past the three men. In his apprehension he found the air in the copse was worse than it had been on Libertador. The mist had become a thick fog; it tasted bitter in his mouth, almost sulphurous. Or is this fear I'm tasting, he wondered.

Nicolás had trouble breathing. The evening light had turned an ominous purple. He stumbled, the footpath under him was unexpectedly slippery. He decided to sprint and slip past the men. But his legs wouldn't respond. He felt inexplicably weak. He moved at a pace that seemed agonizingly slow. Surely, he thought, they must have heard his footsteps on the path, his rasping and heavy gasps for air.

10

Why didn't they turn and glance over their shoulders at him? But they never once looked back at him. Until, just at the point when Nicolás was about to cut through their line, the three men turned upon him with an explosive fury. As they came at Nicolás he saw their faces were wrenched with inhuman rage. They attacked like wild dogs. Their lips curled back over their teeth, saliva ran from the corners of their mouths. Their eyes were savage, blood-flecked. He fought back with all the strength he had, hitting one man in the throat with his fist. He went down. But Nicolás was instantly tackled by the two other men. He could not understand what they wanted. If it had been money they would have demanded some before the attack.

"Why?" Nicolás screamed at his attackers. "Why?"

But they only replied in grunts and curses; their breath vile in his face, as he wrestled with them across the dirt path and into the grass. Nicolás, a powerful man, felt overwhelmed. The men seemed possessed with demonic energy. As soon as Nicolás had subdued one or thrown him down, another would attack.

One of the men wrapped his arms and legs around Nicolás' lower body and held him like a python. The man's grip never relaxed, even when Nicolás beat him about the face and neck with his fists. Another, from behind, seized Nicolás' hair with both hands and pulled him down to the ground.

Then the first man, the one Nicolás had hit in the throat, loomed over him in the half dark. His face twisted in rage and hate, the man pulled an axe out of a canvas bag he carried on his back. Nicolás saw the blow coming. The man began the swing with the axe held high in both hands over his head, then brought it down with all his power. Nicolás, pinned down by the other two men, could not move to escape. The axe smashed him across the left shoulder. Nicolás screamed

11

out as he felt and saw the shiny metal blade of the axe bury itself in his flesh.

The intense pain thrust Nicolás out of this long and terrible dream to hear Guido, the hotel night clerk, screaming angrily in the corridor. But for a few moments Nicolás was paralysed by the agony of his dream; he couldn't get off the bed on which he had fallen asleep fully clothed. His hair was matted with sweat, his clothes soaked. He felt exhausted from the struggle in his dream. His shoulder throbbed painfully. He rubbed the muscles and, in the gloom of his room, tentatively examined his hand. He almost expected to find the fingers covered in blood.

The uproar continued in the passageway outside his room. Nicolás peered at the luminous dial of his watch. It was only five minutes after six. He stumbled to the door and carefully opened it a few inches to find Guido, who must have just started work. He was half-drunk as usual, his skinny body stiff with outrage, screaming in his best military parade-ground voice as he banged with his fist on the bathroom door in the corridor.

"Animals! Pigs! This is the third time this week. Out! Get out of there. The Cruz del Sur is a decent hotel."

A young man's voice shouted through the door, "All right, all right, you crazy old bastard! We're coming out."

Guido stepped back when the bathroom door opened and a dishevelled young couple in their twenties emerged from the corridor bathroom, still rearranging their clothing. The young man, his cheeks flushed, ran a broken comb through his hair. The girl, her face white, stared boldly at Nicolás from behind her boyfriend's shoulder, as she daintily tucked her shirt into her blue jeans and cinched the belt around her waist. She did it with such disarming grace that Nicolás was touched by her pride and sense of self.

12

Nicolás recognized the young homeless couple who had taken to slipping into the hotel to make love in the corridor bathrooms. He rather admired the way they handled Guido. Especially the young man who, under the stark shadows cast by the light of the single bulb hanging from the ceiling, straightened his threadbare jacket with all the transparent dignity of the dispossessed. His disdainful reply was always the same: "You call this cockroach trap a hotel? What a bad joke."

His companion giggled. Guido made a move as if to kick at them. But physically, Guido's tall, skinny body did not intimidate anybody. And there was something sullen and dangerous in the young man's manner; he was lean and muscular, life had certainly whipped him, but not yet into submission. Guido backed down. And with a sly glance at Nicolás standing in the doorway of his room, he fell back on his own cowardly rhetoric: "I am Guido Echeverría, a suboficial mayor of the Tenth Infantry Brigade. I can have you scum swept off the street—"

But the young couple had already disappeared down the stairs. Above the clatter of their shoes on the stone steps, the young man's derisive reply reverberated up the stairwell, "So what the hell is an infantry suboficial doing in this shithole."

The echo of the girl's mocking giggle hung provocatively in the stairwell.

The rebuke cut through Guido's bullying speech, and to the heart of his ever-present self-pity. As Nicolás slowly closed the door of his room, he saw Suboficial Mayor Echeverría slump against the wall of the corridor, a collapsed stork, tears in the eyes of his haggard face.

Guido, Nicolás knew, was a man who slept little. His eyes were sunk in dark blue bruises of insomnia. He always worked a twelve-hour night shift, catching catnaps at the desk in the lobby. And apparently spent most of his days hanging around bars and cafés frequented by military pensioners. From previous conversations that had gone on deep into the night, Nicolás knew that Guido's children would not talk to him, and that his wife had left him to go back to live with her family in Rosario.

Once or twice Guido had seemed to be on the brink of revealing why he had been forced out of the army, where he had spent many years in military intelligence, but he had always held back at the last moment. Guido was a haunted man. Nicolás did not like him much, but humoured him out of a sense of compassion for his obvious and terrible loneliness. And because, Nicolás admitted to himself in more honest moments, he could not overcome his habitual morbid curiosity. He knew that he was really waiting for Guido to confess to him why he had been kicked out of the military.

Alone in his room, Nicolás tried to rouse himself out of the stupor induced by the dream. From past experience, he knew that the corridor confrontation he had just witnessed would inevitably become an excuse for Guido to drop by his room and whine about his bad luck. He decided to go out. He had no stomach for Guido that night. But Nicolás was still washing his face at the sink when Guido knocked on the door, a bottle of Criadores whisky in one hand.

"*Qué personajes!*" Guido complained to Nicolás. "Can you imagine? How is it possible that they could keep a love affair going in a hotel bathroom?"

"They're homeless, Guido. They find privacy where they can."

Guido gestured with his half bottle of Criadores: "The world is going to hell, or maybe we're already there. Have a drink with me?"

14

As always with Guido, the request was more a plea than an invitation. Nicolás hesitated but couldn't think quickly enough of an excuse to keep Guido out. Then, without waiting for an agreement from Nicolás, Guido had slid past him to drop wearily into the chair beside the rickety table that served as Nicolás' desk.

"You're lucky," Guido observed, "to have the only room on this floor with its own bathroom."

Nicolás stepped reluctantly back from the door and sat on the bed. His head was still thick with all the incomprehensible violence and emotions of his dream, and he did not know for how long he would be able to humour this despondent night clerk. *We are all brothers*, Nicolás reminded himself, *in the spirit and in the flesh.*

He watched Guido cast quick furtive glances over his desk. Nicolás supposed these were the uncontrollable lifetime habits of a military intelligence officer.

"Don't you have to be down at the front lobby?" Nicolás hinted.

"No. You can relax. It's quiet. If somebody wants me, all they have to do is ring the bell. I can hear it from here."

Guido waved his hand at the pile of books and papers that littered the little table.

"I can't believe you're still at this junk. No offence intended, but really, *Archetypes of the Zodiac*? *Meditations on the Tarot*?"

As he talked, Guido toyed with the pack of cards Nicolás had left on the table. Nicolás watched him. Incredible! He is a man desperately searching for the truth, when all he has to do is look at his own life.

Guido couldn't resist the temptation. And with a brief "*Con permiso?*" and without waiting for Nicolás' reply, he cut the deck, then turned up the top card – it was the Tower, struck by lightning and in flames. The male and female bodies, thrown from the tower, plunged in an eternal free-fall above the abyss. Guido laughed nervously.

"This doesn't look too promising. What does it mean?"

Nicolás watched Guido who, without waiting for an answer, quickly reshuffled the cards. Nicolás felt he should interfere, but his curiosity held him in check. He waited while Guido cut the deck three times. Guido turned up the face card. His rail-thin body went rigid with tension. He showed the card to Nicolás. Again, it was the Tower. Guido looked up in alarm at Nicolás.

"I don't understand this rubbish. Explain to me what is happening?"

"Everything and nothing," Nicolás shrugged.

"Of course," Guido tried to convince himself, "what do I know about this stuff? It's all crap to me."

Nicolás left his position on the bed to take the Tarot pack out of Guido's inquisitive and nervous hands and carefully put the deck away into a small black velvet bag.

Ramón used to say, "Humanity begins with compassion. We don't know what love is until we participate in the experience of another person's suffering."

Guido couldn't let it go. He laughed awkwardly, his face even more tensed.

"But to get the same card like that one, what do you call it, the Tower? Twice! That's a bad omen, yes?"

Nicolás tried to find a way to calm down the anxious night clerk.

"Guido, that's only what they call synchronicity, events happening in a pattern nobody can quite explain. But by itself it doesn't mean anything. There's a way to do this properly if you really want to get something

16

out of it. First, you're supposed to have a question that you want answered. You concentrate intensely on that question. Then you draw the cards and lay them out within the context of a reading. There's a ritual to it all. And the objective is supposedly to get you to contemplate your inner life."

"My inner life?" Guido repeated sarcastically.

"Yes, you know, those vast landscapes of the imagination that exist inside all of us and which–"

"Wait a minute. Bring it down to earth. I'm a military intelligence officer, or was. But all my life I have dealt with facts, reports, sifting information for the truth–"

"Guido, the simple truth is that you already know the answer to your question."

"So tell me what does the Tower stand for?"

Nicolás reluctantly told him, – "Everything that's already happened to you, and–" Nicolás broke off.

"And what?" Guido demanded.

"Essentially, the Tower is the card of unforeseen disaster."

Guido was impatient. "Then give me a reading? Reveal my future to me?"

"I've told you, I'm not a fortune-teller."

"Then why do you waste your time with all this shit?"

"It's an ancient form of meditation upon the mysteries of life, nothing more."

"Meditation? I don't understand you."

"You go to church?"

"Of course. Mass, every Christmas. That's what the military stands for: God, nation, family."

"Do you pray?"

"For certain! *A la Virgen de la Merced.*"

"Then it is the same thing. Prayer is meditation. At mass you meditate on the mystery of Christ's love."

17

"Then you can't foretell the future?"

"Guido, nobody can foretell the future. But everything you want to know about yourself, why you do what you do, it's all there."

"Where? In the cards?"

"The cards, like prayer, can only lead you to what is already inside you."

"Me?"

"Your psyche, your subconscious, your soul, whatever you want to call it." Nicolás was exasperated. "C'mon Guido. You're twenty years older than me. Don't tell me you haven't thought about these things before. About why you're here?"

"*La gran puta!*" Guido gave up, reached into his voluminous jacket pockets, and produced two glasses.

"I know why I'm here in this crummy little no-star hotel. Because I'm a ruined man. And I have to work at this stinking job to pay my rent, to put food on the table."

Guido suddenly paused. "Why did you choose this hotel, El Cruz del Sur?" he asked in a sidelong glance at Nicolás.

Nicolás felt irritated and responded evasively, "No reason, other than the location is convenient."

And even as Nicolás spoke, so casually, he couldn't believe that he would ever be made to deal with the memory of Lara in such banal fashion. A good time to remind yourself of the truth, Nicolás, he told himself. You walked past the hotel and when you saw the dilapidated sign in gold leaf – Hotel El Cruz del Sur – on the narrow glass doors, the name sent a shiver down your spine. You saw it as an omen. The constellation had been a passion with Lara, a constant motif in her jewellery and clothes. If you were ever going to communicate with Lara again, the information would come to you in this hotel. At least, that is the desperate thought that

18

you had seized upon at the time. And how long was it now that Lara had been disappeared? Eighteen months.

"Just convenience," he repeated. "I like living downtown."

Guido snorted impatiently. "No convenience in my decision. Nobody else will hire me. Because my previous work record is twenty-five years of military service to my country that ended in a dishonourable discharge. But you, a man with your background, do you know what you are doing here? Why have you buried yourself in this fleabag, wasting all your time with this witchcraft mumbo jumbo?"

Nicolás moved from exasperation to boredom. "Don't really know, Guido. Perhaps it's more interesting and less dangerous than politics."

Guido cackled with laughter at what he took to be Nicolás' joke. Before Guido could pour whisky into both glasses, Nicolás took a glass into his own tiny bathroom, really a tiled closet, with a shower head, a sink, and a toilet *à la turque* set in the tiled floor. He carefully washed the tumbler in the sink before bringing it back to the table. He held out a restraining hand as Guido prepared to pour; Nicolás took the bottle of Criadores himself and splashed a modest shot into the tumbler, then raised the glass in silent toast to Guido who, all the time, had intently watched Nicolás' actions.

"You just can't let it go, can you?" said Guido, with grudging admiration. "You can't lose it. Even after you turn your back on your family, your class, and hide out in a dump like this place, you just can't abandon your upbringing. Guys like you always know who they are, what they want. I guess it's the result of all that power and good breeding."

Nicolás smiled with polite amusement at Guido's naiveté. His friend Ramón used to put it differently:

"You can get away with it Nicolás because you have money. You can leave the military, wander around Brazil, take up philosophy, all because you are wealthy. And so the world calls you eccentric. But if a poor person like me behaved that way, they would simply call me nuts." Nicolás had laughed at Ramón. "You're never going to run the risk of being thought nuts Ramón. They think you're dangerous; a psychiatrist who treats the tortured, and on weekends gives basic medical care to the poor in the slums."

Nicolás brought his thoughts back to Guido, who stared at him expectantly. How to communicate with a man who can never move beyond the ideals of a system that has totally betrayed him?

"No. I'm serious," Guido pursued his theme. "You're a Quintana. That's an honoured name in this country. My father was a suboficial in General Quintana's very first command – "

Nicolás waved his hand in an attempt to interrupt and push aside Guido's assertions.

"No, it's true," Guido insisted. "With a name like Quintana, such a name, so much power! Families of generals, ambassadors, landowners – you're protected, nobody can touch you. You don't even have to work for a living – "

What was it that Lara had asked him toward the end?

"Nicolás, don't you ever think about how our families made all their money? How they've used it? Doesn't it make you feel bad sometimes?"

"Nobody gets to choose their parents, Lara," he had replied, a little too glibly.

Lara hadn't been judgemental or angry. She was already on her way to a new wisdom about herself.

"One day you'll have to turn around and face it, just like I'm trying to, Nicolás." And she had held him gently in her arms.

20

Nicolás shook his head to fight off the memories. It was too painful to think about Lara these days. Guido still watched him.

"Guido, Quintana is just a name that I've borrowed for a while in this part of my existence."

Guido was suddenly suspicious.

"You mean it's not your real name? You're not really a Quintana?"

"Sure, but –"

"Well, I'm glad to hear that, because I just knew. And my judgement of people is hardly ever mistaken. The first time I laid eyes on you, when you walked in here three months ago, *'Qué caballero!'* I said to myself. 'Guido, there is a quality gentleman.' And I'm not just talking about the way you always used to dress. Those suits, so" – Guido searched for the word – "impeccable."

Guido offered the bottle to Nicolás, who refused, then poured himself another generous shot.

"By the way, what's happened to you in these last couple of days? Where are all those good clothes you used to wear?"

Nicolás wrenched open the door of the ancient wardrobe to display an almost empty rack on which only two expensively tailored suits hung.

"This is all that's left and this is where they're going to stay."

"*Qué lo parió!*" Guido's face fell. And with a puzzled look, he shook his head and surveyed once again Nicolás' new cheap cotton-polyester clothes.

"You don't like my spring wardrobe?"

"No. I mean, yes. Well, to tell you the truth, I don't understand why someone like you dresses so, to be kind, ordinary."

Ramón had often teased Nicolás about his elegant clothes. "For the sake of appearances, Argentina will destroy itself," Ramón had gloomily predicted.

21

Nicolás examined Guido's close-shaven, exhausted middle-aged face, the meticulously pressed grey flannels and blazer, the white shirt, the neat grey pullover, and carefully knotted tie. He dressed exactly like a million other men in Buenos Aires.

Lara, lying naked on the bed, watching him get dressed, had said, "I'm glad you never wear grey, Nicolás. Grey flannel on a man always looks to me like surrender."

"Tell me, Guido, why do you think clothes are so important to us Latins?"

"Oh no! I'm not going to discuss politics this evening. And I'm not trying to suggest to you that the presentation of one's self is only a matter of clothes."

"In Argentina I am beginning to think that it is everything."

"No, no," Guido objected. "Of course it goes beyond that. And in your case, well, uh, you have a *presencia moral.*"

Nicolás tired of Guido's flattery, and gestured impatiently in the direction of the books on the table.

"There are larger questions to wrestle with, Guido. Why should I worry about what clothes I put on my body when some of the oriental mystics believe our souls are eternal. They simply pass on from one body to another.

"You mean when I die?"

"Not necessarily."

"When I'm still alive?"

"Conceivably."

"What are they saying? They believe several different souls could take turns to inhabit my body during my one lifetime?"

"It's possible, who knows?"

Nicolás was surprised to see that Guido was suddenly excited by the idea. The night clerk drained his glass and eagerly leaned forward on the edge of the chair.

"You know, I'm fifty. When I look back on my own life I feel that there were times when it was not me that did those things, lived out those experiences. That" – Guido explored the words as another person might sample the taste of a different wine – "that somebody else lived that life."

"Well, there you go," shrugged Nicolás, uneasy about what demons he might have liberated in Guido's mind. And he began to move restlessly about the room in the hope that Guido would take the cue that it was time to leave. Nicolás unlatched the French doors to the inner courtyard, where he busied himself taking water from the tap in the wall to fill up the containers for the parrots and the budgerigars the hotel owner kept in cages.

But when he returned to the room, Guido was still there, a man totally self-absorbed. Nicolás watched as Guido agitatedly poured himself another stiff drink. When the whisky spilled over his hand wrapped around the glass, he greedily licked the liquor off his fingers.

"They were awful, horrible things. I mean, those acts that I feel this other person who lived that part of my life – "

"I'm not a priest."

Nicolás interrupted Guido. He had a premonition that he didn't want to hear what Guido had to say. This is another test I'm not ready for, he told himself, as he sat down again.

"Perhaps you should go to the church to confess."

"Priests! How can you trust the church these days. All the intelligent ones are *subversivos*, and the others are too stupid about the world. But you're the only one I can talk to. There's something about you. You're not even thirty – "

Nicolás stirred uneasily in his chair.

"Twenty-nine. And really, it's only something you want to see in me. No, it's need, Guido, simple need.

23

And that's because I'm the only one in the hotel who talks to you."

Despair, a reflection of what might once have been a spark of pride in the man, flickered over Guido's face. Nicolás saw it and, contrite, added more softly, "Besides, for as long as I can remember, people have poured out their lives and their most personal secrets to me."

"You see," Guido smiled tightly, "I was right about that. You should be flattered."

"No, it's a burden."

"A burden," Guido repeated in wonderment.

A silence, charged with tension, filled the room. Nicolás thought, he can't shut up, he can't hang on to this awful guilt that has turned his life into dread.

"A burden," Guido shook his head. "And to think," Guido continued, a terrible pain holding his voice down to a husky whisper, "I had to drive people mad or to their graves before they would give us their real names, let alone talk to us about their lives."

There it was, obliquely slipped out just like that, suddenly out in the open between them: a loathsome evil reptile writhed silently on the carpet in the space between the two men.

Nicolás looked up to see that Guido wept without sobs. The tears flowed copiously down his cheeks. Guido the Torturer weeps. Nicolás felt no compassion. *Judge not and you will not be judged.* The older man continued to whisper huskily through his tears.

"And for this I was dismissed, lost my pension. Not because they thought that what I was doing was wrong. No. You see, someone made a mistake. A stupid mistake. It was as simple as that. Based on information obtained in the interrogation of another subversive, they brought in a young couple who never should have been picked up. From an honourable family. I was told to break them down. Do my job. They were young, very beautiful. As it turned out, she was pregnant. It was one of those nights. Everything got out of hand. They . . . they died on us . . . "

Nicolás kept silent but felt utter loathing, consumed with a cold fury. He thought, what do you mean, they died on you?

Ramón had asked Nicolás: "What is this anima in our national psyche? This passion for self-delusion? Big and small, they've all had it: Perón, Ché Guevara, Evita. And now it is has reached new heights, or should we say new depths? Because this is the time of the criminals – they have the stage."

Nicolás stared into Guido's tormented eyes. He resisted the awful pain and dread that seeped under his skin and moved toward his heart. He thought, nobody "died on you." You killed them. You butchered them.

Guido wrung his hands in rapid washing movements.

"I can see what you're thinking. But it wasn't like that. We, the men who worked with me, all good family men. Loyal. But we were all exhausted. There were just too many prisoners that month. We couldn't do our interrogations properly. There was tremendous constant pressure for results. Look, there's no point in trying to explain that part to you. You'd never understand. So just let me go on. We were told to dump their bodies in the plaza. We didn't find out until it was too late. My commanding officer was seriously compromised. We of course blamed it on the Montoneros. But that wasn't enough. Internally, the army needed a scapegoat. I am the scapegoat. Ruined. My family has abandoned me. No pension. All because somebody had extracted a confession from a Communist and believed it. So idiotic, when we all know that Communists lie, even at the moment of death."

Nicolás felt unable to move, so paralysed was he by this man's stupidity and pain he could barely speak.

Now he knew that this is what he had suspected all along. He thought, I don't want this knowledge, this information. It will be far too painful. I want to live in the hope that Lara is still alive.

"What was her name?"

Guido was startled.

"Her name?"

"Yes. The pregnant young woman you left dead in the plaza."

Guido was frightened. "I could never tell you that. This was a confidential matter, a state secret –"

"You said she came from a good family, I might know her."

Guido shook his head frantically. His sunken grey eyes had almost disappeared somewhere deep inside his head. "No, no –"

Nicolás fought to keep his control. He knew that if he did what he wanted to do, seize Guido by the throat, he would not be able to stop himself from killing the man.

"Let's do it this way, Guido. Did her Christian name begin with L?"

Guido shook his head.

"Did her family name begin with de la?"

Again Guido shook his head.

Slowly, very slowly, Nicolás let the breath out of his body and sank back onto the bed.

Guido coughed and spluttered, shakily poured himself another drink, and wiped away the whisky with the back of his hand when it trickled down his chin.

"You have to help me!" the older man pleaded.

Guido's eyes beseeched him, desperate to reach out to him. But Nicolás refused to give anything to Guido. *Judge not and you will not be judged.*

Nicolás resisted. "I can't help you. This is not my life, it is yours. You have to pay in your own way, and if it is at all possible, find your own peace."

Guido stared in terror at Nicolás.

"You don't understand, I'm ruined. I have no choice but to kill myself or seek revenge. I cannot go on living like this any longer."

Nicolás could only shake his head. Guido became hysterical:

"I didn't do it for me. I didn't even do it for my country. I did it for *your* class. So that spoiled children like you could go on living like none of us could even dream of–"

"No!" Nicolás exploded. "I didn't ask you to torture anyone for me. I never ordered you to kill in my name."

"Your families will always . . . Ah, what's the use." Guido broke off, and covered his face in his hands.

The long and excruciating silence between the two men was gently interrupted by the soft pleading murmurs of a woman in orgasm. The groans floated in over the transom above the door and steadily grew in intensity, despite what sounded like a hand over her mouth to muffle the groans that had now turned to sobs and whimpers.

"They're back."

Nicolás, desperate to extricate himself from the black vortex of Guido's confession, and the agonizing emotions that it had aroused in him, gestured with his head toward the bathroom corridor.

Guido struggled to his feet, and with a contemptuous wave of his hand, dismissed the presence of the homeless couple who had sneaked back into the corridor bathroom. When he spoke to Nicolás again, Guido had made a frightening switch: His face had become a mask, his voice was totally neutral.

"By the way, Señor Quintana, it is my responsibility to inform you that as a guest of this hotel you have twenty-four hours to observe the new military decree on residency. You must update your personal documents within thirty days of change of address and also inform the nearest police *comisaría*. You must be aware that you have been here three months now –"

"Don't be ridiculous, Guido. Don't think for one moment that I am going to put the Cruz del Sur as the permanent address on my identification documents."

"Failure to comply with these new regulations means I will have to inform Sergeant Roggerone, the police officer who daily checks the register of the hotels in this police section."

Then, with elaborate politeness, Suboficial Mayor Echeverría thanked Nicolás.

"I have presumed on your time, and you're a gentleman whose time I realize is extremely important. This was unforgivable of me. I beg your pardon. I can assure you that it will never happen again. Never."

In that moment Nicolás realized he had made an implacable enemy. There was nothing he could do but shake Guido's hand, even though he felt nauseated just by the touch of the man's skin.

"And I thank you for the drink, Suboficial Mayor Echeverría."

As men, they would pretend that what had taken place had never happened. Nicolás formally accompanied the suboficial mayor to the door of his room. Guido moved across the corridor and in a cold rage began to pound alternately with his fist and kick with his shoe on the bathroom door in the hallway.

While the former soldier of military intelligence thumped on the door in the passageway, Nicolás opened the box of Tarot cards, cut the deck, then contemplated the card on the third cut. Again it was the Tower. Incredible, he had never seen that before, three times in a row. His room seemed full of dark and evil energy, the ghosts of Guido's anguished victims had been abandoned in this room along with Guido's confession to Nicolás.

Nicolás spontaneously snatched up an expensive leather shoulder-bag from a corner of the room. He turned the bag upside down and dumped on the floor gym clothes, running shoes, books, and papers. Then he took his last two remaining suits from the wardrobe, quickly folded them into the empty bag. He slipped on a cotton jacket, then, bag over his shoulder, he locked the door to his room. And with a nod to Guido who, in grim determination, still pounded monotonously on the bathroom door with his fist, Nicolás fled the Cruz del Sur for the early evening streets of Buenos Aires.

Nicolás breathed easier as he walked for a couple of blocks along Carlos Pellegrini. After the dream and the horrific confrontation with Guido in his cramped room at the Cruz del Sur, he embraced the expanse of the spacious boulevard with a deep sigh of relief. It was the second week of November. The late-spring weather was sensuous, the evening light soft and luminous. The usually dusty trees along the Avenida Nueve de Julio, cleaned by spring showers, were a rich black-green. A music store filled the evening air with the light playful notes of a *milonga*. In the sky there was the promise of a light shower that would surely freshen the streets, now thronged with people.

Men were in shirtsleeves or carried their jackets. And the women had already begun to dress in the flimsy summer fashions that Ramón laughingly used to claim were responsible for the high rate of cardiac infarction among middle-aged men in Buenos Aires.

"These anxious *viejos* come into my clinic. I advise them: Never mind hyperinflation, the military, or the death squads, these summertime women will get you first. Keep off the streets; stay home at night; draw the curtains. But do they listen!"

Nicolás had an ache in his heart. He missed Ramón's irreverent and irrepressible humour that had lightened even the blackest of moments. Ah, Ramón. There wasn't another doctor like you in the whole of Argentina. Not a day goes by that I don't think about you and Lara, the conversations and the good times the three of us shared.

Nicolás felt hungry enough to stop for a *lomito* sandwich at any one of his favourite cafés off the boulevard, where he could digest the small juicy steak while he lingered over a coffee and attempt to read between the lines of the censored *La Prensa*. Then afterward, he could take a taxi to the affluent Barrio Norte, where he had business with a regular client – in other words, a relaxed and leisurely evening.

But when Nicolás started to walk his hunger left him, even though he had not eaten since breakfast, when he had only had a roll with his coffee. Perhaps it was the sad piercing memories of Ramón and Lara, and animated by the possibility that Lara was still alive, Nicolás suddenly felt possessed, urged on by a mysterious energy. So he passed the Café Vitti with only a casual wave through the glass window to Mario, the ever-watchful waiter. Mario did a second take, gaped, then bobbed his head in a brief half-smile and looked quickly away in embarrassment.

Nicolás had been puzzled for a moment at Mario's reaction, then remembered the waiter had never seen him dressed this way before. Well, they were going to have to get used to it.

Nicolás turned up Avenida Santa Fe. Although surrounded by the chaos of human activity, Nicolás felt that he had recovered his balance. He was calm inside. Composed, he threaded his way through the noise and confusion created by the cars and people that jammed the intersection of Nueve de Julio and Santa Fe.

The route Nicolás had chosen would take him along the crowded sidewalks, past all the smart shops and cafés on Avenida Santa Fe, to the Rivadavia, where his appointment for the evening waited. So seized was he with this strange energy, he actually planned that after the meeting he would walk around the Botanical Gardens. Then perhaps to Palermo and walk through Rosedal and the park and come back along Avenida del Libertador.

To Rosedal? The setting of his bad dream? Was this his morbid sense of curiosity at work again, he asked himself. Why do I want to go back there, especially after a nightmare like that? And where did this spontaneous plan come from? He didn't know, but he felt driven by the possibility that on the streets, that night, information waited for him – there would be answers to his questions.

The evening air stayed warm. And for Nicolás, the walk had became an act of meditation. He surrendered to the turbulent energy of the crowds, watched his thoughts move like a slow train through his head. This avenue in the swank Barrio Norte was like no other in the whole of Latin America. In the shop windows Nicolás could see the latest and most expensive clothes from all over the world: Rome, Paris, West Berlin, New York. He passed a men's store, where in the old days he used to buy most of his clothes. An Italian sports jacket in the window carried a price tag that was the equivalent of three months' salary for a university professor. In the street, drivers of the most recent model of BMWs, Jaguars, and Mercedes Benz automobiles all jockeyed for parking space.

Nicolás entered the cavernous space of the Bar Rivadavia. He walked past the busy tables of people-watchers at the front windows of the bar to the back, where he found his client exactly as had been described in the last instructions given him, right down to the colour of her wig and the design of her dark glasses.

La Señora was seated at a small table for two, a tiny island in a sea of deserted tables. On another island, another table, just out of earshot, sat the man who doubled as her chauffeur and bodyguard, silent and motionless.

La Señora was almost forty, intelligent, her physical beauty fading, wealthy beyond belief, and desperately afraid. She was nervous, excited, in a state of high anxiety. But then, she had appeared that way at the beginning of the last appointment. He wondered what lies she had to tell to those around her in order to take these risks or to explain her absences.

"Do you want the cards today?" Nicolás asked her.

"Oh yes," she replied, "I love the mystery."

Nicolás smiled, "You know, it's only a vehicle, a means to an end?"

She nodded. "Of course." And in eager anticipation drummed her blood-red fingernails on the table.

"It's difficult to work," he told her, "to make any connection, if you keep on your dark glasses."

"I know," she replied. "But it's just too dangerous for me to take them off. I can't run the risk of somebody recognizing me. You will have to do what you can."

"Then give me your hand before I deal the cards," said Nicolás.

La Señora turned to give The Bodyguard a brief reassuring smile, then gave Nicolás her hand. A shiver ran through her body. Her palm was warm and slightly damp. His was cool and dry. This was their second meeting, and she evidently felt comfortable enough to ask personal questions.

"You know, you're an interesting man. So sensitive, so mysterious."

Nicolás smiled. He anticipated her next question.

"Are you married?"

Nicolás shook his head. She moved her fingers softly within the palm of his hand and was surprised to feel the hard callus that ran along the ridge of his palm.

"You work with your hands?"

"No, it's from the apparatus in the gymnasium."

"Another contradiction! A mystic who is an athlete."

"What was the first contradiction?" Nicolás asked.

"Those clothes. A man who walks and talks like you doesn't wear clothes like that."

"The reality remains the same, it's just that our perceptions change."

"The disguise doesn't work. Where is that beautiful cream linen suit you wore last time?"

"I gave it away."

"How did you get into all of this?"

"A medical friend of mine introduced me to mysticism as a way to deal with a deep personal tragedy."

"I would like to meet this doctor."

Nicolás nodded. Then suddenly felt a powerful surge of energy from the woman.

"Did you feel that?" she asked excitedly.

"Yes, now we can begin." Nicolás released her hand.

"Are you not married because you're too busy with these – what do you call them?"

"Talks," Nicolás shrugged.

"How many people do you *talk* to in a day?"

"Depends, but usually not more than two or three a week."

"I like that."

"Why?"

"Makes me feel part of an exclusive group. And so it should, because you cost me more money than my psychiatrist."

"Does this mean you want to stop the sessions," he asked her, completely without anxiety.

"No! no! Why? You're five times more helpful than my psychiatrist."

Before Nicolás dealt the cards, she reached forward and put her heavily ringed left hand over his. "I still don't know your family name."

34

"And, officially, I don't know yours. But it's not important. To you, I'm just Nicolás. Now close your eyes and think about the question you have in your mind."

To myself and the rest of Argentina, Nicolás thought, you are simply La Señora del Barrio Norte. Rich, uneducated, and completely self-absorbed. The spoiled wife of one of the most powerful investment bankers in South America, a man at this moment suspected by the military of laundering the millions of dollars taken as ransom by the revolutionary groups in their political kidnappings.

"Show me the Significator you have chosen?" asked La Señora.

Nicolás laid down the Queen of Cups. Voluptuous, she sat on her throne, radiant and crowned. "Love and pleasure," smiled Nicolás.

The ritual had begun and, as always, it created its own mysterious psychological momentum. Nicolás shuffled and cut the deck, then drew the first card to cover the Queen. It was the Moon. He heard her gasp in fright.

"The Moon covers the Queen," he said calmly. "Hecate, the moon-queen hangs above the path of blood and tears."

From the other side of the table, he could feel a wave of panic emanate from La Señora and surround him in a palpable flow of dread.

"This is the road you travel," Nicolás continued, "and upon which fear and hesitation must be overcome."

La Señora's eyes were fixed on the card: the two wild dogs howled at the moon, as it hung above and between the two grim towers. In the foreground, a crayfish crawled from a stagnant pool. It took an enormous act of will on the part of Nicolás to deflect the tension, push it away from himself, so that he could deal the cards in the Grand Cross spread and focus on the Tarot reading.

"This crosses her," Nicolás said and drew the second card, which he laid across the Moon. "The Two of Wands: power, wealth, and good fortune."

La Señora breathed easier. But then the uneasy smile tightened in her face when Nicolás drew the third card.

"This is above her." And Nicolás drew the Eight of Wands, reversed. "Argument and jealousy in the marriage, provoked by an infatuation with an outsider."

La Señora stole a look at her bodyguard and seemed relieved that he was out of earshot.

"This is below her." The fourth card was the Star. The naked woman poured water from a jar into the river. "The Mother Goddess provides you with unexpected help to enable you to overcome all your tribulations."

Nicolás could feel the tensions dissipate.

"This is behind her, the Two of Swords; a state of harmony reigns. This is before her, the Sun." Nicolás laid down the sixth card with positive emphasis. The sun beamed down on the naked couple in the idyllic meadow, the woman opening her legs for the man. "Happiness on all levels of being and consciousness."

By the time Nicolás got to the sixth card, which was the Nine of Pentacles – "Great material good fortune" – La Señora exuded warmth and confidence. The seventh to tenth cards were all positive, and Nicolás realized the session was going to be hard work, but in the end, indisputably beneficial. He was confident that he would be able to move La Señora away from all her anxieties, and have her ask herself why she did what she did. Perhaps even why she believed what she believed. Once again, she took his hand in hers, but this time unconsciously.

•   •   •

36

La Señora was ready to leave, she looked ten years younger. Nicolás felt as if he had been on a long voyage. They had travelled back through her memory and probed her psyche more deeply than before. The reading had been successful, La Señora appeared vitalized by the process. As before, with this particular client, Nicolás had been left enervated, but transcendent. For Nicolás, these were the moments he lived for: when he was transformed, the karma transmuted into dharma, and he was highly sensitized to everyone and everything around him. In those moments Nicolás perceived the world with an incredible clarity. Not that he revealed any of his feelings. This awareness was a special secret he held to himself.

"Whenever you want to make a lot of money," La Señora told him, "I'll give you your own special show on one of my husband's radio or television stations. With your talent, we could make millions."

The idea amused Nicolás. "How?" he asked.

"With advice!"

"For who?"

"For everyone. Businessmen, politicians, factory workers, the lovelorn, the lost."

"Thank you for the offer, but I don't think I have been put on this earth to make money."

"Whenever you find out what it is that God has intended for you, I'm sure that it will be quite extraordinary. You are a remarkable man. Where were you educated?"

"All the best schools, but I really didn't learn very much."

La Señora smiled. "Don't worry, I'm not going to try and find out who you are. It would be easy enough for me to do so. But I enjoy mysteries, especially this one."

She took an elegant blue envelope out of her purse and gracefully pushed it across the table toward him.

"Next week?" she asked. "You'll find the time and place in here with the money." She tapped the envelope on the table.

Nicolás nodded. He didn't like meeting in these bars. "These aren't the best places to talk. I don't find them private enough for –"

"You can't come to the villa. It's out of the question. Officially I'm still supposed to be under house arrest. There is an arrangement with the police, but we know that the villa is watched by military intelligence."

"Perhaps we could meet at the house of a friend?"

"Worse. You're too handsome to be inconspicuous. You know what this city is like. Everyone will immediately assume I'm having an affair. Military intelligence will open a file on you. And the tabloid paparazzi will have your face all over their pages."

Nicolás smiled. La Señora lingered. She glanced over and nodded to her patient bodyguard, a man who sat so still he was invisible. He rose to his feet and approached their table.

"Before I go, I promised my chauffeur he could ask you a question."

Nicolás waited. The Bodyguard, a fit, broad-shouldered man in his mid-thirties, deliberately sat down at the table. His movements were calm, studied; the image of a man totally in control of himself. But Nicolás, still in a heightened state of sensitivity from the reading with La Señora, could immediately sense the tangle of repressed tension inside the man. When The Bodyguard took off his dark glasses, Nicolás was not surprised to find himself looking into the beautiful, gentle eyes of a troubled dreamer. From their body posture and the energy that flowed between the woman and her employee, Nicolás also understood immediately that The Bodyguard was her lover. So the Tarot cards had been true. He came straight to the point, but not before a brief wondering visual check of Nicolás' attire. I suppose I'm the one that will have to get used to this, thought Nicolás.

"La Señora has spoken so highly of your abilities, I would be deeply moved if you could help me. You see, my brother is a *desaparecido* and–"

"You want me to tell you how and where to find him?"

"Yes señor. Quite simply, that is it."

"I'm sorry. But I'm not a psychic. I don't have visions."

"Ah," he breathed politely. "I understand, señor."

Nicolás could see the man didn't believe him.

"Señor, if it's a question of money, my family–"

"No, believe me. If I could do this thing you are asking for, I would do it for nothing."

La Señora nodded in agreement. "The señor has never asked me for anything."

"Ah," again the gentle outburst of breath. "Now I understand. I apologize for the implications I might have made. As you can see, we're desperate. Clutching at straws. I hope that you can empathize with our concern. You're not angry?"

"No. I wish I could help. But you know, if such a person exists" – Nicolás broke off, searching for the right words. He did not want the man to misunderstand him and think he was indifferent to his pain – "I think they would very quickly go crazy."

"I don't understand, señor?"

"Let's say, even if I had such a gift. Can you imagine how much pain and suffering I would bring to everyone who sought my help?"

The Bodyguard reflected in silence for a moment, then observed, "Of course, you are right. But with all respect, señor, the pain of not knowing whether our family members are alive or dead is driving us all crazy."

Then, with the unspoken communication of lovers in harmony, they rose together from the table. At the same moment a tremendous commotion broke out among the crowded tables at the front. The Bodyguard, in swift fluid movements, stepped protectively in front of La Señora, his gun out and discreetly ready under a folded issue of the tabloid *Clarín*. Now what woman in these times, thought Nicolás, couldn't use a man like that for her lover? Nicolás turned to see three young people, a man and two women, students by their dress, their faces covered by black cloth masks, scatter handfuls of yellow leaflets over the customers as they ran among the tables yelling: *"Abajo la dictatura! Abajo los militares!"*

"Ah," Nicolás heard The Bodyguard murmur reassuringly behind him, "it's only a demonstration, señora."

Nicolás turned in time to see The Bodyguard slip a large note to the waiter and lead La Señora discreetly out through the kitchen to the back door. The students, after their lightning-strike protest, had also disappeared out the front door. For the most part, the clients pretended nothing had happened. Only one or two appeared to read the leaflets. Two waiters quickly went to work, picking the yellow leaflets off the tables and the floor.

Nicolás had given La Señora and The Bodyguard a few minutes to exit the Bar Rivadavia before he casually opened the envelope. Nicolás was wryly amused. La Señora had left a more than generous payment. Given his frugal way of life, there was enough money in the envelope to live on for the next two months. Nicolás felt uncomfortable, watched. He looked up. His eyes met those of the man who had been their waiter, and Nicolás knew immediately he was looking into the eyes of a police informer. The waiter turned away, and

Nicolás discreetly slipped the envelope of money into a hidden pocket at the bottom of the leather bag. He left casually, placing with great care exactly the correct amount for a tip.

When Nicolás returned to the street, it was almost dark and Santa Fe was more lively than ever. Just outside the door of the Bar Rivadavia, he found and picked up one of the yellow leaflets. The expertly printed message on the handbill called upon the military command of the city to release two student leaders who had been disappeared a month earlier. Nicolás looked up from the leaflet to find his waiter had followed him to the door.

"This must be love," Nicolás said. The waiter didn't blink. Nicolás handed him the leaflet. "Seems you missed one."

Nicolás strolled easily, floated unseen, he felt, through the crowds on Santa Fe.

But not, as it turned out, unnoticed by everyone. Just as Nicolás was about to cross Libertad, a dirty blur of green metal sliced across the plane of his consciousness with a squeal of tires. And he was brought back into this world. The car, a Ford Falcon, engine racing, pulled in tight alongside the curb, effectively blocking his passage. In his peripheral vision, Nicolás caught the glint of a gun barrel, and sheer terror exploded the inner calm he had experienced since he had left the Rivadavia.

A dark chubby hand emerged from the passenger window of the Falcon and urgently beckoned Nicolás to look down. Nicolás leaned forward and found himself face-to-sidelong-face with the man awkwardly half-turned in the passenger seat. He wore thick glasses. A thin lipless mouth moved in a slow broken line across a dark round face. Ugly festering warts speckled the lower part of his jaw and neck. A toad, thought Nicolás. Spectacles on a toad.

"Don't move!" said The Toad. His voice was high-pitched. Not comical, but scary, because it was just this side of control.

From his height and three-quarter angle of vision, Nicolás could see the hate in The Toad's eyes, distorted and enlarged by the lenses of his glasses. Nicolás looked down into the man's lap and saw The Toad held a sawed-off shotgun pointed at him, the double barrels resting on the sill of the car window.

"Put your hands on the roof," squeaked The Toad.

Nicolás slowly leaned forward. Mentally he searched for some handle to hold on to, but fear loosened the inside muscles of his thighs and crept into his gut. What form of dark energy had pulled him through the crowded streets to this evil confrontation? He shuffled to keep his sandals on the edge of the curb, then reached out and felt the roof of the car, warm and grimy under his palms. They didn't wash this car very often. He could see other smudged hand marks, etched by the acid of human sweat into the film of scum on the paint. Blood, splattered on the chrome around the window and down the door panel, had dried dark brown.

Nicolás turned his head from side to side to search among the blur of faces in the crowd. He tried unsuccessfully to fight his rising panic. There had been no time to prepare for this moment. Who could he recognize? Who would know him? Who would choose to see him? The every-night sidewalks of Santa Fe, noisy, crowded with the well-dressed and elegant residents of the Barrio Norte, had suddenly become a no man's land for Nicolás. As always, the crowds slipped past the Falcon as if it was not there, just another rock in the urban river, dangerous and to be carefully navigated around.

Everybody, Nicolás understood, pretended that they hadn't quite noticed what was happening right in front of their eyes. The fear crept up under the skin of Nicolás' back and neck and into his brain. The crowd blurred to an unfocused curtain, against which the driver, as he emerged from the other side of the Falcon with a cut-down Itaka shot gun cradled on the underside of his huge right arm, became the sharply edged image of Nicolás' total concentration. He wondered, will they shoot me right here on the sidewalk? Or will they throw me in the back of the Falcon? That's how they had disappeared Ramón two months ago, without even first asking him any questions. What had Ramón done in those initial few seconds? Was this the way he had felt, a great strange emptiness under his chest?

The driver, a tall, big man, with mirror shades over his eyes, a tight yellow T-shirt that revealed his belly, and saggy blue jeans, moved swiftly around the front of the car in a pair of Adidas running shoes, and quickly and professionally ran his hands over Nicolás' body. His right hand stopped with an interest all of its own on the bulge in Nicolás' jacket pocket. Big Man cautiously took out the black velvet bag that held the deck of cards and put them on the roof of the car.

"Okay, stand up now and turn around slowly," ordered Big Man.

Nicolás carefully took his hands off the car roof, where they left two sweaty palm prints, and turned to face Big Man.

"What's in the shoulder-bag?"

"Two suits."

"Open it carefully."

Big Man held the Itaka under Nicolás' chin. Nicolás carefully unzipped the top of the bag, and showed Big Man the suits. He whistled.

"Where did you steal them from?"

Nicolás didn't answer.

Out of the corner of his eye he saw The Toad reluctantly put down his gun and awkwardly heave himself out of the Falcon. He was short, heavy, and reeked of cheap cologne. Great patches of sweat circled the armpits of his rumpled white cotton suit jacket. Underneath the jacket, a huge belly pushed against a knitted green golf shirt that sported an alligator insignia on the front. Designer medals for military intelligence. Nicolás knew that he would never again be able to see one of those alligators on a shirt without thinking of this man.

Big Man reached out and examined the black velvet bag he had left on top of the car. His huge hands fumbled with the drawstring. Right behind Big Man, no more than half a metre away, a shoeshine boy, a skinny teenager in shabby clothes, squatted at his boot rack, intensely involved in reading the *Clarín*. When some of the illustrated cards fell on the sidewalk, the bootblack's eyes briefly slid in their direction. But then he quickly turned the page of the tabloid.

"What the hell's this?" asked Big Man.

"A deck of Tarot cards."

"Huh! You a fortuneteller?"

"No."

"Pick them up!"

Nicolás stared over Big Man's shoulder and down Santa Fe. He didn't want to be on his hands and knees when they shot him.

"*Qué boludo!*" shrugged Big Man. "All right then, asshole, leave them there."

Big Man ignored the half-dozen cards spilled on the sidewalk, and shoved the velvet bag that contained the main pack of cards back into Nicolás' pocket.

"Well, well, what do we have here – *un chanta o un subversivo?*"

44

So that's what it has come to, Nicolás thought, wise guy or revolutionary? These men would kill you if they suspected you of being either; it was all the same to them.

"Or maybe," The Toad continued, "even a Montonero?" Nicolás could see and hear that The Toad's irritated mocking demeanour was permanent. Understandable. That face and personality would not attract much positive karma.

Nicolás imagined that The Toad, a short man, probably felt it unjust that he always had to look up to suspects. The top of The Toad's head came only halfway up to Nicolás' chest, so he had to reach high now as he rubbed his forefinger and thumb together wordlessly in front of Nicolás' eyes, then impatiently snapped his fingers under Nicolás' nose. Nicolás understood and silently handed over his *documentos*, contained in a plastic sleeve with the ever-present U.S. ten-dollar bill.

The Toad expertly palmed the bill. A toad that could do conjuring tricks. He pocketed Nicolás' I.D. and nodded to Big Man. The Toad opened the door to the Falcon, and Big Man violently shoved Nicolás from behind. Nicolás landed heavily and awkwardly on the metal floor behind the front seats. The rear seat had been removed and replaced with a single makeshift jump seat. Big Man threw the shoulder-bag on top of him.

Nicolás struggled to sit up. Just above the line of the rear window, he caught sight of the only person on Santa Fe who seemed willing to bear witness – a tall slim woman with black hair tied in a short thick braid. She wore a simple cotton dress. She stared directly at Nicolás. She was calm. Her eyes took in everything. When she shook her head, it was not in despair but in frustration. Nicolás understood her desire to help him.

The Toad scrambled to take up his position on the single jump seat. He had trouble handling the heavy

Itaka, even though the barrel had been cut down. He waved the shotgun in Nicolás' face.

"Lie down!" screamed The Toad. And kicked at Nicolás with his small pointed leather shoes.

Big Man was already behind the wheel. For several moments the Falcon's whining starter motor would not catch. Nicolás was seized by a ludicrous hope: If the car won't start, they will have to let me go.

"*Qué auto de mierda!*" Big Man swore. Then the Falcon's motor fired, and the vehicle left the curb with sudden acceleration and a squeal of rubber burned from the tires.

Nicolás was too big for the space.

"Get your head down!" The Toad stamped his feet on Nicolás' back.

Nicolás scrunched his head below the line of the window and jammed his knees up to his chest. Is this how it was with Ramón? he wondered. Would they take him to the same place out by the highway near Ezeiza and shoot him, and let him bleed to death, just as they had done to Ramón? That is how he had found Ramón when he had driven out with Ramón's father to identify the body. The old man, overcome, had fallen down in the long grass beside the corpse of his son. Who will come and identify me? wondered Nicolás.

Big Man leaned on the horn in impatient bursts as he raced the green Ford Falcon through the narrow brick and concrete valley that is Alvear, when Nicolás suddenly heard The Toad order Big Man: "Go back to where we picked him up."

"*Ah, no! Por qué —*" began Big Man in disgusted protest. But The Toad screamed at the top of his lungs, "WHERE WE PICKED HIM UP!"

Big Man cursed under his breath and spun the steering wheel into a violent turn. His action was greeted by a crescendo of klaxons in protest. Against the din, The Toad turned to Nicolás.

"You can sit up now," he said in a grudging but more normal voice.

When Nicolás levered himself up into a sitting position on the metal floor of the Falcon, he saw that The Toad studied his I.D. as if it held some new secret of the universe. Big Man examined Nicolás in the rearview mirror, finally aware that something might have gone wrong.

A couple of minutes later they were back at Santa Fe and Libertad. The Toad let Nicolás out of the back seat with a sullen and silent formality. Nicolás was surprised to see his Tarot cards still lying untouched on the sidewalk, exactly as they had fallen. The three of them stood on the sidewalk in almost exactly the same positions as six minutes earlier.

The Toad read the identity card one more time and again closely compared the photo with Nicolás. He let his flabby arm fall to his side in exasperation. His plump little hand slapped the I.D. several times against his thigh. His fat toad's head rolled around on his narrow, hunched shoulders.

"Shit!" he squealed in his weird high-pitched voice at the darkened yellow fume of the Buenos Aires sky. "Shit! Why the fuck do I have nights like this?"

The Toad turned to Nicolás, his arms held theatrically apart, the palms of his hands turned up and open in a gesture that implied both resignation and error.

"Señor Quintana," said The Toad, as he handed the I.D. card over for Big Man to examine, "we apologize, profusely."

Ah, that magic Quintana name and the enchanted address in Palermo Chico. What wonders they always worked! Nicolás let go of the tension that had held him in such a tight grip, and he felt a great part of the fear slide off his body. He could breathe again.

Big Man pushed his mirror shades over his forehead to peer at the I.D. card, and then absentmindedly saluted Nicolás in military fashion. He threw his right hand up across his forehead and brought his heels casually together in the old paratrooper style. So much, thought Nicolás, for the attempt to disguise themselves as civilians in street clothes.

"We had been given a description of a subversive and ... " The Toad's voice trailed off as he gestured with his fat little hand to take in Nicolás' presence and to imply that Nicolás in his cheap cotton-polyester clothing had fit the likeness.

Nicolás didn't see respect, just institutional conditioning. He could still see the hate, now tinged with caution, in the men's eyes. To them, Nicolás came from a strata of society they as foot soldiers would never enter. And he could tell by the way they looked at him that they thought Nicolás, with his longish hair and cut-rate, ill-fitting clothes, had really betrayed their idea of what he should be.

"My nephew," said Big Man conversationally, "told me he was at the Military Academy with you. Daniel Moreno? "

Nicolás shrugged.

"No, I guess you wouldn't remember the little prick. He would've been two years behind you. He won a scholarship," Big Man added, almost apologetically, as if to offer an explanation of how such a piss-poor kid like Moreno would ever get into the academy. "The first one in the family to ever win anything," Big Man added gloomily.

Nicolás did indeed remember Moreno, a tall skinny kid who was bullied relentlessly by his classmates. He had been completely without the will or ability to fight back. Moreno, Nicolás concluded, must have been paying for his uncle's history of abuses and transgressions.

The two of them, Nicolás and Big Man, their social exchange in suspension, turned to watch The Toad. Their eyes locked on his clumsy chubby little fingers, one puffed up with a thick gold wedding band, stuff the ten-dollar note and the I.D. back into the plastic sleeve. Incredible! Could The Toad really have a wife? Someone who held him close, opened her legs for him at night? It would have to be, could only be, another toad.

"You were his hero," Big Man added as an afterthought, "because of all your jumps as a cadet. How many?"

"Twenty-five." Nicolás answered truthfully.

Big Man worked a massive index finger inside his left nostril, withdrew it, but unsatisfied with the result, inserted his forefinger to rummage inside his nose.

"I'm an old paratrooper," Big Man divulged with a dumb grin.

Nicolás nodded noncommittally. He had always found it difficult to maintain a conversation with a man who was picking his nose.

"No hard feelings?" The Toad tried unsuccessfully to smile. With the ironic suggestion of a bow, The Toad ceremoniously handed back the little plastic package containing the I.D. and money to Nicolás.

"You don't say much, do you?" said Big Man, resentfully, as he carefully examined at the end of his finger the mucus he had extracted from his nose and then flicked it away.

"Perhaps you should get a haircut," said The Toad. "You know how things are these days. Details like that make our job much easier, Señor Quintana. Especially with those clothes, you, uh, could be easily mistaken for a day-labourer from Lomas de Zamora."

"Yes," added Big Man, "you'd be surprised to know how many of these subversives are stupid enough to let their hair grow. Makes it real easy for us to spot them in a crowd."

Nicolás nodded without expression. He understood the veiled threat. But he wasn't going to give anything to these idiots.

"Your father is one hell of a soldier," said The Toad.

Actually it's my uncle you're thinking of, Nicolás could have replied, but he didn't think it necessary to correct The Toad. A nephew, especially an ill-dressed nephew, as he had just learned, isn't necessarily held in the same esteem as a son. But Nicolás had found his balance again, and when he heard his voice he was glad to hear that he spoke in a flat neutral tone.

"Next time I see the general I'll certainly mention it to him, but may I have the honour of your name, señor, so that I can pass on the compliment?"

But The Toad and Big Man immediately backed off.

"Ah, it's of no significance," squeaked The Toad. "I'm sure the general has more important things on his mind."

No matter, thought Nicolás, it would be easy enough to find out the identity of Daniel Moreno's uncle. ("Remember me, Danielito? I saved you from many a shit-kicking at the hands and feet of your vicious brethren at the academy. Well, I finally figured out why you had such a lousy time of it. The Lords of Karma decided you had to carry some of the freight. You see they couldn't absorb into their humanity all the ugliness and pain caused by your uncle, the one in military intelligence. I bumped into the miserable bastard the other day. What's his name again?")

The Toad turned with a casual wave to collapse back into the passenger seat of the Falcon. A beach ball in a sweaty white suit, armed with a shotgun. Big Man noticed the fallen Tarot cards on the sidewalk and, after a moment's hesitation, squatted clumsily to pick them up. Nicolás winced when he saw Big Man use the same fingers he had had up his nose to gather the cards together. Big Man dusted and wiped the cards against his yellow T-shirt. When he handed them back to Nicolás, they both noticed the top card face-up was the Ten of Swords, a man's corpse, impaled with ten swords. Nicolás could see that Big Man didn't like it.

"What the fuck does that mean?" Big Man asked, with a taunting grin.

"The card is right way up for you."

"What does that mean?" asked Big Man again, now with a sheepish not-quite-so-sure smirk.

"Exactly what you see," replied Nicolás.

Big Man frowned and chewed his lower lip, then with a nod returned to his unmarked Falcon. He fished Nicolás' shoulder-bag out of the back and tossed it over the roof of the Falcon to Nicolás, then, with a last casual wave of farewell, drove slowly away. Nicolás could see that within a few seconds they had already begun to scan the crowds on the sidewalks – two fishers of men working the reeds close to the shore.

Only when the Falcon had moved out of view did the pedestrians on the Avenida Santa Fe suddenly regain their vision and awareness of what was happening around them, and turned to glance speculatively at Nicolás. But nobody talked to him.

Then Nicolás noticed the slim young woman in the plain cotton dress. She had just come out of the pharmacy on the other side of Libertad. In one hand she held one of those gaily woven bags from Peru or Bolivia. She stared at Nicolás in amazement, then shook her head gently in complete puzzlement. Nicolás raised his hands and shrugged to communicate his own gesture of disbelief. He wanted to cross the street to talk to her, but the light had changed and a river of cars separated them. Their eyes seemed locked on each other. She smiled gently, a smile of intrigue, threw the bag over one shoulder, then turned and quickly walked away into the crowd on Sante Fe. She moved with a simple grace and elegance Nicolás found quite breathtaking.

Nicolás looked longingly after the young woman. There was something about her that stirred a profound memory deep inside him that he recognized with a stab of anguish: the way in which she carried herself reminded him of Lara. He wondered exactly what the young woman had wanted to say. For a moment he had been tempted to try and follow her. His interest had been fuelled by his relief at finding himself still free after the encounter with the military, and had immediately transmitted itself into desire, a hunger to celebrate the flesh. But he had held back because, although he understood that the smile from the woman in the blue cotton dress had been intended as an invitation, he had business to do that evening. And now he felt, at some deeper level, there were even more questions to be answered.

"Señor?" Nicolás turned to find the bootblack's thin pockmarked face looking up at him.

"Señor, I didn't let anyone pick them up. I told the people the cards are *malditas*. Nobody would touch them."

Nicolás enjoyed the irony. Here in the heart of Buenos Aires' street of most conspicuous material consumerism, no passerby would touch a Tarot card that an impoverished bootblack described as cursed. He gave the boy all the money he had in his pocket.

"Señor, you really must be a *brujo*. The *milicos* disappear you, then five minutes later they bring you back. This has to be some kind of record."

Nicolás laughed. "No, I'm definitely not a wizard," he said, shaking his head.

"Señor, you don't remember me, do you?"

Nicolás shook his head again.

"Two years ago, I worked in the Plaza Alsina. God must have smiled on you more at that time. You always wore such fine clothes. I shined your shoes. The beautiful señorita, the one with the long blonde hair, was always with you."

Nicolás was stunned. The awful pain he always felt when a third person remembered him and Lara together seized his whole body.

"I will never forget her name, Señorita Lara. She worked in an office near Alsina. She was so kind to me. Whenever I was giving you a shine, she would go and buy me the most expensive *lomito*, and . . ."

Nicolás had begun to walk away.

"Please señor, what's wrong? Have I offended you? *Discúlpeme.*"

Nicolás turned back. He spoke with difficulty.

"No, *che*. No offence. And I am pleased that you remember my fiancée and speak of her so well."

Nicolás fumbled with the strap of his wristwatch, an expensive Rolex.

"Here, I want you to have this."

Nicolás handed the watch to the astounded bootblack, and began to walk away again. He had only gone a dozen paces along the sidewalk when the boy tugged at his sleeve.

"*Con permiso*, señor. I can't take this watch." He showed the back to Nicolás. "See, it says 'For Nicolás, from Lara.'"

Nicolás nodded. "I know, but I'm sure she would like you to have it."

The boy's narrow little face suddenly tightened in understanding.

"Señor, what happened to the Señorita Lara?"

Nicolás could not answer.

The boy turned away to hide his stricken face.

"*Suerte*, señor," he murmured. He clutched the watch in his hand, constantly gazing at it as he slouched back to his shoeshine box.

Nicolás quickly melted into the crowd. Externally, his face was impassive and his body posture serene. But internally, the encounter with The Toad and Big Man, followed so swiftly by the piercing reminder of Lara, had left him in chaos. He walked and struggled to bring his emotions under control. As always, Nicolás found the solution was to move outside of himself. Again he moved with the energy of the many until he abruptly connected with another human being – a ragged old man in a scruffy green felt hat, singing a tango in a mall near Santa Fe and Callao.

The old man had a wild brilliance in his eye, and the gleam caught and held Nicolás for a moment. The old guy's shirt was torn, and his greasy black pants were held up with odd pieces of string clumsily knotted together. His ruined face poured with sweat. The unvarnished guitar, which he clutched so tenderly against his own wreck of a body, was hopelessly worn. A battery-driven amplifier had been amateurishly patched into the belly of the guitar. A shabby guitar case, lid open, with a few coins and notes inside, lay strategically on the sidewalk in front of the street singer. The lid of the guitar case was precariously propped open with a sepia-toned portrait of the singer, many years younger. The glass of the frame that held the photograph was badly cracked and held together with yellowed Scotch tape. But the power of the personality in the photograph radiated through the barriers of cracked glass and tape to reveal a beautiful young man in his early twenties, a real seducer with hypnotic, enchanted eyes. He was dressed in a fine suit. In his hands he held a polished and finely crafted guitar. Below the sepia print, a battered hand-lettered sign identified the street singer only as Felipe, no family name, from el barrio de Matadevos. This is a man, thought Nicolás, who has changed direction and turned to meet the karma he created for himself in his early life. What a voyage it must have been; a tango singer now reduced to croaking out boleros and popular songs on the street.

His audience kept changing; a group of maids on a coffee break, then a gang of teenagers, all dressed in flashy nylon sports clothes and tracksuits, pushed around. They snickered in derision as they mimicked the old man's cracked and quavery voice. The old tango singer seemed unaware of the hostility and snobbish glances cast his way, almost as if he did not see the wealthy crowd that hesitated and then swarmed past him. But when an elderly woman with a mothy fur stole around her throat, despite the warm weather, dropped a coin in Felipe's open guitar case, he bowed gallantly and swept off his shabby green felt hat in mid-song. Felipe's brilliant eyes held the old woman's face for a moment, and Nicolás read the communication and compassion that passed between them and was deeply moved.

So absorbed was Nicolás, it took him several minutes to recognize that behind the old man's shoulder, and a little to one side, stood the young woman in the plain cotton dress. Was she with the old man? Hard to tell. There was something very different about her. She certainly wasn't the usual Señorita del Barrio Norte. She would have been beautiful, Nicolás thought, if she had not been quite so slender. Nicolás watched as she impatiently jiggled the connections of a battered portable tape recorder hanging from her shoulder. She was taping the old man and the recorder wouldn't work. Their eyes met. Nicolás nodded, and she returned a smile that dazzled him. The young woman then walked straight toward him. He waited, unsure. She turned aside at the last moment to pass by him. Secretively her hand sought his. Her touch was delicate, her skin cool; the contact sent little shock waves along the flesh of his arm. She deftly pressed into the palm of his hand a tiny square of folded paper.

"Don't read it now," she whispered in his ear. "I'll meet you in paradise." Then she was gone.

The conspiracy of the moment demanded he keep his eyes on the old street singer, so he was unable to see in which direction the woman had gone. When he finally turned his head casually to glance around, she had disappeared once again among the crowds on Santa Fe. He slipped the folded wad of paper into his shirt pocket.

Felipe coaxed a few recognizable and sweet notes out of the impossible guitar, and launched with a courageous struggle against the noise of the traffic, against the disbelief of his audience, and against death itself, into the venerable tango, Uno. Nicolás listened and knew immediately that at one time the old man must have really had the magic, possessed the mastery. But now, the words, "*Uno busca lleno de esperanzas, el camino que los sueños, prometieron a sus ansias*" were ghostly, sung in a ruined hoarse old man's voice, and poignantly followed Nicolás as he turned and shouldered his way back into the stylishly dressed crowd on the Avenida Santa Fe.

Nicolás discovered the gates to the Botanical Gardens were locked for the evening. Of course, what did he think? The gates were always closed at dusk. But then this wasn't his usual visiting time. Between two and three in the afternoon was the best hour. He even enjoyed the walk from Malabia, where the fence around the gardens started. That six-hundred-metre walk was part of the anticipation of the peace he would savour inside. From outside the wire one could see the solitary souls break from their meditative strolls around the plants, flower beds, and trees, to pause and peer at the tidy little signs that identified and gave the origin of the plant species. Nicolás was disappointed. He stopped to watch two elderly ladies feed a group of cats that had collected on the other side of the fence. The old women called and scolded the motley collection of street cats by name. He understood that he was witness to a nightly ritual.

Nicolás was distracted and drawn by the laughter and music from Plaza Italia across the street. The square was thronged with people. Groups of young girls laughed and flirtatiously eyed passing young men. It must be Thursday thought Nicolás, the traditional night off for the housemaids of the barrio.

He found a place on a bench in the plaza. Beside him a young couple ignored him as they negotiated with each other in a mixture of Spanish and Guaraní. The girl wanted to go to a dance. The young man had other things on his mind. As he idly gazed around him, Nicolás remembered. He put his hand into his shirt pocket and found the tiny square of folded paper given to him by the strange young woman. He was surprised. He had half expected some banal clandestine political message from the underground left. Instead, it was with delighted wonderment that he read the hand-printed note:

The word is our sign and seal. By means of it we recognize each other among strangers, and we use it every time the real conditions of our being rise to our lips.

He wondered about the mysterious young woman who had handed him the note. And why did she quote from Octavio Paz's *Labyrinth of Solitude*?

"I'll meet you in paradise," she had whispered.

Now what did that mean? How and where would he find her again? Paradise in Buenos Aires? Paradise in hell?

Ramón had refused to take him seriously that evening at the Tivoli Gardens restaurant in Florida.

"This is a living hell, this life we lead in this country," Nicolás had observed, as they talked late into that awful night while they had waited for news of Lara.

"Nicolás, do you remember Dante's idea of hell?"

Ramón's big misshapen face had broken into that craggy smile that everyone found so irresistible. No one could be afraid or resist the charm of a man who was that homely but had such a beautiful smile. And Ramón had been trying hard to cheer Nicolás up. There had been no word from Lara since she had left the day before for her trip to Rio.

"Yes, Ramón. You are given for eternity that which you thought you most wanted on earth."

"So then paradise could also be hell?"

"What are you trying to tell me Ramón?"

"Well, that you should perhaps think more about this obsession of yours."

"And how would you describe my obsession?"

"To marry Lara and have a normal life."

Nicolás had had enough. He called for the bill.

"I've known you for more than ten years, but sometimes, Ramón–" He had got up from the table annoyed with his best friend.

Ramón immediately apologized.

"I'm sorry. It was insensitive. Relax! I'm sure Lara is okay. We know she was met by friends at the airport in Rio."

"No, Ramón. In my bones I feel that something has gone wrong this time."

Ramón had studied Nicolás for a long moment, put out his cigarette, then hurriedly pulled his lanky body out of the chair.

"Then we should trust your bones. Come! Let's go to Rio. We have to hurry. If Lara is there, we will find her and bring her back."

Nicolás remembered the dread of that moment, and to escape the agony of remembered pain, he got up from the bench in Plaza Italia and walked south again on Santa Fe. Decision and action were sometimes his only release.

Nicolás found Felipe still at work. He had moved out of the mall to the intersection of Callao and Santa Fe. His stage was the doorway of a locked bank building. In the stark shadows of the doorway, Felipe's ravaged face looked even more like a death mask. The man could be anywhere between fifty and seventy years of age. He should be dead, thought Nicolás. Then Felipe turned to look directly at Nicolás. In that eerie moment Nicolás saw that those dark mad eyes, now caught and sparked by reflections of the streetlights, revealed Felipe's body was driven by the will and soul of a young man.

Felipe had pulled around him a small crowd of amused idlers. And above the roar of the traffic, he was trying to make Discepolo's "Yira" be heard. Nicolás, fascinated and held by the insight he had just received, listened for a sign in the words:

> "Verás que todo es mentira,
> verás que nada es amor,
> qué al mundo nada le importa.
> Yira! Yira!"

The bystanders didn't even try to hide their derisive laughter. Nicolás slipped the elegant blue envelope of money La Señora had given him from the secret pocket in his leather shoulder-bag. He circumspectly removed and pocketed a bundle of notes, and left about a third of the money in the envelope. Nicolás stepped out of the crowd, moved close to Felipe, and gently pushed the envelope into his shirt pocket.

"You sing like an angel, señor," Nicolás told him in a voice so low nobody else could hear.

The old man never stopped singing, as with one hand he felt the roll of money against his chest. The gleam in the old man's eyes turned even more intense, and he bowed his head toward Nicolás. In a break in the tango's refrain, he hoarsely whispered to Nicolás, "What goes around comes around."

For Nicolás, it was the perfect answer to reflect upon as he turned and once more made his way back up Santa Fe.

Suddenly weary, Nicolás abandoned his walk and descended into the subway at Callao to return to the Cruz del Sur. On the subway train Nicolás stared unseeing out the window. He remembered the flight to Rio with Ramón. They had travelled first class. The only seats available. Nicolás had paid. They had been quiet, tense. He had stared out the window then, too. Ramón, reflective, had tried to distract him.

"Nicolás do you know what my patients want most of all in the world?"

Nicolás, deep in his own thoughts and not particularly interested, murmured politely, "All kinds of things, I suppose."

"Oh yes. They say, 'If only I was beautiful, if only I was young, if only I was rich, et cetera, I could be what I want to be.' But deep down, do you know what they're all looking for, what they all really want, Nicolás?"

"True love?"

"Exactly!"

"Tell me, Ramón. Why are we so drawn to certain individuals?"

"Simple. Because we like them."

"No, there has to be more to it than that. Why do I connect so profoundly with Lara, and other women leave me indifferent?"

60

"Every relationship between two people has its own magic, its own phenomenology: how certain men and women seek each other out, where they miss, where they make contact, why they become lovers," Ramón shrugged. "It's all a mystery."

Nicolás was disappointed. "That's the best you can do as a psychiatrist?"

Ramón laughed, "I can go the next step, Nicolás, and tell you that half the men and women I know, no matter how deeply they are in love with each other, do not know how to live out that love in happiness."

"Why do they try?"

Ramón threw up his hands. "Am I old? Am I wise? Listen! This continent is full of love stories, Nicolás. Do you know the great unresolved love story and political mystery of our time?"

Nicolás grinned, "Perón and Evita."

"No."

"Marilyn Monroe and John Kennedy."

"Let's not be trashy. Leave it to the gringos, they're better at it. I said a great political mystery and a love story."

"I'm not interested in politics."

"Everything is political, Nicolás."

"Oh, you know what I mean, Ramón. Anyway, what's the love story?"

"El Ché and Tania."

Nicolás had to think about that one for a while.

"Strange. Other than the media images and all the mythology, I really don't know anything about them."

"Everybody thinks Tania was Latin. She was really East German. She just happened to spend the first few years of her life here in Argentina."

"How did they meet, then?"

"Ché Guevara met her in East Germany just after the triumphant overthrow of Batista. The Cuban revolutionaries were being lionized by the intellectual left in Latin America, Europe, North America – everywhere."

"And what about Tania?"

"Tania was beautiful, a brilliant student of languages. They fell in love. Or perhaps she was overwhelmed by Ché."

"I remember the photographs," mused Nicolás.

"Yes. He cut a glamorous figure. At that time the world wanted to see him as a handsome bearded rebel, an intellectual and a man of action. Ironically there were many Argentines who resented the world's attention."

"Why?"

"Because we're such a chauvinist nation, we can't stand the world saying anything about one of ours, good or bad. And here was Ché, an Argentine who had pursued his dream of revolution all through Latin America, who met up with Fidel in Guatemala. And then as a guerrilla, tested by war, he had come down from the Sierra Maestra probably more popular than Fidel himself."

"What was he doing in East Germany?"

"Head of a trade mission. He was actually president of the Bank of Cuba at the time. Then he became Cuba's minister of industrial development. At which, I add, he was an economic and political disaster. But the catastrophes had not yet sunk in. Those were still heady days."

"How old was Tania?"

"She was twenty-two when she met Ché. She was dead at twenty-nine."

"What happened?"

"Ché invited her to Cuba. She did some things for him in Central America. Then she became his advance organizer in South America."

"I thought you said it was a political mystery."

62

"Better, a political thriller. Because afterwards the Americans said Ché didn't know that all the time Tania really worked for the KGB. The Russians wanted to keep Ché and Fidel on a leash, and her mission was to sabotage Ché's attempt to pull off a revolution in Bolivia, an uprising that would set Latin America afire. Remember Ché's slogan? 'Many Vietnams!'"

Nicolás had laughed, "El Ché and the revolution betrayed by a woman! That's too tacky, Ramón."

"Hey, what would Perón have been without Evita?"

"Exactly what he became after she died—just another general.

"So, there's your answer."

"That's too glib, Ramón. I was eighteen when all that happened, and in another world, but I can remember the press stories. Ché and his guerrillas went through a very difficult time in Bolivia."

"No doubt. He also gave the Cuban revolution a certain international style that Fidel could never project."

"Was it just a question of style?"

"No. Ché was one of us. An Argentine. And you know how we look down our noses at the rest of Latin America. And here was Ché, intelligent, well educated, an intellectual. He was also a macho. He had gone to Cuba, a backward little Third World country in a pathetic state of bondage to the United States, and had emerged as one of the most important leaders in a war of liberation."

"If that was the style, then what was the promise?"

"At the time, for the rest of us in Latin America, the promise was that everything and anything was possible."

"Well, if he can see us Argentines now, he must lie uneasy in his grave."

The plane banked out of the clouds, Rio sprawled below them. And somewhere down there was Lara.

"Why didn't Tania just shoot Ché?" asked Nicolás. "I mean, why go through all that hardship in the mountains of Bolivia?"

"I told you it was a mystery."

"No, you said it was a political thriller."

"And so it is. We know how it all ended, or at least so we're led to believe."

"C'mon, Ramón. There were photographs. I remember that famous one of Ché, half-naked. It looked like Mantegna's *Dead Christ*. There is no doubt that Ché died."

Out of the window, they could see the arms of the giant statue of Christ the Redeemer reach up for them.

"Of course. The Bolivians even cut off his hands and stuck them in a jar of formaldehyde before they cremated his body. But we don't–"

"Why did they cut off his hands?"

"Oh, to have his fingerprints on file, so to speak. Just in case somebody tried to claim the real Ché was still alive. But we really don't know why it all came apart the way it did, and why Tania ended up in the mountains with him. Except that if sabotage was her assignment, she did a good job."

"That doesn't make sense, Ramón. If Tania was in love with Ché, why would she destroy him?"

"Because Ché became her emotional obsession. Because Tania was deeply in love with him. Because Tania wanted to die with him."

"How do you know all that?"

"I don't. Just guessing. *Deformacion profesional.* I'm a psychiatrist, remember? But really, nobody knows."

"I remember now, Ché kept a journal. It was published all over the world. And there were other diaries, weren't there?"

"Sure, but have you ever kept a diary? Remember how difficult it was to get the whole story down? The important things? Everything is reduced to a kind of shorthand perspective to aid your memory. And have you ever looked back a couple of years later at a journal you kept, and weren't you struck by how cryptic it was? How unrevealing? Just imagine how much of everything you would get down if you were fighting for your life in the Bolivian mountains."

"Just the essentials of the day. Everything else would have to wait."

"Well that's exactly it. That's why Ché and Tania remain so much of a mystery."

Nicolás had found it hard to focus. He had stared out of the plane window.

"I didn't want Lara to go this time, Ramón. When she told me she had to go to Rio for three days, I told her it wasn't a good time to travel. When I found she was travelling alone, I offered to go with her. But she said no. The group, she said, had decided she had to travel by herself. Why did you let her go to Rio by herself?"

Ramón had taken him firmly by the arm and looked him directly in the face. "This is not the moment for selective amnesia, Nicolás. You've told us all along you're not interested in politics. And that was the agreement, right?"

"I know, I know. But this is hard, Ramón. Not knowing."

Ramón had moved his hand to cup Nicolás affectionately by the back of his neck.

"If it makes you feel any better, these operations are even harder on couples who work together inside the revolutionary groups."

"At least they share the knowledge of the risks. I'm sure Ché Guevara and Tania were happier when they fought side by side."

"I don't think it was quite like that. Besides Ché had a wife and kids at home."

"You're cynical about true love aren't you, Ramón?"

"I've learned from experience. You see, in my life there were two women with whom I agreed to be monogamous. But both betrayed the agreement before I did."

"Were you hurt by these betrayals?"

"Yes, of course! Deeply. Oh, I know what you're thinking, but you're wrong. I've had too many women tell me what a beautiful lover I am to worry about the performance aspect."

"Is that why you live alone now?"

"Yes. I'm trying to get to that place in my head and my heart where if betrayal happens it is not important to my–"

"Please, señores! Your seats?" The Brazilian flight attendant had interrupted them to ask that they set their seats in the upright position for landing. She noticed Nicolás' emotional tension and asked Ramón, "Is your friend nervous about flying?"

"Terrified," Ramón smiled.

"Strange, isn't it?" she had smiled reassuringly at Nicolás. Her dark slender many-ringed fingers had reached out and patted Nicolás' wrist. Then confidentially to Ramón, but loud enough so that Nicolás could hear, she had said, "The big beautiful ones always are."

She had come back in a few seconds with a folded napkin and a paper cup of water for Nicolás.

"I've got something to calm your nerves," she had told him with a wonderful hungry smile. "Welcome to Río."

Amused, they had watched her drift away. When Nicolás had unwrapped the serviette he had discovered an aspirin and the woman's name and phone number written on the napkin.

Ramón had been delighted. "Pure Hegel," he had murmured. "Something for the mind, the body, and a little something for the soul."

66

"I'm beginning to feel like an actor in everyone else's little drama except my own," Nicolás had protested.

"One of my patients," Ramón had observed, "told me she has finally figured out sex and power. If you want to fuck someone, she said, right away they've got the drop on you."

On the subway Nicolás decided he couldn't stand to go back to the Cruz del Sur and deal with Guido. At least not then in his agonized state of mind. He would try later. He abruptly changed at Carlos Pelligrini to take Línea B up Corrientes.

Seated in the swaying car, he glanced about at the anonymous faces, and thought, ah, Ramón, what I would give to see your homely middle-aged face right now, and meet you in one of these joints along Corrientes for a *cortado* and a chat. What would they talk about? Their failure to find Lara in Rio? The rumours they had chased down – that Lara had been kidnapped and secretly flown back to Buenos Aires; then the Candomblé priest with whom Ramón had left Nicolás. They could certainly talk about that. Nicolás felt a moment of such terrible devastation and loneliness that he thought, perhaps it's time to leave this country. All your closest friends are either in exile, dead, or disappeared. You don't even have one friend left to meet for a coffee and chat with for a couple of hours.

Lara had gently warned him, "One day, Nicolás, you will have to turn around and deal with the enormous protection and privilege your family bestows on you."

"I am, Lara. I am. I am paying now!" He spoke out so loudly and fervently on the subway car that his nearest fellow passengers nervously moved away from him. Self-conscious and unable to bear the weight of these thoughts any longer, Nicolás lunged off the train at Callao and Corrientes.

When Nicolás emerged from the train, deep in thought, head down, and began the climb to the top of the stairs from the subway, he heard The Stammerer's harshly whispered stutter before he saw him, "*Che!* I'll t-t-t-rade you for what-t-t-t ever you h-h-h-have in your b-b-b-ag."

The Stammerer, impeded by what seemed like a serious limp, struggled to ascend the stairs beside Nicolás. With a surreptitious nudge, he discreetly held out a worn blue plastic shopping bag. Because Nicolás' thoughts were still back at the Cruz del Sur, pondering what to do about the potentially dangerous problem of Guido's newly expressed hatred for him, The Stammerer had to try his opening gambit a second time, "What-t-t-ever is in there for w-w-w-what's in the b-b-b-bag," before Nicolás understood.

Nicolás smiled. He began to feel more and more like a spider, constantly at the centre of a web of karmic anticipation that he had woven: create karma and there will be an opposite and equal reaction. He had set out earlier that evening from the Cruz del Sur with the intention to rid himself of the last of his expensive suits, the ones his father had paid for, and the symbolic attachments they held to his past life. And here, right beside him, a complete stranger had anticipated his need and found him on these steps, a man who wanted the suits he had to give away. This was truly the path of satori. His only regret was that he hadn't brought along a pair of shoes, too, because he now realized that what he had first taken for a limp was really an adjustment the man had to make in his gait to compensate for the sole flapping free from his broken left shoe.

With a lighthearted smile of recognition and acceptance, Nicolás held out the leather shoulder bag.

"I should have known that you would be here waiting for me."

The Stammerer appeared to relax somewhat. "Sorry I'm late, usual p-p-p-problems." He took the leather bag with one hand but, with an expectant look on his face, refused to let go of the plastic bag when Nicolás grasped it in exchange.

"*Está bien, che,*" grinned Nicolás. "It's a fair exchange."

Panic broke up The Stammerer's face and triggered a nervous tic that tugged frantically at his left eye. By this time the two men had surfaced to the street exit of Callao. Passersby had begun to cast inquisitive glances at Nicolás and The Stammerer, as they struggled for each other's property. There is a comic aspect to this, thought Nicolás, that with luck will not transcend the karma.

"P-p-p-p-password?" demanded The Stammerer, in a fierce whisper that sprayed saliva into the night air.

"The word is our sign and seal," Nicolás smiled, optimistic that the words, pulled instinctively from the Octavio Paz quote mysteriously handed to him so recently, would appease this eccentric. If the man wanted the leather satchel and the plastic bag, too, so be it.

"*No te preocupés, che.*" Nicolás let go of both bags, and stepped away with a benign smile. The Stammerer became even more upset. Nicolás had not given this strange intermediary what he wanted to hear or see. He glanced around suspiciously, then in classic *porteño* style The Stammerer decided he was bored with this street negotiation.

"F-f-f-f-f-uckit!" In the manner of a true dweller of Buenos Aires, he impetuously thrust the plastic bag into Nicolás' arms, and with one hand on the stair rail, the other holding onto Nicolás' expensive shoulder-bag, The Stammerer scuttled down the stairs, the sole of one shoe flapping, into the subway. At the bottom of the staircase, he paused to yell up to Nicolás without a single stutter to impede his angry imprecation: "God-damn Peronist Youth! Why the hell can't you ever get your act together?"

The wild accusation bumped Nicolás out of his quixotic state of mind. Perhaps, Nicolás thought, he just might have overestimated his ability to generate positive karma. Who was the spider and who was the fly in this particular net? he asked himself. He consoled himself that it was a good thing he had removed from his shoulder-bag what remained of La Señora's money. The plastic bag was heavy with an odd sort of lethal weight to its heft. In fact, as he realized in a matter of seconds, the bag was actually three bags layered inside each other to sustain the weight of the contents. Nicolás, aware that he was being observed by the usual late-evening idlers who always hung about the corner kiosk, began to walk along Callao. And, because of the The Stammerer's final outburst, Nicolás was also suddenly suspicious he might have been set up for a street arrest by military provocateurs. For that reason, he decided to wait until he was almost at Avenida de Mayo before he casually examined the inside of the bag. Three rolled up shirts, he decided, should not be that heavy.

A series of possible worst-case scenarios raced through his mind; they all ended with, what if it is a bomb given to me by some mentally deranged stranger?

Open yourself up to the world, he noted wryly, and paranoia rushes in.

He passed a newspaper kiosk. The tabloid headlines boomed out at him: "ANOTHER BOMB ATTACK IN LANUS! THREE DEAD." The information quickened his decision.

Nicolás nervously turned in front of the Congreso Nacional and found an empty bench in the Plaza del Congreso. He sat on the bench and gently deposited the bag on the ground. After he had checked carefully to see whether he had been followed, and with one hand casually inside the bag, Nicolás slowly felt his way through the folds of the shirt. He didn't have to take them out, he recognized the familiar surface and shape through the fabric of the shirts. My God! That's one. That's two. And there's the third. Sure enough, three. Incredible! His years as a military cadet told him they were live, with the pins in position.

Now what the hell to do? Nicolás wondered. Here you are, he lectured himself, in a day-to-day struggle for survival within a military dictatorship, in a country where, by decree of the junta, you can be shot without trial if found in possession of a weapon or explosives – and what do you do? You wander along one of the main thoroughfares of downtown Buenos Aires – Look there! His attention was caught by a Ford Falcon that circled the plaza at a snail's pace. The side streets must be crawling with Ford Falcons! And here you are with three live grenades that some madman has planted on you. What a crazy city. What fucked-up people. There's no great mystery as to why we're all killing each other, we're simply all mad.

Nicolás ran through several possible ways to get rid of the grenades. Dump them in the garbage cans behind the Congreso? Slip them into the back of that military truck parked by the curb? Jettison them in that litter basket in the plaza? But what if some homeless person

71

rummaged carelessly through the trash? They could blow themselves up and anyone else who happened to pass by at that moment. He discarded all of these alternatives either as too risky or too irresponsible, and finally decided to make his way to the Riachuelo, four or five kilometres further south, and dump the grenades in the canal.

Nicolás crossed the Plaza del Congreso to where Callao becomes Avenida Entre Ríos. And as he walked south through the city, he speculated that the grenades The Stammerer had inadvertently passed to him had been intended for use in an attack or an assassination, and at some point he had blundered into the weapons delivery and distribution system of the group that was organizing the attack.

Nicolás was struck by an intriguing thought. He had been given the opportunity to participate in "the other face of karma," the collective karma. Nicolás, the former military cadet, member of a distinguished military family, had been selected to be an instrument of intervention. To him, this was the karmic law of compensation at work.

He came to the conclusion that he should feel honoured to have been chosen as the unsuspecting medium to neutralize the karma that would undoubtedly have added only more pain and suffering to this world. Only one problem remained – how to get rid of the damned grenades. He must relax, not force the situation.

Nicolás decided, as long as he continued to go with the flow of this incredible night, the solutions would become apparent and be offered to him. All he had to do was remain open to the possibilities. Let the action flow through me, and I will meet whatever happens with grace, he decided.

• • •

72

Nicolás could have taken a *colectivo* or a taxi, but for some reason he had kept on walking. Weary and thirsty, he found himself outside an ill-lit and miserable bar, El Paraíso, somewhere on the mean streets of the lower part of the Barrio Barracas by the South Canal near the railway yards of the Buenos Aires station.

When he entered he found no surprises, the interior was as unprepossessing as the outside. Instead of individual tables and linen, the bar was furnished with long scrubbed wooden trestle tables bounded by an assortment of benches and dilapidated chairs. The palpable despair of too much work and never enough money hung heavy in the air and on the faces of the group of men who, despite the late hour, wore the coveralls of railway workers. They appeared to be engrossed in a card game at a table in the back. They eyed Nicolás briefly, without apparent interest, then went back to their game. Another shitty night in paradise.

The only other clients Nicolás could see in El Paraíso were a surly couple at a table near the bar. Gaunt, dressed in worn, threadbare clothes, they were lost in an intense and desperate argument conducted in angry, whispering hisses. In the chair between them sat a tiny girl of about five or six. In a transparent attempt to block out the words and hatred between the two adults, the child sat with her back to them. She talked with total concentration in a continuous loud singsong to the cheap cloth doll she held cradled in her arms. A bomb could go off, Nicolás thought, and the little girl wouldn't even notice.

So despondent was the atmosphere that Nicolás was about to leave when the waiter made a surprise entrance from the kitchen. He was a huge man, Falstaffian and friendly. The worn floorboards creaked under his weight. Despite the waiter's smiles, Nicolás was not sure that he wanted to stay.

73

"Are you about to close?" he asked the waiter, hopefully.

But the fat man replied in the grand tradition of Buenos Aires waiters: "No señor, we're open for as long as there are customers. And we're pleased to be at your service."

The waiter had a professionally trained voice, with a somewhat affected delivery. Nicolás moved to the opposite side of the room. The waiter politely followed and with great courtesy offered a chair to Nicolás. But before Nicolás could sit down, the waiter found some defect in the chair and, with a gesture, held Nicolás back. The waiter cursed, impatiently pushed the first chair aside, took another, and went through a complicated test for structural strength of the second chair. He grunted as he leaned his great weight upon it, rocked the chair back and forth, pushed the chair this way and that, until finally satisfied, indicated to Nicolás with a grand flourish that the chair was trustworthy, and that he could sit down, *"Síentese, por favor, caballero!"*

After such a performance Nicolás thought he should keep it simple and ordered coffee and a brandy.

But the pleasant fat man was not about to give up easily. "Something to eat?" he asked. "A sandwich? You look hungry. A big man like you should eat to keep his strength up. Try the ricotta pie," he coaxed." It's fresh."

Nicolás nodded in agreement, more to appease the man. The grenades, not food, were on his mind. He asked for the washroom.

"Caballero! Your coffee, brandy, and your torte"–the waiter enthusiastically smacked his meaty hands together–"will be on the table when you get back."

In the washroom Nicolás carefully checked the grenades to see if the pins were properly locked in place, then gently wrapped them up in the shirts again.

74

When Nicolás returned to the bar, he instantly sensed a strange tension in the air. The card players were still grouped at the back; the sullen couple continued to argue furtively; and the child sang to herself in a non-stop chant. Then, from the other side of the dimly lit bar, he saw the back of a woman at his table.

Nicolás glanced at the waiter, who was now behind the bar. The fat man avoided his gaze. The other men in the room stared back at him without expression. Nicolás had the notion they were all in on this and were waiting to see how he would handle the situation.

At first he thought she might be a prostitute on the prowl, but as he drew closer to the table Nicolás recognized with surprise that it was the woman who had pressed the note into his hand on Avenida Santa Fe. She still wore the same dress, but now had a light black nylon jacket over her shoulders. As he approached the table he could see that she had almost finished the slice of ricotta pie that he had ordered. Without the least intimation of embarrassment, she stood up from the table, offered a firm handshake, and graciously introduced herself with a certain flourish, "Tania Gutiérrez Bauer."

"*Mucho gusto*, Nicolás Quintana."

"Oh, please?"

With another courteous wave of her hand, Tania Gutiérrez urged Nicolás to take his seat. The intensity with which she peered into his face made Nicolás realize he was supposed to recognize her name. For a moment the name stirred something uneasily in his memory, but before any meaningful fact surfaced, Nicolás was distracted by the arguing couple. The woman stood up abruptly to leave, her heavy wooden chair scraping harshly on the floor. The man grabbed her by the arm and roughly shoved her back onto her seat. The

75

woman, aware that all eyes in the room were on her, made a discernible attempt to control her emotions. She sat up, her head erect, and proudly stared straight ahead. Only her mouth quivered in betrayal of the humiliation she surely felt.

"*Qué macho!*" exclaimed Tania under her breath. She stood up and went over to the couple's table, where in a clear assertive voice she suggested the woman come and join Tania and Nicolás for a coffee. The man ignored Tania, but stared with open hostility at Nicolás who, knowledgeable of the code that the lower-working class lived by, knew that if the woman accepted the invitation, he was almost certainly in for a fight. But the woman shook her head and declined Tania's offer. Tears welled up in her eyes and ran down her face. She appeared a careworn forty years of age, but was probably in her mid-twenties, Nicolás judged. Poverty had robbed her of her youth but not her dignity.

"Thank you, señora. But this is a private matter of small importance to anyone except us. Certainly not worth having your friend cut with a knife."

Tania touched the woman sympathetically on the shoulder, and returned to sit down opposite Nicolás.

"I hope you didn't mind," she said. "I thought that a big strong man like you could easily deal with whatever might happen."

"Well, you've got the wrong man. I don't believe anything is solved by violence."

"So, a pacifist? How interesting!" Tania's voice took on an immediate edge. "Do you think we should sit and watch the woman take shit?"

"No. But you saw a man punish a woman, and I saw two defeated human beings."

"Even at the lowest end of the social scale, the man has the power. Top or the bottom, the struggle is the same. All relationships – everything is political."

Everything is political. Ramón had said that too. One of his favourite catch-all phrases. He must remember to ask her if she had ever known a psychiatrist named Ramón Ochoa.

"Yes, and everything is moral. Tell me, do you think you diminished the conflict in any way between those two people?"

They both looked across the room: the couple were frozen in a tableau of tension and anger; their child babbled on in self-imposed oblivion.

"That wasn't the point. Even if, when they are alone together later, he beats her, she will remember that there was at least one woman who stood up for her. Perhaps that will give her the courage to take her child and leave him, or even fight back."

Nicolás shrugged. He found this rhetoric too self-indulgent. It carried all the ugly echoes of what was most wrong with Argentina and the rest of Latin America.

"Is this your Marxist speech A or speech B?" he asked.

"I like this puzzle," she mocked. "It gets better and better. A pacifist, built like an oak tree, and with a sense of humour."

"I hope you're not like this all the time, because you're beginning to get on my nerves," Nicolás replied.

Tania's answer was a burst of laughter. That was better, thought Nicolás. Besides he was more curious to hear what intriguing explanation she would offer as to why they had encountered each other for the third time in twenty-four hours. Had she followed him? Possible, but not likely. But then in a city of nine million people, it had to be more than just coincidence. What kind of synchronous process had unfolded and pulled them together? But if she was surprised to see him again, she revealed nothing. Tania behaved as if this evening had somehow been arranged. Did this mean she worked for an intelligence organization? He felt even more intrigued. Perhaps, Nicolás thought, she is simply quite mad, and the best course would be just to humour her. He ordered a bottle of good Mendoza red wine and steak sandwiches from the waiter.

Tania, as it turned out, knew the waiter and, in an amicable exchange of introductions, Nicolás learned that his name was Máximo Medina and that he was also the proprietor of this unassuming bar. Máximo seemed delighted with the whole business, although Nicolás had the impression that a large part of Máximo's good humour spilled out of a perception that the joke was on Nicolás. If so, Nicolás didn't mind.

Nicolás watched Tania eat. She ate in quick, greedy bites, her eyes sensuously half-closed in the unconscious passion of the starved. He could see now that her body was not as fragile as he had first thought. Rather it was supple and lean, and emanated a tenacious energy and drive. It was good, he thought, to have that kind of power to get through the normal demands of any day on the streets of Buenos Aires. She wore no makeup on a face that was tanned from exposure to the sun, as were her arms and legs. Obviously she spent a great deal of time outside.

She had that classic Argentine oval-shaped, fine-featured face. Her hair was jet black and tied back in a thick braid. But as she bent over her food, he could see that the roots of her hair were a light brown. Why, he wondered, would she dye her hair? She looked up and caught his gaze, and laughed, a little embarrassed.

"I can't remember the last time I ate," she offered by way of explanation. The wine and food had already brought a glow to her cheeks. With some rest and a bit more weight, Nicolás decided, she could be a beautiful woman.

"Are you working?" he asked.

"I've had jobs as a freelance gardener. But things are a bit slow right now. I pick up a little money here and there teaching languages or music, but there's a lot of competition these days. Too many educated young people and not enough work."

"Why did you follow me here?" he asked.

She looked puzzled.

"We arranged to meet, remember? On the street I said to meet me in Paraíso. Everybody worth knowing knows Máximo and El Paraíso. So here we are. I was hungry and thirsty and I just knew you would be here to share with me whatever you had."

Nicolás felt humbled. He was convinced powerful forces had shaped the seemingly coincidental events of this evening.

"Where do you live?" he asked.

She was evasive. "Oh, most of the time I rent a room around the corner. I travel when I can. From time to time, I stay with friends in other barrios."

"No. What I'm trying to ask is how is it that out of the millions of possibilities in this enormous city – well, let's not take the whole city of Buenos Aires, but just the barrios I've walked through today, which must hold at least a million inhabitants – how is it that this is the third time in less than twenty-four hours I've bumped into you? You see, until half an hour ago. I never knew this bar existed."

"It was simply meant to be." She shrugged and called out, "Máximo! Do you think we could have some more coffee, please?"

Máximo brought a beautifully engraved silver coffee-pot and placed it with great ceremony on the table between Nicolás and Tania.

"I feel," Máximo said, in a tone that was half-serious, half-parody, "that this is one of those auspicious occasions. My horoscope tells me that today I should be generous, to share my life, and reach out to a stranger. We must not deny our destiny. For this reason, I would like you to use this coffeepot. My grandmother brought it with her from Italy, as a sweet and innocent immigrant girl, as part of her hope chest. You can understand I only use it for moments of special sentiment."

"Is the lady still alive?"

"No señor. She came to South America for the same reason millions of Europeans have come here–in search of a better life. She was a teacher of languages, French and Italian. She had dreams of becoming an actress. But she fell in love and married a young printer with whom she had nine children. Tragically only one of them, my mother, survived their first year of life in this difficult continent."

Tania applauded his speech.

"Bravo! Máximo. I swear you should never have left the theatre."

"The theatre, my dear," Máximo lowered his voice, "thanks to Caesar and his centurions, no longer exists in this heartbreaking country."

"And your mother," asked Nicolás, "did she have a better, happier life?"

The question made the smiling Máximo suddenly pensive. He sat down with them for a moment, his elbow on the table, a beefy forearm and hand supporting his large head. The carefully brilliantined and slicked-back hair shone as an iridescent black halo under the hanging lamp above the table. Tania made an impatient movement. Nicolás sensed she did not appreciate this intervention. Neither did Nicolás. He felt oddly attracted to this woman. Máximo ignored them.

"She would say yes. But as her son, I have my facts on this side of the river, so to speak. As I watched her live out her life with my father, I was made exhausted by their constant state of war with each other. Not physical but psychological warfare. And so it was not until I was a man that I realized she always knew, always, exactly what my father needed to feel emotionally secure and at peace with her."

"She probably wouldn't go to bed with him often enough," interjected Tania, with a conspiratorial smile to Nicolás.

"No, Tanita." Máximo nodded gravely. Nicolás was surprised to hear him use the familiar diminutive of her name. They must know each other well, he thought.

"That was not the case," Máximo continued. "In fact, my father was proud and used to brag about what a passionate physical relationship they had. And as a boy I – accidentally, you understand – often saw and heard evidence of that."

"Then, if it wasn't sex, did you ever find out what she wouldn't give him?" asked Tania.

"Yes. Very early, when they were both quite young, there had been another man. A short-lived love affair, my dear. I don't know the details. But the important element of this story is that my parents were reconciled. I think my father loved my mother very much. I know that he worked hard to make her happy. He was completely loyal to her. And she – "

"Treated your father like shit? It's an old story, Máximo."

She definitely wanted Máximo to finish his story and leave. But Nicolás was now captivated, he wanted to hear the end.

"No, Tanita," Máximo continued gently. "No, she was correct in everything. There is no other word for it, *correcta*" – Máximo curled the tips of his sausage-like finger and thumb together to form an O and emphasize the word – "and respectful. But never again, even though she lived with my father for thirty years, did she ever tell him that she loved him."

"Not once?" asked Tania. "Or maybe she never said it in front of the children. A lot of parents are like that."

"No, not once, not even in private, so my father told me. This refusal drove my father crazy. It was the one thing he wanted to hear and she wouldn't give it to him. Consequently, for thirty years my father lived in a state of insecure jealousy."

"He believed your mother loved the other man."

Máximo turned up his hands in bewilderment.

"Or she let him believe that. As I say, I never understood this until recently. Two years ago my father was dying. On the last night my father asked my mother, 'Julia, before I go, tell me in the name of the *Virgen de Luján* that you have loved me all these years?' My dears, she sat there with her mouth closed. All the years of refusal sat like a stone on her lips. She refused to tell him. My father heaved that sigh of exasperation I knew so well, and died."

Tania was about to speak, but Máximo held up a hand.

"*Con permiso*, the story is almost finished. A few days after the funeral was over and all the relatives had left the city, I took my mother to her favourite restaurant for a meal. She has a strange passion for Chinese restaurants. Not the food, just the restaurants. You see, she never travelled, but had a fascination for the Orient, and so in later years just visiting a Chinese restaurant was an extraordinary excursion for her. She often said it calmed her nerves.

"At the end of the lunch she told me, 'Máximo, out of my four children you are my favourite. You have always been the kindest to me. And I know that you will never abandon me because you will never have children of your own.'" – Máximo rolled his eyes heavenward – "How is it mothers always know these things? Given the sentiment, I assumed that this was a time of shared intimacies between mother and son. 'So tell me, Mother,' I asked, 'I need the answer to something that is very important for me to know. Did you love Papa?' You know what she said?"

"That, of course, she had always loved him!" offered Nicolás.

"No! My mother said, 'I don't wish to talk about it.' "

Máximo repeated the phrase, "I don't wish to talk about it," with the emphasis on each word. "*Es lo que me pone loco.* And that was it. Even though I said, 'C'mon, Mama. It's been thirty years. The man is dead. His soul has gone wherever souls go. His body is in the sanctified ground of Our Lady of Eternal Sorrows in Villa Adelina. You can tell me, Mother. I'm a grown man. I have a right to know. I want to know if I, your first born son, Máximo, am the product of a union without love? Did you love my father, yes or no?' *Me puso loco.* Nothing. Silence. She refused to hear another question on the subject."

Tania sat quiet for once, lost in her own thoughts.

"That's an extraordinary story," said Nicolás.

Máximo shook his massive head.

"*Creo que sí.* But, if you will permit me to say, I think it is unusual only in the details. I believe we are all the same as my mother. Each of us knows very well what that other person wants, needs, to make another person emotionally and psychologically secure. As individuals we know it, as communities, as societies, as states, we know it. There's no big secret. But each and every one of us refuses to give it. Why? Because to do so is to relinquish power."

"So what is this *it*?" asked Tania.

"Exactly what my mother refused all her life to give to my father–"

"Love?" exclaimed Tania.

"No. What is more important than love?" Máximo demanded rhetorically. "The acknowledgement of love!" he answered himself.

"Ay-yi-yi-yi," exclaimed Tania. "Only a Latinoamericano would argue that the declaration and acknowledgement of love is more important than love itself."

"Of course," said Máximo. "If you want to understand love, war, and revolution in Latin America, then you first have to understand that."

"Every Latinoamericano understands that –"

"No!" Máximo was emphatic. "Not even your beloved El Ché understood that. And that's why he failed –"

"*Escúcheme!*" Tania looked as if she was about to explode. "Speaking as a woman, if your father seriously wanted to find out if your mother loved him or not, all he had to do was leave. If she had loved him, she would have come after him. If not, he would never have heard from her again. Just think, your mother waited her whole life, for what? The real problem was your father. He didn't have the balls to take the risk and find out one way or another. And that's the way it is with most men in this part of the world when it comes to women. They still want us to carry the burden of their lives for them."

This time Máximo burst into applause. "Bravo Tania!" He clapped, whistled, and stamped his huge feet. The floorboards trembled. "*Qué feminista!* A couple of years in France and Germany and she talks down to us dumb *porteños* of Buenos Aires like a real gringa – our new leader, who wants to take us on to a better world." He turned, his face full of good-humoured laughter, to Nicolás, "And you thought Bar Paraíso was just another crummy little joint. Oh yes, Quintana. I saw it in your eyes when you first came through that door. No insincerity in El Paraíso, please. But tell me, *che*, where else in Buenos Aires would you get a show like this – free?"

Nicolás didn't get a chance to answer.

"Mamaaaaa!" The child's wail rent the atmosphere of Paraíso with a heartbroken keening. The three turned to see the singsong child, her face pressed into the seat of the chair, her hands gripped the back struts, her feet drummed in futile hysteria on the floor. All alone. The man and the woman had vanished.

"Oh no!" exclaimed Máximo. "This is the third time this week."

Máximo moved surprisingly fast for such a big man. He swept up the child and rushed out the door, but returned in a few seconds, deeply exasperated.

"They've gone. Just like that. Left their kid behind like it was a piece of dog shit on the street. What's wrong with them? What's wrong with these people?" he yelled at everybody and nobody.

Then just as quickly, Máximo let go of his anger and focused his attention on the heartbroken child in his huge arms, smothering her with affection. "*Ayee, cariño*, no more tears. No more crying. El Gordo is going to find a nice pastry for you. The tastiest pastry you've ever eaten in all your unhappy little life. And then we'll call the good Sisters of Mercy from around the corner, and they'll come and take care of you."

Strangely, Nicolás noted, through all of this Tania had remained silent. Cold would be the correct word. She had not even offered to take the little girl to comfort her. Nicolás followed Máximo to the bar.

Máximo gently placed the sobbing child on the counter, where she slowly curled up into a foetal position. He fetched a sweet pastry for her from one of the covered cake stands. Nicolás noticed the men in the back barely looked up from their card game. Máximo followed his gaze and understood.

"Ah, those guys, they're used to it." He waved a dismissive hand in the direction of the card players. "The problem with El Paraíso is that there is an orphanage four doors away. So I go through this at least half-a-dozen times a month. I've got it down to a process now. *Discúlpame* – " Máximo broke off and turned to the phone.

Nicolás gently stroked the child's hair, which was wiry and grimy to the touch. He noticed that the hair roots had that telltale reddish tinge.

"You see the hair, Nicolás?" He had driven Ramón out to the Barrio San Francisco Solano, a slum barrio, where Ramón was giving one of his free weekend clinics in a concrete-block building with a dirt floor. Ramón had pushed back the reddish hair of the skinny little boy who stood beside the table. "That red is a sign of serious malnutrition. That is what you see in children starving in Ethiopia." The child had stared dully up at Nicolás. He thought, whose karma do these children have to carry?

"What did the parents order to eat while they were here?" Nicolás asked.

"Nothing," Máximo replied. "Just coffee and a sweet drink for the kid."

Nicolás glanced over at Tania, who continued to sit by herself. She had refused to become involved. Instead of a political confrontation, thought Nicolás, the couple had needed a meal. It might have just kept them together as a family, for at least one more day. And who knows, the father might have found a job later today? Tomorrow?

Again, Máximo intuited his thoughts, "*Cuidado con ella*," the fat man whispered. "*La Tania es un tango, largo y complejo.* I have known her for a long time, but frankly I'm still not sure if her elevator goes all the way to the top floor." Nicolás had the impression that

Máximo was testing him. For what? He didn't understand.

The little girl's clothing was poor and patched. Nicolás found a serviette and wiped away the mucus and tears from her face. She accepted his ministrations without looking at him. He saw the girl had retreated into deep emotional shock. The light in her eyes had closed. This moment in her life has been sealed off, he thought, put in that place where children put these emotions when they have nowhere else to place them. Until something terrible happens, twenty, thirty, or forty years later, then they have to deal with these wounds. There was already a numb expression on her face, as she absently began to chew on the pastry. On the phone he could hear Máximo finish his matter-of-fact conversation with a Sister of Mercy:

"Yes, Sister. I know it's inconvenient, but I don't arrange these disasters. God does," he reminded her. "Thank you. You'll be around right away? *Perfecto.*"

Máximo put down the phone and turned to Nicolás. "You know, by now I should be able to, but I can never get used to it. Never." And it was true. Nicolás could see that, under the permanently jolly soft face, the man was genuinely upset. "This kind of circumstance makes me understand revolution. If I was a different kind of man, I would," he continued, as he leaned confidentially to whisper across the bar to Nicolás, "be like our friend, La Tania, a militant. But where has that got us today? As a nation? As a people? Everyday people blown up with bombs. Men and women disappearing from the street. *No, che! No soy esa clase de tipo! Pero simpatizo, porque lo entiendo perfectamente.*"

Nicolás found Máximo's muddled and emotional political analysis a bit too ingenuous. Again, he believed he was being felt out. But Máximo's observations reminded Nicolás of the three grenades in the

87

plastic bag that he had forgotten by his chair. He left Máximo to deal with the child, and returned to Tania. As he sat down he discreetly hefted the plastic shopping bag. It was too light!

Tania eyed him with that curious mocking mien in her eyes, and gently patted her woven Bolivian bag. "*Pobrecito. No te preocupés, che. Tengo tus huevos a qui,*" she murmured with a knowing wink, as she enjoyed the outrageous pun she had made in the slang reference to Nicolás' balls, "*en mi saco, che.*"

Despite his chagrin, Nicolás felt a familiar slight burning sensation at the base of his testicles.

"So tell me," she continued seductively, "why does a handsome young pacifist like you, Nicolás Quintana, run around Buenos Aires with live hand grenades."

"You wouldn't believe me if I told you."

"The question, if you will forgive me for being so blunt, is what did you intend to do with these three beautiful little eggs?"

"A small pacifist operation. I was on my way to dump them in the Riachuelo–"

"A likely story," she teased. "No doubt, after a minor counter-terrorist provocation on the way, hmm? Tell me Compañero Pacifista, under whose authority do you act?"

"The Lords of Karma."

"Aha! This is a new death squad put in place by López Rega?"

"Higher intelligences, the Lords of Karma, had decided to absorb a destructive and painful act and enfold it within their own consciousness."

"Imagine that!"

"Why don't you come to the Riachuelo with me and see?"

"I wouldn't miss this for the world. But before we go, let's have some more of Máximo's sentimental coffee."

As she poured the coffee, two Sisters of Mercy arrived to take away the abandoned child. They looked like no-nonsense nuns: cheerful middle-aged women, in ordinary blue work dresses and simple scarves for their heads. They came to the table to ask for a contribution for the abandoned girl.

"You will have a charmed life," smiled the older nun as she took the large note that Nicolás had folded up to give her. "God smiles on the generous of heart." The child now dozed in her arms.

"Do the parents ever come back?" asked Nicolás.

"Not in this lifetime," the Sister of Mercy answered matter-of-factly.

"Did the little girl tell you what her name was before she fell asleep?" asked Nicolás.

"Iemanjanita." The nun raised an eyebrow, and departed with the child to solicit contributions from the card players.

"I guess she recognized the name and didn't like it," Nicolás mused.

Tania raised her eyebrow to mimic the nun, and pulled down her mouth in bizarre fashion. She seemed to use frequently these peculiar enigmatic grimaces that twisted her face up in a rubbery way, the way a small child would. Hard to know how to read these facial contortions. Does she want an explanation or not? wondered Nicolás.

"Iemanja, among those Brazilians who practise Macumba, is the black goddess of the sea."

"Ah yes, voodoo. All that mumbo jumbo."

Nicolás gave up. This woman really did have an extraordinarily unpleasant side to her. For relief he watched the two nuns say goodbye to Máximo. To Nicolás the scene was bleached of colour, a movie tableau shot in sepia tone, but the action in the frame was warm and vibrated with human emotion. Máximo, in his brown tent-like shirt, stood behind the plain bar of unvarnished wood. Over his head a fan turned lazily. He listened intently to the two nuns in their drab clothes, his eyes never left their worn but animated faces. He shook his head in commiseration as the sisters passed the sleeping child from one to another. Then Máximo punched open the ancient and rusty cash register. He reached into the back of the cash drawer and withdrew a handful of notes, which he pushed into the nun's hand. Behind the counter, Máximo poured himself a quick shot and, with the heel of his hand, wiped a tear from the corner of his eye.

"Poor Máximo." Tania shook her head. "Gay, radical, with a heart of gold, and he still can't shake all of the fatherland's patriarchal bullshit values that were stuffed in his head."

"And what's in your head?"

Tania ignored the question. "Examine his story for a moment. Where was the hidden political bias, Señor Quintana?"

Nicolás shrugged. "When do I get my eggs back?"

She waved his question airily aside, "Lots of time for that. The hidden bias is that Máximo's father never wanted to really forgive his wife for having had an affair."

"How do you know she actually betrayed her husband?"

"All women betray their men, Quintana," she mocked him again. "Or are you still too young to have learned that yet?"

"All women?"

"Of course, in sexual politics, betrayal is the only real ace women have to play. The other cards revolve around the sex and power game. Every woman with two brains to put together knows that if a man wants to fuck her she's got the drop on him. Taken aback, *hijo?* Well, I can see you've led a sheltered upper-class life, Quintana. And you've certainly got a lot of growing up to do."

"I recognize that I'm in capable hands," replied Nicolás drily, but thought, she is beginning to get under my skin. I'd like to do something to her. When he felt that familiar burning sensation again, he realized exactly what it was that he wanted to do to her. He remembered Máximo's whispered warning that Tania was unbalanced. This, in turn, made him think of Ramón's old saying:

"Nicolás, it's from the crazy ones that you really learn the important stuff." Yes, that was where he had heard Tania's cynical observation about sex and power before, from Ramón on the flight to Río.

"So did you dance?" Tania asked abruptly.

"Dance?"

"Yes, with the Macumba zealots in Bahia Maranhao?"

"How did you know? Oh, I see. This is your style. You pretend ignorance, that you don't know what the other person is talking about, then you come back in with your expert knowledge."

"Oh, I get what I want," she shrugged. "But that's beside the point, did you dance, or 'writhe with the gods,' as they say?"

"I find it dishonest, manipulative, to treat other people like that."

"God! You're boring."

"Yes, I danced in Minas."

"With which sect, Candomblé or Umbanda?"

"I writhed with a Candomblé group."

"Were you possessed by one of the gods?"

Nicolás paused for a moment, "Yes."

"Male or female?"

"You must know that one doesn't have a choice."

91

"Did the *orixá* speak through you?"

"Yes."

"What did the god say?"

"You're trying to trick me again. You know that when you're possessed you remember nothing."

"Congratulations, you've just passed the Bar Paraíso bullshit test. I'm impressed, Quintana. At least you know what you're talking about."

"You're impossible."

"I know, but tell me, which *orixá* entered into your soul? Something makes me feel it was an *orixá feminina*."

"They never told me."

"Now I know you're lying." She was relentless. "You're a man who was possessed by Iemanja, black goddess of the sea. And you're too much of a macho to admit that you were possessed by such an important female *orixá*."

Nicolás refused to let himself be baited into any further admissions.

"You're a very fortunate man," she told him. "Did Iemanja give you the power of visions?"

"No. I'm not a psychic."

"Who got you interested in the Macumba?"

"A friend of mine, a psychiatrist. Did you dance, 'writhe with the gods,' too?" asked Nicolás politely to change the direction of the conversation.

"No. They wouldn't let me. Nobody would tell me why." She said it with such sadness, Nicolás knew she had spoken the truth.

"Probably a good thing for all of us. You would have made an absolutely relentless *ajibono*."

"Oh, I never wanted to be a believer. I just desperately wanted to be seized, penetrated by Ogun. To be given all the mystical protection of one of his soldiers." In frustration, she pounded her fist on the table.

"Perhaps you were," Nicolás speculated.

Tania suddenly smiled her dazzling smile at Nicolás and simply became another woman, soft, playful:

"No. I'm no warrior. Ogun, the god of war, could not have helped me. I'm a folklorist, I have my doctorate in music folklore. And I've made beautiful tapes of the music played in the Macumba rites. Remember the drumming? So you better be careful, Quintana. I may yet put you under a spell."

Nicolás was amazed at her sudden switch in mood. Yes, she's quite mad, he decided. But if she was mad, she was also intelligent. Nicolás decided to push away the mild hostility he felt toward Tania and try to get past her psychological defence. He didn't believe for one moment their meeting had been simply accidental.

He found her speech curious. Like many Argentines her age, she peppered her speech with English and French slang, using words like "groovy" and phrases such as "j'ai eu mon voyage." Nicolás, who spoke both languages fluently, realized their usage strangely dated her conversation. They were all terms from the sixties. He also recognized she never once referred to the current political crisis – not that many people did on first acquaintance. These days it was just too dangerous.

Tania was somewhere on the left, but where? When Nicolás tried to feel out where her sympathies lay with a couple of humorous references to the disastrous economic plans the military had put in place, she reacted as if the jokes went right over her head. Nicolás had the impression that Tania had been away. Locked up, perhaps, in a prison or in a mental institution, as so many intelligent young leftists had been neutralized by the military in the past few years. He was curious, but at the same time did not want to blunder.

"Máximo mentioned you had been in Europe?"

"Oh," Tania dismissed it, "that was ages ago."

"Have you, uh, been away, travelling since?"

Tania was too smart. She knew what he was fishing for. She stared directly at him for a long moment to consider the question.

"Perhaps you could call it that," she finally answered.

He thought, why not? Try it. "Did you ever know a psychiatrist called Ramón Ochoa?"

She thought carefully for a moment.

"If you are ever interrogated by the military or the cops," Ramón had told him, "never answer too quickly. I've managed to get hold of their interrogation manuals. And they all operate on the premise that if the suspect answers too quickly or, conversely, takes too long to think about the question, the interrogator can proceed with the assumption the suspect is lying. These are of course primitive applications of theories in psychotherapy. So the answer, Nicolás, is to try and keep everything conversational."

"No, the name doesn't mean anything to me."

The studied way in which she replied confirmed his intuition: he was convinced that Tania had been one of Ramón's patients. The recognition excited him, especially as it came on top of the cynical quip about sex and power. He was convinced that she represented a connection to Ramón. But he decided not to push the subject with her at that moment.

Nicolás moved the conversation to art and music. When Nicolás challenged Tania to a quiz on Discepolo's tangos she was far more knowledgeable than Nicolás on the subject. And he had to laugh when she showed him how little he really knew.

"I don't understand, today in Argentina most women under thirty don't want to hear anything about the tango. And here you are, a militant of the tango."

"Well I have an advantage, you see. My doctorate is on music folklore as a part of Latin American culture."

And it was true, she had travelled all over Bolivia, Brazil, Peru, Chile, and had recorded hundreds of hours of indigenous folk music.

To Nicolás this seemed the most attractive and healthiest part of Tania. She dropped her mocking manner and inquisitorial tone of voice. Somewhere along in her voyage, Nicolás realized, she had been seriously damaged emotionally. But when she was in the world of her music folklore, all her positive and most attractive energies came to the surface.

Nicolás found himself fascinated by her stories and the adventures she had experienced in her travels. She was also rightfully proud that she had done so much travelling alone.

"Here, listen to this. A tape I made north of Oruro a few years ago. I can only play a few minutes because I have to save the batteries for recording."

From inside the brightly woven bag on the chair beside her she pulled out the battered old tape recorder he had seen earlier on the Avenida Santa Fe, when she had tried to tape Felipe, the street singer. Tania carefully inserted a cassette. The guttural sounds of Aymará, and the strange drums, whistles, and flutes of the Bolivian altiplano magically filled the space around their table. The card players in the rear of the bar applauded, and Máximo came over.

"The guys in the back would like to send over a cognac. Would that be acceptable?"

They accepted and in return Nicolás bought two bottles of wine for the card players.

To Nicolás it seemed that the gloomy all-pervading despondency that had first marked the ambience of this shabby bar had slowly dispersed and had been gradually replaced with a lighter, more mellow atmosphere. Máximo showed Tania an electrical outlet in the wall

95

into which she could plug her tape recorder. She put in another tape, and soft Brazilian sambas filled El Paraíso. Máximo gave them another cognac on the house. A few more people, artists and students, it would seem, filtered into the bar and brought with them a different energy. Some couples began to dance to Tania's music.

The tone between Nicolás and Tania had become quite easy. They both spontaneously rose at the same moment and danced for a few minutes to one of the sambas. Nicolás showed her a variation on some steps. Tania laughed delightedly and picked the moves up with a quick facility. They found that they danced smoothly together, without hesitation. They had made a connection that both tacitly recognized was loaded with sexuality. They felt themselves to be in that place of sensual promise that sometimes happens between men and women on a first encounter. To Nicolás it seemed that they deliberately toyed with the moment, took the luxury of time to explore in which direction these emotions could develop.

Tania was playful. "I like the way Brazilians think about sex."

Nicolás waited.

"They say every couple in love believe they have invented sex for the first time."

Nicolás slapped his forehead in mock surprise. "So that's why the Brazilians never had time to discover the microchip!"

But then as they danced the conversation moved back again to politics, in an irrational and sudden shift in gears that left Nicolás bewildered.

"In Brazil, as everywhere in Latin America, the 'country surrounds the city,'" she said. "This simple fact will support the theory of the revolution which one day will sweep the South American continent."

Nicolás chuckled. "Drop it Tania, that's the political jargon of the sixties."

When she talked like this, he wondered, was it a manifestation of her mental illness? Or was it just the alcohol?

But Tania hotly replied, "And Mao's slogans are still correct: Power still does come from the barrel of a gun!"

Nicolás became alarmed. "Careful," he warned, as they returned to their seats, and with a nod to the people around them in the bar he added, "Just in case you've forgotten, we live under military rule. People have been disappeared even when they have used much more humorous political language than yours."

Her face went into one of those rubbery childlike grimaces that expressed blank incomprehension whenever the realities of the present were introduced.

Nicolás wondered if he could ever get Tania to move from the general to the particular. Then he could get Tania to drop all this political rhetoric and reveal more about the other side of herself, and perhaps disclose the source for this obsession with the sixties. Strangely, the opportunity came when she tried to pry his political tendencies out of him.

"So tell me, Quintana. When you're not running around with live grenades in a shopping bag, what is your agenda? An intellectual," she tiresomely lectured, reaching for another one of those sixties' slogans, "especially if he is a bourgeois, should speak of strategy before all else."

"Who said that?"

"Régis Debray, *Revolution in the Revolution.*"

Nicolás laughed. "He's the wealthy French intellectual who got caught in Bolivia with Ché Guevara."

"There was a bit more to it than that."

"Listen, I know a guy in Buenos Aires who spent time in jail with Debray in Bolivia."

97

"Who?" Tania tried unsuccessfully to hide her eager interest.

"Tania, you know better than to ask questions like that. Anyway, he has nothing but shit to say about Debray."

"There were only five men who shared a Bolivian prison with Debray. The only Argentine was a revolutionary named Ciros Bustos."

Nicolás was impressed with her detailed knowledge. Why does she carry all this stuff around in her head? What is her karma? Am I, he asked himself, talking to another intelligence expert?

"Well I don't think it was Bustos."

"Debray is an honourable man. Even today, he does more than any Frenchman for Latin Americans forced to live in exile in France."

"Perhaps. But in jail in Bolivia he wouldn't even share with his cell mate the food baskets sent in daily by his rich family."

"Malicious gossip," shrugged Tania.

"You're weakening. I'm surprised you didn't say 'fascist propaganda.'"

"More and more you come across as a reactionary."

"Oh no! I have gone beyond politics, I practise controlled abandonment," Nicolás told her.

"What does that mean?"

"I have walked away, step-by-step, from all the expectations my illustrious family had of me."

"Which were?"

"A military career, the pursuit of politics, and money."

"What interests you now?"

"The occult."

Tania smiled tolerantly.

"The religious rites of the Candomblé are one thing; black magic is another opiate for the masses. I hope you haven't spent too much time on it?"

"Oh, the occult has its uses. For example," he continued, "I can probably tell, within a few days on either side, your birth date."

He could see that despite herself she was intrigued.

"Give me your hand."

"This is silly." She was flustered, but nevertheless gave Nicolás her hand.

Nicolás assumed a trance-like state.

"Scorpio," he said with great confidence.

Tania's lips parted in a surprised smile. Nicolás watched her through half-closed eyes.

"Mars and Pluto: the eighth house of death, transformation, and rebirth." Tania held his hand even more tightly. "The lower end, closer to Sagittarius. Perhaps on the cusp. So let's say between the eighteenth and twenty-fourth of November."

"The nineteenth," said Tania, in a whisper.

"That's only a few days away," observed Nicolás. "How old will you be?"

"Twenty-nine." Tania took her hand away. "How do you do that?"

"Simple. I've listened and talked with you for a few hours."

"So?"

"Almost anyone with a grasp of psychological archetypes and a knowledge of the zodiacal signs could do it."

"Then you didn't really need to hold my hand?"

"Oh yes, that's very important."

"Why?"

"Energy, and I wanted to touch you," he laughed.

Tania was amused. "Why do men always have to do this flirtatious nonsense?" she asked, but entered into the spirit of the occasion. "First, tell me your sign?"

"Cancer."

"I don't know enough about this, you have to tell me what that makes you."

"I don't believe you. But anyway, I'm supposed to be deeply intuitive."

"All right, you want to play? Take my hand again, close your eyes," she ordered.

"I'm not a psychic, and you've lost your sense of humour."

Tania insisted. "Keep your eyes closed. And empty your mind. This is your big chance, Quintana. What do you see?"

Two images came into his mind, in and out, very simple, but as in a slow-motion film sequence. First he saw the body of a drowned woman, fully clothed, with a *mochila* on her back, caught under a fallen tree by the side of a fast-flowing river in the mountains. In the second image the woman had been pulled out of the river and lay on the bank surrounded by a group of men, soldiers in uniform. Except for one man, small and dark. He wore civilian clothes but carried a pistol in a holster on his belt. And an automatic weapon on his shoulder. He wore a peaked cap. The man knelt beside the woman's body, pulled some documents from a plastic pouch on the woman's belt and began to examine them. To hide his deep sense of unease, Nicolás casually let go of Tania's hand and slowly sat up in his chair.

"What did you see?" she asked.

"Nothing. I told you, I'm not a psychic. I don't have visions."

He maintained a relaxed composure, but he inwardly felt considerably disconcerted. He had never experienced a moment quite like the one in which images had been thrust upon his mind. More unnerving still, he realized that he had blocked out the face of the drowned woman. Instinctively he knew he had done it because it was Tania he had recognized.

"What was I thinking about?"

"I have no idea, nothing unusual came into my head," he lied.

She seemed disappointed.

"Oh well. I had a passing thought about my namesake, Tania the Guerrilla. No matter."

Her admission pushed Nicolás into himself again. The amazing synchronous events of the evening unwound themselves again like a movie in his head.

He came out of this reverie to hear that Tania had returned to her obsessive theme, and was once again rattling on about the promise of the sixties. God! She had begun to get on his nerves.

"Cuba," Tania asserted, "is still the new political power centre for Latin America."

This woman is out of touch, thought Nicolás. Do I humour her or bring her up to date with some gentle reality maintenance?

"That may have been the promise way back. But today, Tania, ever since El Ché died in Bolivia, Fidel has been isolated, the Cuban economy is in ruins. He depends on the Soviets and tourists to stay alive. And it is only a matter of time before Fidel is abandoned by – say," Nicolás interrupted himself, "what is this fascination you have for Ché Guevara and for this woman you describe as your namesake. Or is Tania just a coincidence?"

Nicolás recalled Ramón's words: *"The great unresolved love story and political mystery of our time."*

Tania's face abruptly set in a fixed way.

"It's a common name in Argentina. I'm sure that's why she chose it as her *nom de guerre*. There must be a million of us. Besides, let's not even talk about El Ché," she said. "It's just a waste of time to remind Argentines of their greatest contemporary hero."

"Okay," said Nicolás equably, "then let's talk about

Tania. Listen, I was just a know-nothing kid in a military academy when all that was—"

"Ché was a phenomenon. For a brief moment in history he held the conscience of the world in his hands. This happens perhaps every two or three hundred years."

"I've never thought of it that way, but I suppose you're right."

"Well, what way did you think about it?"

"I always thought Ché Guevara got caught in a symbolic predicament. And that's not very healthy. Look what happened to Jesus Christ."

"This is a very cynical age."

Nicolás tried to reach back through the fog created by the brandy and the late hour.

"I'm trying to remember. I had a friend who knew a lot about it. Is Tania still alive? I mean if she is, she'd be in her forties?"

"Tania? Yes, that would be about right."

Tania had taken on that amused and distant look that comes from the power of information. She watched Nicolás flounder in front of her.

"Why do we know everything about Ché, and almost nothing about her?"

Tania was indifferent, "Oh, probably something to do with sexual politics."

"A political thriller," Ramón had said.

"She was East German, right?"

Tania was now tight-lipped, "Yes, but everyone forgets, she was born right here in Buenos Aires, and lived here until she was a teenager."

So Ramón had been wrong when he had said she spent just the first few years of her life here.

"I didn't know that. But in South America she was also called?"

"Laura."

"Yes, and she had another name, a German name."

Tania was not willing to help him any further.

"And where is she now?"

"Nobody knows. She was reported killed by the Bolivian Rangers. Shot down in an ambush at Vado del Yeso, the Masicurí Bajo, on August 31, 1967."

"Well, then she's dead, right?"

Tania raised her eyebrows slightly.

"What's the mystery? Is Tania dead or not?"

"Five days after she was reported shot, the military said they found a badly decomposed female body downriver. The military identified her as Tania from documents they found on the body and then quickly buried her."

"Where?"

"Not far from where they found her. In a bleak little cemetery in Valle Grande, itself a tiny impoverished village. I went there to pay homage. It's the usual collection of badly made concrete crypts. I discovered some mysterious person from the village regularly puts flowers on the tomb." Tania raised her eyebrows noncommittally. "Her name is on the grave."

Nicolás once again received the two images he had seen earlier: the drowned woman in the river, and then on the bank, surrounded by soldiers and the man in civilian clothes. But that woman had the face of the Tania who sat opposite him in El Paraíso.

"What are you suggesting," Nicolás asked. "That Tania is still alive?"

"No, I'm just telling you what happened. Besides, would you believe in a military report anywhere in Latin America?"

Nicolás suddenly had a difficult time concentrating. His head echoed with the buzz of white noise. He had the impression there were two radios in the bar tuned to the same station, and one was just off the frequency.

He looked around to see if there was indeed a radio playing, but it was Tania's recorder playing one of Gardel's tangos. Nicolás discovered with a shock that El Paraíso had filled up with a strange assortment of artistic types. When did that happen? Máximo held court behind the bar, surrounded by a group of laughing and joking men and women. The atmosphere was transformed.

Tania was solicitous, "Are you all right? Perhaps you should go to bed, you look quite tired."

"I'll walk you home."

"No, I'll stay here. I haven't paid my rent, so I have no place to sleep tonight. No really, it's all right. Máximo doesn't mind. I wash the floor before they open for the evening. That's my payment. And I can sleep on here" – she patted the long wooden table – "I've done it many times."

Why, Nicolás wondered, couldn't a woman with a doctorate in music folklore come up with enough money to pay the room rent? Just one more sign of the times, he reflected.

"Come to my hotel. I can get you a room for the night."

"All right, thank you."

He liked the way she was quite matter-of-fact and didn't put up conventional polite protestations. They called Máximo for the bill and Nicolás left a huge tip, which led to much handshaking and demands that Nicolás return soon. In farewell, Máximo reminded them, "Be careful in this barrio. *La noche es siempre peligrosa*. But then, you are with Tania," he laughed and added, "and she has more lives than a cat."

As they left El Paraíso through the front door, an old man brushed past them as he went into the bar. He turned and caught Nicolás by the jacket.

"Be careful, *hijo. Este es un país fascista.*"

Nicolás took a moment in the darkened doorway to realize it was Felipe, the street musician. The old man laughed at Nicolás' surprise, then greeted him warmly. Nicolás thought it odd to see the old man by himself on the streets at such a late hour. They shook hands and exchanged greetings as if they were old friends.

"You're alone. Don't you worry about being robbed on the street?" Nicolás asked Felipe.

"*No señor, éste es mi salvoconducto.*" He replied in his hoarse old man's voice, and proudly patted his battered old guitar. "They recognize me as an artist and have respect for me. Even the gangs of boys who control *las villas miserias* at nighttime don't try to rob me."

Nicolás wanted to go back into El Paraíso with Felipe, but Tania took his arm and pulled him along the street.

"I have to talk to that old guy. I just know that he has some information I need," Nicolás protested.

"You're such a romantic, Quintana. You can talk to Felipe another time. He's always here," Tania assured him.

They went in search of a taxi and soon found themselves on Avenida Don Pedro de Mendoza. Then Nicolás remembered. "My pacifist operation! You see, now you get a chance to observe truth in action. Karma becomes dharma. The action becomes the law. Come with me."

They followed the avenue into the industrial zone along the South Canal. The street was deserted. Nicolás had lost track of the time. Somewhere between three and four in the morning. He felt uneasy. He didn't know this barrio. He remembered Máximo's warning: *The night is always dangerous.* He had a premonition of danger, and a desire to fulfil his mission as quickly as possible.

A huge full moon hung low over the city. The Riachuelo was a lustrous sheen of black. All floating objects were profiled and thrown into stark relief, with intense deep black shadows. This is how Nicolás remembered night in the altiplano when he had travelled in Bolivia, bright and black.

He asked Tania in a whisper, "Does this remind you of Bolivia?"

"There's too much city," she whispered back, as if she too had absorbed his apprehension of immediate danger.

"The country surrounds the city," he reminded her. Then he suddenly recalled, "El Ché's compañera, Tania. There was something mysterious wasn't there? Didn't she betray him? Didn't she work for the Russians?"

"No," Tania whispered fiercely. "No. None of that's true." She said it with such pain in her voice that Nicolás was taken aback. If they had been talking normally, her outburst would, he realized, have been a cry of anguish. What offence was there in the question? Why had she taken the suggestion of Tania's betrayal so personally? Before he could ask, Tania had wrapped a hand around his mouth and pulled him into the dark shadows of a doorway. Nicolás, surprised, misunderstood her intentions and folded his arms around Tania in an embrace. She impatiently pushed his arms away and silently pointed to the navy launch in the Riachuelo below them.

For a moment Nicolás felt sheepish, but then his attention was caught by the action on the launch. Two crewmen carried out of the cabin, one by one, three inert bodies with hoods over their heads and placed them on the fantail of the boat; the heads of the bodies hung limply over the stern. Nicolás took Tania by the hand and, bent over double, they raced across the street. Crouched down behind a low wall they could look into the launch below, no more than thirty metres away from them, and drifting closer all the time. The three people who had been laid out facedown on the deck, a man and two women, moaned and made slight twitching movements. One of the enlisted men who had carried out the bodies stepped forward in what seemed like an involuntary act and decorously pulled down the dress of one of the women to cover her bared thighs.

Then a handsome marine lieutenant, his insignia flashing in the moonlight, stepped out of the cockpit. He took off his cap and gave it to one of the enlisted men to hold. In the moonlight, the lieutenant looked no more than twenty-five. He was strikingly handsome with clean chiselled features. His blond wavy hair shone like gold. He paused for a moment. Nicolás could have sworn it was a moment of prayer. Then the lieutenant took out a revolver from the holster on his waist belt and in rapid succession shot each of the three hooded bodies in the back of the head at point-blank range.

The lieutenant then indicated with a wave of his hand to the two sailors that they should dump the bodies into the canal. Nicolás had been aware of Tania rummaging around in her Bolivian bag. He was astounded to see her take out a grenade. He had forgotten that she still carried the grenades. He reached out to stop her, but she rolled away and pulled the pin. Fearlessly, she stood up to get a better position to throw.

"Throw it," he urged her. "Don't hold it any longer."

Tania lobbed the grenade into the moonlight. They heard it drop with a heavy thunk into the hull of the launch. A moment of silence. Then another thunk as she threw the second. The third went into the Riachuelo with a splash. Then unintelligible yells from a sailor on board the launch. A uniformed arm pointed in the moonlight toward them. The grenades must have been duds, Nicolás thought. The crew reached for their weapons to fire, when the grenades exploded and a split second later, a secondary explosion from the fuel tanks on the launch enveloped Tania and Nicolás in a wave of heat. The boat was a pyramid of fire. A sailor, his clothes in flames, leaped into the water. Ammunition on the boat exploded in heavy bursts.

Tania was beside herself. She jumped up and down, her fist pumped over her head into the night as she screamed in triumph. Nicolás was amazed at the transformation in her. He had to grab and hold her for a second to get her attention. Then he gripped her by the hand and dragged her away with him.

"Run!" He implored. "Run!"

They alternately ran and walked for several blocks through dark deserted streets lined with warehouses, machine shops, and run-down houses. Tania ran like a deer for short sprints, but would have to stop every two hundred metres to walk and catch her breath. Nicolás was furious with her.

"You had no right to involve me in that–"

"Why, is this too real for you, Señor Místico?" she panted, as she slumped against a wall for a moment.

"I just want to be asked first, so I can decide if I want to take the risks attached to your harebrained stunts." He yanked the woven bag off her shoulder.

"Excuse me, but I have to make sure you don't have any more little surprises in here."

"Remember, Quintana–you were the supplier."

"No! I betrayed myself. I let you manipulate me."

Tania watched without protest as Nicolás dumped the contents of the bag onto the sidewalk. He found only a few items: underwear, some makeup, a blonde wig, the old tape recorder, a score of cassettes, and an envelope file stuffed with typewritten pages and newspaper clippings.

"What's this?" he demanded.

108

"My research. Be careful with it."

He threw the wig at her, and scooped everything else back in the bag.

"Where are your *documentos*? Show me. I want to know who you really are."

"I don't have any. They were stolen." Her fingers shook with fatigue as she tried to pull the wig over her head.

"Why haven't you reapplied?"

"With a name like Tania Gutiérrez Bauer?" She finally had the blonde wig in place.

"You're completely mad," he told her. "Don't you know that under the state of siege it's automatic imprisonment if you're caught without identity documents. You're lucky if they don't shoot you on sight. At least buy some phoney ones."

"I don't have enough money to eat, let alone buy false documents."

Nicolás pulled out his wallet and took out a wad of notes, and held them up for her to see before he stuffed them into her bag.

"Buy some."

Nicolás hauled Tania to her feet, threw her bag over his shoulder, and began running with her down the street again. Nicolás prayed for a taxi. At any other time, Buenos Aires seemed to have more taxis than private cars, and now they couldn't even find one.

Finally they flagged a taxi on Dias Goncalves near the Sola railway station. They flung themselves into the back seat and Nicolás gave a fictitious address in Barrio Belgrano. Tania couldn't control her heavy panting. The *taxista* was suspicious and began to ask questions. He had heard shots and explosions and had seen the fire on the South Canal as he had crossed over the bridge onto Avenida Velez Sarsfield. He wanted to know what they had run away from.

"Drive!" yelled Nicolás. "The military have gone crazy back there. They're killing people without asking questions."

The *taxista* panicked, threw the car into gear and lurched off without any more queries. Nicolás and Tania didn't exchange a word about what had taken place in the South Canal. Nobody talked in taxis any more. It was too well known that many of the *taxistas* worked for the military or the police. Reports had circulated that some of the *taxistas* were actually used to kidnap citizens off the streets. But Nicolás saw that this driver made an effort not to look at them. If anybody questioned him later, he didn't want to know anything.

Nicolás watched the monochrome five-in-the-morning streets of Buenos Aires, grey and dark, slide by the taxi window. From the radio came an ancient recording of Gardel singing *"Mentiras."* Tania slowly recovered her breath and no longer panted so desperately for air.

Forced into silence, Nicolás reflected on the events of the night. And instantly the realization fell in on him. Of course, Tania! That Tania! The woman who had been with Ché Guevara in his impossible Bolivian adventure in 1967, her full *nom de guerre* had also been Tania Gutierrez Bauer. God! How slow he had been on picking up on that full name. Now much of Tania's strange behaviour – even her fixation on the language and politics of the sixties – became more understandable, even if he disagreed with it.

But the more Nicolás brooded over the implications of Tania's adopted identity, the deeper the chagrin he felt. This was another one of life's bad jokes. Nicolás felt let down. No matter which way you turned in this country, you got caught up in the web of somebody's fantasy life. And the fantasy he had been caught up in that night was another one of those stupid national obsessions, in which individuals abandoned their given names and assumed the names of their heroes and heroines. They then spent most of their lives in a dreamworld where they tried to emulate the life and work of their heroes.

Nicolás felt the joke was on him. He had spent the better part of the night with a madwoman who had assumed the name of one of the Third World's supposedly great and forgotten heroines. A woman who now spent her time roaming the streets of Buenos Aires, lost in a surrealist fantasy in which she lived out her assumed namesake's past. Well, he thought, better go carefully here. Now that he had blundered and had allowed himself to be entrapped in a stranger's delusion, he had better try to withdraw as gently and delicately as possible.

Nicolás startled both the *taxista* and Tania when he burst out with uncontrollable laughter. But yes, he thought, the joke was really on him. The taxi driver scowled in the mirror. Tania took his hand nervously in hers. Nicolás told the driver to stop. He pulled over without question, even though they were only halfway to the destination Nicolás had given him.

When they got out, Nicolás went around to the driver's window to pay, but the driver refused to take the money and raced off in a great burst of speed. Nicolás understood. If later they were caught and arrested as terrorists, the *taxista* didn't want to be implicated as an accomplice. They walked across the street and took another taxi to the Retiro station, and then changed taxis twice again before they got out two blocks from the Cruz del Sur. By that time it was already six-thirty. The streets had begun to fill up with people. In another thirty minutes the rush hour would begin.

Nicolás started to walk toward the hotel. He still had Tania's bag on his shoulder. Tania held back.

111

"Give me my bag, and I'll go."

Without a word Nicolás handed her the bag, and turned to go on his way. Tania held his arm.

"You are right, what I did was outrageous. I acted spontaneously. It was extreme. I committed you to an action that has serious consequences for you, and did so without your agreement."

Nicolás turned and regarded her for a long moment. She looked forlorn and frail and very much alone in the street. It was the first time that he had ever seen her appear vulnerable. Then the image of the triumphant guerrilla on the canal bank flooded into his mind. He relented.

"Whatever I might think, you were very brave."

"I don't feel very brave right now."

Nicolás took her arm. "C'mon. Let's get off the street and get some rest. You know that without documents it's impossible to get you a separate room." She nodded.

He sneaked Tania into the Cruz del Sur without problems – it was simple. At the front door they found the mentally retarded young man who cleaned the floors at the hotel mopping the lobby tiles. He recognized Nicolás and with a smile unlocked the front door for Nicolás and Tania.

Retired Suboficial Mayor Echeverría, now underemployed night clerk, had drunk himself into oblivion. He lay sprawled in the office chair, his mouth open, heaving deep snores. He didn't even stir when Nicolás leaned over him to take his room key off the row of hooks.

In the room, Tania insisted he have the first turn in the shower. When she came to the bed, Nicolás was almost asleep. She slipped into his arms.

Nicolás was surprised at how effortlessly they moved into emotional intimacy. Tania knew her body well. She had no inhibitions as she softly told Nicolás exactly what she needed, what pleased her. The effect was as if they had been lovers for years; they made love very gently, very naturally. Against his better judgement, Nicolás felt even more closely drawn to Tania. He was almost asleep when he asked her, "What was your name before you changed it to Tania?"

If Tania replied, he didn't hear. Because Nicolás fell asleep.

In mid-afternoon Nicolás and Tania woke up in each other's arms. The light, filtered into the room through the curtains and shutters across the windows, was dim and green. Here and there slender shafts of daylight entered through a broken shutter louvre or moth hole in the curtains. The thick and ancient walls of the Hotel Cruz del Sur kept the sounds of the city distant and muted. From the interior courtyard came the shrieks and whistles of the two tethered parrots and the cage of budgerigars.

"I feel as if I'm in the jungle," whispered Tania.

Wide awake and curious, Tania made Nicolás lie on his stomach while she carefully examined Nicolás' naked body. She ran her fingers gently over his skin, delicately tracing and exploring the huge muscles of his back, where they curved and overlapped into the base of his spine. With the palms of her hands Tania followed the flow of sculptured flesh from the buttocks and into the powerful thighs.

"*Qué bello cuerpo*," she murmured.

"This is only flesh," smiled Nicolás.

Silently, Tania gently tugged on Nicolás' shoulder to indicate he should turn over on his back. She crouched on her knees and ran her hands in light circular stroking movements from his feet, up over his thighs, pausing to softly caress his groin, then follow with the tips of her fingers the clearly defined muscles of his stomach and chest.

"Only flesh," she echoed.

Tania threw off the loose shirt she wore, and naked sat astride his hips. Her body was so slender and supple he could hardly feel the weight of her on top of him.

"Really, Nicolás?" Tania smiled dreamily down at him. "Coincidentally that's what I used to tell my lovers, too. This is only flesh." And she reached behind her with her right hand and began to stroke his cock lightly. "But this"–she turned in her left hand the small white cloth bag that hung from a slender leather cord around his neck–"this, Nicolás, if I'm not mistaken, is not of the flesh but of the spirit."

"You know what it is?"

"Yes, Nicolás. And I am impressed. That Candomblé sect in Brazil must have thought highly of you to have given you a *kpoli*. Did the *babalorixá* write in the dust the name of the god that possessed you?"

Nicolás nodded.

"Then he put the dust with some sacred leaves in this bag and gave it to you as a personal *odu*, yes?"

Tania seemed suffused with sexual tension. Her words came tightly from her chest.

"What did he tell you when he gave it to you?"

"He said that it would assist me in divining the mysteries of my dream life."

She had let go of the *kpoli* and lightly balanced herself with her left hand on his chest. The index finger and thumb of her right hand expertly circled his scrotum at the base of his cock, and with deft little downward tugs urged even more blood into his penis.

"I'm jealous, Nicolás. So tell me, what was the name of the god who spoke through you and whose name was written in the dust." Tania slowly and rhythmically shifted her hips so that with every tug the head of his cock beat rhythmically against the lips to the entrance of her own body.

Nicolás laughed gently, "You're cruel. You know as much as I do about all this. Most of all, you know I can't reveal the name of the *orixá*."

"Perhaps it was Ogun, Nicolás, the god of iron and war, because what I have in my hand here feels like iron."

"No, it wasn't Ogun, and –" But Nicolás didn't have a chance to finish his sentence, as Tania adroitly took him inside her. Tania stayed on top of Nicolás for a long time. He felt detached, unlike the first time they had made love, when it had seemed intimate and natural. This second time it was as if this act of passion was happening in another and separate space, where in his mind's eye he was able to watch himself as Tania took her pleasure, repeatedly. Tania must have sensed the distance. She gently disengaged herself from his body.

"All right, my beautiful friend," she said. "I'm going to give you something I've never given any other man."

In a few swift movements she took a cassette out of her bag and placed it in Nicolás' tape deck.

"Nicolás," she whispered, before turning on the tape, "this is a present I bring especially for you, all the way from Brazil's Río Grande do Sul. Perhaps you can remember, my sweet friend?"

The moment Nicolás heard the familiar drumming, the beat sent shivers across the top of his scalp. Then, still naked, Tania began to dance the batuque for Nicolás. Her flesh surrendered completely to the inner rhythms of the music. This was not the way she had danced the intricate stylized steps of the Brazilian samba in El Paraíso. The erotic and sensual movements of her hips in the batuque were completely spontaneous. The forms Tania's body moved through as she turned and twisted in and out of the shafts of sunlight that pierced the dim room took on an ancient beauty. This, thought Nicolás, was the way women danced at the beginning of time. Her eyes locked on Nicolás. Her hands lifted her hair off the back of her neck, her fingers interlaced and clasped together across the back of her head. Bare feet flat on the floor, knees bent, thighs apart, and her hips lowered, Tania shuffled with carnal thrusts to the beat of the drums, across the floor to entice Nicolás into the primal dance. They moved together, flesh against flesh, through the simple lustful movements of the batuque. The drumming entered their bodies and their souls. They never lost contact, even when Tania had to reach over to the machine and replay the tape. They became lost in each other's energy and motion. They danced until their skin was wet with sweat and glided and slipped across the planes of each other's flesh. They danced until the sexual tension became unbearable. They fell onto the bed and into another long hedonistic dance of lovemaking that ended only when they finally collapsed in each other's arms.

Long minutes of immobility passed. Tania finally struggled to sit up on the bed. She placed pillows behind her back so that she could lean more comfortably against the wall. She reached over and turned down the volume of the drum tape to a bare murmur. Then, from behind, she took Nicolás' languorous body tenderly into her arms. She rested the back of his head against her shoulder. She hooked a leg over his thigh and with her hands gently stroked the front of his body, his chest, his face, and hair.

At first it seemed that Nicolás had fallen into a heavy sleep, but when he opened his eyes to speak Tania could see that Nicolás was in a deep trance. He began to speak in an eerily calm voice.

"This is strange, Tania. I am walking with you through the streets. Except that I'm not really there."

Tania started in astonishment. For a moment her body tightened in fright, then she made a visible effort to relax and enter this new state with Nicolás.

"If you are not there, then who is there with me?" Tania asked.

"Jorge is there. You are walking through the streets with him."

Tania stiffened, then made another obvious effort to calm herself. "Anybody else?" she asked.

"No. Just you and Jorge. I think you are afraid of him. Just a little."

Tania grimaced at the memory Nicolás had given back to her. But she continued to hold his naked body close to her. Still seated behind him, Tania wrapped her arms around his chest, and laid her head against the side of his neck so that she could whisper into his ear.

"I'm going to think about that time, and I want you to tell me what you see in your head," she told him softly.

"Where are we?" Tania wanted to know.

"I'm not sure," replied Nicolás. "It's not Buenos Aires. For some reason you find it very hard to breathe. Ah, now I know. A group of campesinos pass us in the street. They speak Quechua. This is La Paz and you are uncomfortable with the altitude."

"Why am I in La Paz?"

"To kill the sergeant," Nicolás answered with difficulty.

There was a long silence as if Nicolás had lost contact. But then when he spoke again it was with an easier flow of words that triggered strange internal memories and images that had never been his and could only be Tania's.

"You are in a restaurant. It is dirty, squalid. The name is La Góndola. The worst kind of Latin American rock music bangs on your ears."

118

"Why am I in this restaurant?"

"You are waiting. This is the afternoon of the second day that your group has hung around."

"What are we waiting for?"

"A car, and a man called Ruiz."

"Why?"

"Ruiz will drive your group to Los Altos."

"How many are there in this group?"

"Besides yourself, two men: Jorge and, uh, a Peruvian called Puentes."

"What kind of mood am I in?"

"You are angry and bored. You feel everything is going wrong on this operation."

"What do I want?"

"You want to go back to La Panama, the restaurant where you waited the whole day before."

Tania would never forget La Panama, a clean and pleasant bar. The owner was an expatriate Argentine, a kind man from Ushuaia. He had a large collection of tapes and an excellent sound system. She had spent the afternoon listening to soft Argentine zambas and boleros.

"Who am I talking to? Jorge?"

"No. Jorge is still there. But you are arguing with Puentes. He won't let the group go back to La Panama to hang around for another day. He says it's too dangerous."

Tania remembered: La Gordita, she had countered, was risky because it attracted all the petty criminals. Even though it was three days after Carnival, four or five sodden drunks were stumbling around the room, cadging drinks.

Nicolás spoke, dreamily but clearly, "You recognize one of them as the police detective who put the squeeze on you a week ago when you and Jorge left the hotel in La Paz."

"What kind of squeeze did he put on us?" Tania asked.

Nicolás was silent for several moments. "I don't understand that part of it."

"What did this guy look like?" asked Tania, fascinated by the detail and texture offered up by Nicolás in his trance.

"Squat, heavy. That's all I can see."

"What happens when I see the detective again in La Gordita?"

"For the moment, nothing. But you are afraid the cop will recognize you and put the bite on you again. More dangerous, you think the cop will perhaps remember your group together in this place. You worry that it might jeopardize future operations. You begin to badger Puentes again to find another driver to take the group to Los Altos. But Puentes is obstinate."

"What does Puentes say to me?"

"I don't know."

"Wait. I'll try to remember and see if you can get it, too."

Tania remembered Puentes saying, "It has to be Ruiz. He is the only one who knows the sergeant."

And that's all he would say. Puentes was from Cuzco and uncommunicative. He had been in the Cochabamba for a long time as a guerrilla. Tania thought that he probably picked up his habit of morose silence in the jungle. Puentes sat brooding in the corner, hunched over in a rickety wooden chair, staring through everything and everybody, the ever-present unlit black cigarillo in the corner of his thin mouth.

"No, I don't get anything," said Nicolás.

Jorge was on her side in the argument. At Puentes' response he had sucked disgustedly through his teeth, and cursed long and eloquently under his breath in the best Cuban slang. Jorge, Tania had discovered, had the interesting ability to suddenly generate the most frightening kind of tension. It was a quality that made Tania afraid of him, and at the same time aroused her sexually in a way that alarmed her.

Nicolás suddenly spoke again. "Jorge is your lover and Puentes is annoyed. For this reason they don't get along very well, but they respect each other's abilities."

"Why? Is Puentes jealous?"

"No. It's because he and Puentes have often worked together and . . . I don't know all of this part. It feels confusing."

"What about the cop, is he still there?"

"Oh yes. You warn them about the cop. Jorge takes one look at him and sends over a bottle of pulque. The detective –"

"You still don't get his name?"

"No."

Tania remembered the cop, Mendoza was his name. He was already so drunk he couldn't even get off his chair to come over to thank them, but waved vaguely in the direction of their table. In ten minutes he had downed half the bottle and then quietly passed out, face flat on the table, arms hanging down.

The bartender came out from behind the bar, picked the detective out of the chair, and threw him out into the street.

"That guy used to be a cop," the bartender explained. "But he got fired last week. Now I don't have to pay him off any more."

"Okay, okay." Tania blew gently in Nicolás' ear. "Tell me," she whispered, "what happens when Ruiz finally shows up at La Gordita?"

"He offers no explanations for his two-day delay, and you are too exhausted to complain. The three of you, Puentes, Jorge, and yourself, climb into Ruiz's taxi. No one speaks."

Tania remembered: When they finally left La Paz it was almost dark. Ruiz drove south through sudden showers toward Calicoto. Fat heavy raindrops splattered against the windshield. When it wasn't raining, the cold bitter wind off the altiplano covered the old Buick in dust. After half an hour the dust hung like an invisible veil in front of her face. She could taste it every time she licked her dry lips with her tongue.

Nicolás interrupted her memories. "You can't understand what had possessed Guevara to start a Latin American revolution in this godforsaken place."

Tania was startled. "I don't remember thinking that at the time," she murmured. "Go on."

"There's nothing more."

No, there's lots more, thought Tania with a sigh of relief that it wasn't all getting through to Nicolás.

She remembered that a few kilometres outside of La Paz the highway deteriorated. The suspension shocks in the Buick were gone, and the springs in the back seat had collapsed in unpredictable places. She could feel every rut in the road, but she had still managed to fall into an uneasy sleep.

"You dreamed of German winters and tobogganing on the slopes around Eisenhuttenstadt."

"No. That's wrong. I was never on toboggans," Tania said emphatically. "But I do remember that I had the dream. Please, go on."

"You wake up. The car has stopped. Outside, total blackness. You feel disoriented, feverish. You have trouble remembering where you are. The air inside the Buick is stale. In the front seat Puentes argues with Ruiz about money. Puentes insists on the original agreement: a third now, a third after the group has been led to the sergeant, and the final payment when they are back in La Paz.

"Jorge sees you are awake. In German, Jorge mutters to you: 'The asshole thinks we're so dumb that he can take us outside, lose us in the dark, then fuck off back to La Paz without us.' "

Tania remembered: Ruiz heard Jorge talking to her. The driver turned around to appeal to them in the back seat. But he fell silent in mid-sentence when, in the dim interior light of the car, his eyes fell on Jorge who had taken his nine millimetre pistol out of his shoulder bag and was calmly loading the magazine clip. Ruiz understood and shrugged.

"All right. You want to meet the madman who shot Ché Guevara," he paused and smiled viciously. "Then you have to walk for one hour. Follow me."

Ruiz opened the door and without hesitation plunged into the blackness. They all quickly scrambled out of the car after him. Puentes grabbed the driver by the arm and expertly slipped a pre-knotted cord around his wrist. The other end was already attached to his own wrist. Ruiz laughed, but there was fear in his voice.

"Relax, guys. Everything is going to be all right. I just wanted to see if you were serious."

While Puentes held a flashlight on the driver, Jorge quickly searched him. He found a huge knife tucked in the man's boot.

"Try anything," Puentes warned him, "and we'll kill you. All of us are armed."

Tania's early feeling of disorientation accelerated into panic. For a reason that she couldn't understand, she had no night vision. Lack of Vitamin A? She blamed it on the poor Bolivian diet. She had been in this impoverished country too long, Tania told herself. She tripped and fell on her knees as she stumbled along the path behind the others.

Nicolás softly picked up the thread of her story again: "Jorge tells you to hold on to the back of his poncho. Gratefully, you hang on. You go along like this, then it begins to rain, very heavily. After a long time your eyes adjust somewhat to the dark."

Nicolás stirred uneasily in Tania's arms.

"Los Altos," Tania murmured. "Don't stop now."

When Nicolás moved restlessly, as if to break away from her, she held him tightly in her arms, her back against the wall. Tania's fascination with this bizarre, unfolding communication was tinged now with fear and apprehension.

But Nicolás couldn't continue, even when Tania urged him on again.

Los Altos! Tania remembered a large sprawling hacienda. Oil lamps glowed softly in some of the windows. The outer walls of the hacienda were surrounded by a clutter of lean-to shacks, a mini barrio of alleys and instant houses had sprung up around the hacienda.

"The out-patients department for the psychiatric hospital," Ruiz explained.

The three followed Ruiz through the slimy alleys between the shacks. He stopped outside a particularly tumbledown structure. Suddenly, from out of the darkness, a pack of snarling mongrels leaped upon them. Tania kicked hard with her boots. Puentes lashed about with the heavy walking stick he always carried. The dogs yelped in pain, and whining, retreated.

"They smell woman," chuckled Ruiz.

Tania took her machine pistol from out of her shoulder bag.

"Ruiz," she had told him in a curt whisper. "You're an asshole. Don't provoke me any further. Nobody here shares your sense of humour."

"Let's get on with it," whispered Jorge.

"Frightened voices are calling to you from inside the shacks," whispered Nicolás.

Ruiz yelled. "It's only me, the driver for El Doctor Hernandez."

In a low voice Ruiz called out a few words in Quechua and pushed aside a primitive door made of corrugated iron. Behind it hung a sack curtain. Ruiz tried to slip the cord from his wrist and dodge away, but Jorge grabbed him and pushed him ahead through the opening. Puentes produced the flashlight. The beam of light fell on the frightened face of a girl of about seventeen. She peered out from under mosquito netting. Ruiz spoke to her again in Quechua, and the girl relaxed a little but remained wary.

"Tell her we're friends and we're here to talk with the sergeant," commanded Puentes.

"I already did and–" Ruiz began, but was interrupted by the girl replying in Spanish, "He's sick. He can't talk tonight."

Tania had the impression that the girl had been through something like this quite a few times. Puentes' flashlight probed the mean little room. A few clothes hung from nails in the wall. A table nailed together out of scrap pieces of wood stood on the dirt floor. A couple of wooden crates served as chairs. Everybody jumped at a sudden rustling movement under the bed. The girl calmly reached down, pulled out a cardboard carton, lifted out a three- or four-month-old baby, and put the child to her breast.

All this time the large shape on the bed beside the girl had remained motionless under the blankets. Puentes quickly stepped forward and pulled back the covers. The face of the executioner of Ché Guevara stared at Tania. It was a face made ugly with fear. The terrified eyes were wide open. They all recognized immediately that the sergeant was not just hiding out, but was a man who had passed a long time ago into the world of the mentally ill. Jorge cursed angrily.

"How can we go through with this?" he asked.

"Be careful" said Ruiz. "He understands that you have come to kill him."

"Compañera Tania has her orders," said Puentes.

125

Tania shifted her position on the bed. She laid Nicolás down on his side, still in close contact, but supported herself on an elbow so that she could watch his face.

Nicolás spoke. "Before you leave, you ask the girl if it is his child. She shakes her head. You give her a roll of money. She snatches it from you and hides it inside her clothing. Then you leave her in the shack with her baby. Outside it is raining heavily. You follow the others as they hold the sergeant by the arms. You all come to a drainage ditch. The sergeant shakes and cries unintelligibly. Jorge begins to argue with you and Puentes. You ready your machine pistol and tell—"

Tania could not bear to hear any more. She wrapped her hand around Nicolás' mouth. Blew hard in his ears. Pulled away from contact with his flesh. When she spoke her voice had a rapid sharp edge.

"Nicolás! No more now. Time to stop. You must wake up."

Nicolás came drowsily to the surface of consciousness, barely sensible.

"You were dreaming."

"I was?"

"Yes, talking in your sleep. Can't you remember?"

"No, nothing.

"Not a word?"

"Absolutely nothing."

Tania sat on the edge of the bed, emotionally drained. Nicolás quickly fell back into a deep sleep. But this time he remained silent.

Nicolás and Tania, hand in hand, clattered cheerfully down the ancient twisting marble staircase of the Hotel Cruz del Sur to the tiny lobby, where a grim-faced Guido stood calculating the accounts behind the ornate turn-of-the-century cashier's booth, a grotesque glass and polished-brass affair that, according to the hotel owner, had been imported directly from a Paris brothel in the 1920s. The sight of Guido reminded Nicolás that they had slept all the day. Through the glass lobby doors he could see that it was already dark on the street.

Tania brushed her lips against Nicolás' neck and whispered, "I'll wait for you outside on the sidewalk, but be quick, I'm starving," and went ahead through the narrow glass doors, leaving Nicolás to deal with the hostile Guido.

"This is the rent for the woman who is staying with me for a few days."

Nicolás counted out a pile of bank notes on the counter in front of Guido. He watched, towering above the flimsy glass partition of the cage, as the night clerk wordlessly took the pile of pesos and methodically recounted the money. Nicolás had purposefully given twice the normal rate. Guido created two piles. This certainly made the transaction a lot more straightforward, thought Nicolás, believing the night clerk would pocket his share immediately, but the former suboficial hesitated.

"This is not possible, Señor Quintana. The policy of the Cruz del Sur does not allow for prostitutes in the rooms."

"Guido, don't try to goad me into some act we will both regret. My friend is a serious person, going through a difficult time –"

"Then if she has become your companion," Guido sneered, "she will have to register and show her personal identity documents as the law demands."

"Guido, I know that you are angry, because when you confessed to me why you were thrown out of the army I could not give you whatever you were looking for –"

"I want nothing from you."

Now that's not true, thought Nicolás. But instead, he said, "No. You still haven't heard me. I have nothing to give you, except money. And about *that* you have to be practical."

Nicolás impassively added more bank notes to the two stacks of pesos already on the counter. He remembered Ramón's words: *We do not know love until we participate in the suffering of others.* Ah, Ramón. I cannot enter into anything with this man, except to acknowledge his anguish. Ramón, I am not bribing this man to silence his pain, but as an insurance premium to stave off for a little longer Tania's inevitable and certainly violent death.

Guido fixed his eyes on some point beyond Nicolás' shoulder. His voice was embittered with calculated disappointment. "I had always thought of you as an officer and a gentleman, Señor Quintana."

"Only the Americans still pretend to believe in that nonsense," replied Nicolás.

Nicolás could see that Guido's heavy burden of guilt had paralysed his ability to think or act. But Nicolás also knew that because of his desperate financial straits, Guido in the end would not refuse the money that he had offered him.

Guido swept up the pile with the haughty air of a general who had been called upon to clean out a toilet.

"Do you know, Señor Quintana, what is the worst humiliation one suffers in poverty?"

"Yes, I think it's quite simple, Guido – lack of money."

"No señor. My daily bread is lack of respect."

"Don't be theatrical, Guido. And don't be so stupid as to think of betraying me. It would do you no good to kill the goose who now lays the golden pesos."

Externally calm, inside Nicolás was in a sudden rage. For the safety of those around us we now have to negotiate with self-confessed torturers.

"I cannot give you any assurances, you understand," warned Guido. "If the military decide to conduct a search, and they find this woman unregistered and without full personal documents, then I will have to deny all knowledge of her, and they will treat her like a prostitute."

"These days," responded Nicolás, "that might not be so bad."

Nicolás looked around the dilapidated little lobby, with its faded velvet curtains, its rococo décor, worn marble staircase, and moth-eaten carpet. This is no stage on which to be intimidated and surrender to the likes of Guido, he thought. And mindful that it was not a moment too soon for Guido to start paying compensation for his past crimes, he decided not to let him off the hook.

"I have paid you this money on one condition, Guido: it will be your responsibility to give us adequate warning."

"I couldn't do that," said Guido, shocked. "Lie to the military authorities."

"Guido, you and I know the army. No matter what you do from now on, they will never take you back. You have been court-martialled, with a dishonourable discharge. To the military mind this means you have become a non-person. Your years of service mean nothing. Your existence only means trouble. So they have written your name down in a book, sealed it, and tossed it away into a military filing cabinet, never to be reopened in your lifetime. So don't think for one minute that turning my friend in to the authorities will open those closed doors for you."

Guido was devastated by Nicolás' assertion. As if he had never considered this obvious fact before. "I've dreamed and lived for the day when I will be reinstated," he muttered desperately.

Time, Nicolás thought, to deal with Guido for what he was, a not-too-bright noncommissioned officer.

"No, Guido. This is a reality maintenance briefing for you. Under the guise of the Program of National Reconstruction, you and your commanding officers have committed some of the most horrific human rights violations. You think nobody has noticed. But we know. A lot of people pretend they don't know, but the truth is that really everybody knows. Outside, in the larger world, what has been done here in Argentina has already been called barbaric and worthy of Hitler's worst butchers. And if this country is ever to survive, there will first have to be a day of reckoning when all of you sadistic bastards must stand trial. And you will be one of the first, Guido. You want to know why? Because the army has abandoned you."

"To stand trial in a military court?" Guido was dazed at the thought.

"No doubt about it," Nicolás bulldozed ahead, "and only then will Argentina be able to evolve with some basic moral concepts. In the meantime, Suboficial Mayor, try to behave decently and make amends in some small way for the terrible damage you have done."

Incredibly, Guido stepped back, clicked his heels together and saluted. More evidence, Nicolás thought, of Guido's psychological state. With a curt nod he accepted Guido's conditioned response to class and authority. Before he turned to leave, Nicolás took one last look into Guido's haunted eyes and glimpsed a shocking image – the huge long-tailed black rats of the Buenos Aires docks, crawling among a pile of dead and mutilated bodies in a rain-drenched park. Nicolás thought he recognized the location, somewhere near the Boulevard de Los Italianos near the harbour.

Deeply disturbed, Nicolás left the lobby of the Cruz del Sur for the street to find Tania had watched his encounter with Guido through the glass doors. She took his arm, and they began to thread their way along the crowded sidewalks, a pedestrian battleground where no one respected anybody's privacy or right of way. It must be only in Buenos Aires, Nicolás suspected, that pedestrians took on the behaviour of colonies of ants travelling across the urban wasteland. Eleven million people! That's too many in one place, Nicolás thought. Perhaps that's part of the problem. They say that even rats start to kill each other if they are overcrowded. Tania finally interrupted his silent brooding:

"That was bizarre, Nicolás. I didn't hear a word, but I can see that hotel clerk hates you. He will betray us."

"No, I don't think so. At least not yet. In the psychological struggle that exists between us, I, at this moment, hold his conscience."

Tania let go of his arm. Not, Nicolás felt, because she wanted more freedom of movement but because she didn't want to touch him. There was something fearful in her withdrawal. Ever since he had woken up and found her dressed and ready to go out, he had sensed that she had wanted some distance between them. Why? What had happened between them, the lovemaking, the batuque, had been profoundly intimate. Strange, he had thought, after the unique events they had experienced in such a short time together, that

131

Tania should erect this barrier. What was her point, he asked himself, in creating these emotional stews of alternating resistance and vulnerability? He sensed that she was one of those people who craved intimacy, worked hard to create the possibility, then fled in terror from its realization. Tania did not have to worry. He had certainly not developed overnight the intention or need to anchor her life. Not as long as the possibility that Lara was still alive existed. The memory of Lara connected a loop of memories in his brain that instantly led Nicolás to the location of the nightmarish image he had seen a few minutes earlier in Guido's eyes. The connection was so powerful Nicolás could not doubt it.

"Wait here for me," he hastily told Tania, and without explanation he abandoned her beside a telephone kiosk. He raced back to the Cruz del Sur. Guido, the surprised stork trapped in his glass cage, looked up nervously from his paperwork as Nicolás burst through the front doors of the lobby. Nicolás moved around the counter to contain Guido in his glass box.

"The plaza where you said you dumped the body of the pregnant woman and her companion?"

Guido nodded in apprehension.

"You lied about one thing. It wasn't a plaza."

Guido looked panicked and spluttered incomprehensibly.

"I could have been misinformed."

Nicolás was relentless, absolutely certain of his information.

"No! You were there."

"I'm not sure . . . lots of things happened—"

"You left their bodies along with five or six corpses down by the docks in a small park?"

"Who told you this?" Guido was pale, in shock.

"Near the School of Fine Arts. Where Calabria meets Brasil."

Guido's hands trembled as he put away the bills and receipt books. They shook uncontrollably as he locked up the cash drawer. He dropped the keys on the floor, then regained them with difficulty. By using both hands wrapped around the key, he finally managed to unlock a small cabinet under the counter. He took out a half-full bottle of Tres Plumas brandy and shakily poured himself a drink into a china cup. Nicolás interrupted Guido's intention; he reached out and covered the cup with one hand and held the bottle of brandy in the other. Guido could not bring himself to look at Nicolás.

"I'm right, aren't I?" asked Nicolás very softly. "This is why your children won't talk to you any more? Why your wife has left you?"

Nicolás waited a long moment. "Yes. Everything you've said is true," mumbled Guido finally, his eyes fixed on the cup and the bottle in Nicolás' hands. Nicolás slowly let go of both and withdrew. When he looked back from the door Guido had sunk into his seat and was staring blankly at the bottle of cheap brandy and the still untouched cup.

As he threaded his way again through the crowds on the street, Nicolás felt deeply disturbed by this new ability that was being imposed on him. At the same time he was thankful, because now he was almost certain that the dead woman he had seen in the terrifying image transmitted to him by Guido was not Lara.

Nicolás found Tania had moved halfway down the block and was in a ferocious argument with the impatient owner of a newspaper kiosk. He had apparently suggested she buy the Paris fashion magazine instead of trying to read it at his kiosk. She greeted Nicolás calmly and without questions about his brief absence, a reaction that he appreciated, given his own inner turmoil. Nicolás remembered that Tania had no money, so he absentmindedly paid for the magazine, even though she protested in a slightly embarrassed way that she didn't really need it. But the wistful expression on her face, as she flipped through the pages of the fashion magazine while they strolled along the street, told a different story and unconsciously revealed a latent part of herself. Nicolás had to smile at the contradiction of Tania the revolutionary in her plain cotton dress, and the woman who harboured the fantasy of being strikingly modish. He was about to tease her, ask her if she thought she was entering another stage of the revolutionary conflict, but kept silent when he perceived how vulnerable she really was. She interrupted his thoughts.

"I love to dress up, ever since I was a kid. Fancy dress parties are what I lived for. I'm sure it's something I share with my namesake. I read somewhere that when she was still Tamara, she always dressed up in the East German uniforms, the Young Pioneers, Communist Youth. And then later when Ché invited her to Cuba, it was more of the same: militia uniforms –"

Nicolás interrupted her, "Perhaps we should get you some better camouflage."

They found a store that had stayed open late. Tania picked out some simple clothes: jeans, a cotton skirt, two blouses. Still, Nicolás had to talk her out of buying the cheapest quality clothes.

"You can afford to dress eccentrically like me," he whispered in her ear, "only if you have my I.D. and family name."

Then Nicolás waited inside a grubby little photo studio near the busy downtown intersection of Maipú and Lavalle while Tania had some pictures taken for new *documentos*. Nicolás bribed the photographer not to record the negative and file photographs as demanded by the junta's regulations.

They ate in what used to be one of Nicolás' favourite haunts, El Bar Windsor, behind the Teatro Colón. The bar was a traditional establishment of dark and polished wood. The waiters knew Nicolás from his old days and treated him warmly but with deference. Nobody was presumptuous enough to ask why he had been absent for so many months. His clothes were not such a problem because he had decided to wear a good white cotton shirt and jeans. But Tania's new jeans and blouse, and the arresting sight that she offered as she once again ate like a famished wolf, eyes half-closed and humming to herself, drew stares from the decidedly upper-class clientele, some of whom were in evening gowns and tuxedos. Tania became aware of the stares and showed her discomfort.

"Why did we come to eat here Nicolás?" she asked.

"There's safety among the upper classes. They know me here. And you have no documents. Besides, there's usually a man here who would be able to take care of the problem for you. Ah, there he is."

Nicolás raised his wineglass and signalled to a man in a suit standing by himself at the bar. When The Suit came over to their table, Nicolás smiled and graciously asked him to sit down.

"I don't want to know any names," he said.

"How is my father?" Nicolás asked, noticing Tania's hostile reaction.

"The same as ever. He has energy to burn. I know that he misses you. Nicolás, my boy, life is too hard and too short to hold grudges against your own family."

Nicolás smiled. He remembered his father: "If you have the usual filial concern of turning out like me, Nicolás, don't waste your energy on rebellion. We're as different as any father and son could possibly be."

He discreetly passed the photos of Tania to the stranger. The Suit, who had ignored Tania until now, took a quick look at the photos, then studied Tania for a moment without speaking to her.

"Occupation?" he finally asked.

Tania refused to reply.

The Suit shrugged, "I need some basic information to fit the documents."

"Education?"

Nicolás answered, "A doctorate in the liberal arts."

The Suit grunted unpleasantly. "Lots of those documents around these days in search of a living identity. It won't be a problem." He nodded to Nicolás. "Tomorrow then. Old Favourites at 10:00 P.M. The young lady or you can meet me there."

Nicolás passed the man a cheque.

"Oh no," said The Suit, as he saw the folded cheque in Nicolás' hand, "cash only."

Nicolás reassured him, "It's in U.S. notes, made out in cash and drawn on a U.S. account."

"In that case, I'll accept, happily. But please, tomorrow, have the other half in U.S. notes?"

Nicolás nodded in agreement. Before the man slipped away, he said, "You should really make peace with your father. Remember, we're all dead a long time."

Nicolás nodded again. One more Argentine cliché about life and the family, he thought, and I might just drop dead from boredom myself.

"Why are you doing business with a policeman?" Tania wanted to know, as she silently accepted the wad of U.S. notes Nicolás handed her.

"This is the second payment. Why, you know him?"

"Of course not. But after a while you can just smell them. C'mon, Nicolás."

"Do you object on principle?"

"No. My only concerns are about my security."

This is a self-centred woman, thought Nicolás.

"We have to deal with him for two reasons: the military have either imprisoned or employed all the best professional forgers; secondly, he has access to computerized files. So if he supplies you with a new identity, he'll make sure there are no compromising problems left in the police records."

"Such as?"

"When he gives you a new identity he will destroy the source files. If you are checked, the files won't show that the person whose name you have been given in your new I.D. is in prison, or was killed last September while carrying out a bank holdup for the treasury department of the Montoneros, or that your new name is not on a registry of suspects in the Army of the Poor.

"I still want to know if you have an alternative?"

"Not really, this is as secure a way to obtain documents as it is possible under the circumstances."

"Why?"

"The policeman owes me. Last year his own son had problems with the military. I hid the boy on a friend's ranch in the country until arrangements could be made to get him out of the country. Then I drove him to the airport and put him on the plane, while his father pretended to be hunting him down in another city."

"I just get nervous when we have to collaborate with the police, even the renegades."

"If you have a better idea, I'm listening."

"Oh, it's so difficult to know any more," Tania observed archly, "who is on what side. There! Did I sound enough like one of your Barrio Norte matrons?"

"Yes, it's a strange country we live in, isn't it?"

"Yes, and you're a strange man, Nicolás."

Nicolás remembered Ramón saying: "As a psychiatrist, Nicolás, I can put the nation, the whole of Latin America on the couch. I call it *golpe* syndrome. Our history is tied to unending cycles of military dictatorships. After each coup the people resign themselves to another period of rigid military oppression. But a mass surrender requires a multitude of personal surrenders.

137

Each person has to suppress his individual emotions: guilt, anger, hope. The result? Mass hypocrisy as a means for psychological survival. But underneath this passivity all the preconditions for rebellion are fermenting – frustration, anxiety, homicidal hatred – held in check only by the temporary paralysis of depression. Basically all the same unhealthy emotional and psychological ingredients of the average marriage."

Tania continued, "You must be careful, Nicolás. In Latin America men like you quickly become the leaders of cults, then political movements, and end up dictators."

"Don't worry," replied Nicolás, "it's not in the cards, nor in me."

"No, Nicolás. Latin America is the wild card. What happened to this part of the world? How did this madness begin? I mean, there seems to be no end to it. How did it happen to us?"

"There's a lot of blame to go around. The generals say we, the civilians, are to blame. Your idol Ché Guevara said we should blame the United States. Freud said we should blame our parents. Marx said we should blame the ruling class."

"Okay, wise guy. And who do you blame?"

"Nobody, because I don't live in faith or hope."

"Then what do you live in?"

Nicolás smiled and toyed with his glass of wine. For some reason, as he listened and responded to Tania, his eye was constantly held by the Mendoza label on the wine bottle. He didn't understand. Most of the wine sold in the city had the name Mendoza on the label. He had seen this same label many times but some possibility, the memory of something he had forgotten to do, kept nagging at his mind.

Ramón had his own concept of freedom: "If it cannot be constructed, then it cannot be destroyed."

"And that's it? That's all?" Nicolás demanded.

138

Ramón had replied, "Think about it, the concept is all pervasive."

"No," Nicolás answered Tania, "I live in experience."

"What kind of experience?" Tania persisted. She had switched to the persona of the prim intellectual, as she sat in the restaurant in her plain clothes, hair tied back. He could easily imagine her lecturing a class of future music ethnologists. Nobody would believe, looking at her now, he thought, that underneath this studious woman, was the same libidinous spirit that had exploded in the batuque dance of last night.

"In the past twenty-four hours I have experienced anger, lust, passion, love, hatred, compassion, all inspired by larger energies than myself. That's my experience. It is my good fortune that in some way these energies balance themselves out and hold me in a state of equilibrium."

"You are too young to be this wise."

"That's only because at this period of my life wiser, more profound intelligences, souls, powers, whatever, have taken up residence in me. Who knows if tomorrow, next month, or next year, I may be seized and driven by all manner of self-destructive forces."

"Oh, Nicolás. You are so naive. So full of these romantic bourgeois contradictions. Listen! Talk about the ruling class, can we leave this place? These women keep staring at me. They make me nervous."

"Yes, I can understand. This is not El Paraíso. No, I'm not being sarcastic. You see, I don't take any notice. Because I grew up surrounded by the attitudes of wealthy women, I forget how obnoxious they can be. Where to?"

"I want to show you something."

"Another dance?"

Tania blushed and suddenly melted at the memory. Her chameleon spirit had moved into another climate. Her eyes shone warmly, a woman in lust.

"Oh, Nicolás, you were beautiful."

A scruffy young girl with a dirty face wandered in from the street, selling flowers from a basket. Nicolás bought three roses from the child before the waiters shooed her out. He presented the roses to Tania. *"Para mantener la atmósfera tropical."* He smiled and stroked an imaginary moustache. Tania managed to look faint and startled the matrons at the next table by emitting a deep groan of sexual pleasure.

Nicolás paid the bill and they left the restaurant, conscious that the wondering eyes of the waiters followed them to the door.

On the street Tania heaved a sigh of relief. "At least now I can breathe again." She took his arm. "Walk with me this way."

"Tell me," asked Nicolás, "last night something happened after the dance? There is something between us that was not there before."

Tania instantly did another shift. She became matter-of-fact, cool.

"You had a long dream. You talked a lot in your sleep. Don't you remember?"

"Back in the Bar Windsor I kept reading the name Mendoza on the wine bottle, again and again. It had something to do with my dream. That's all I can remember."

Tania flagged a taxi. They climbed into the back of the tiny Fiat.

"Where are we going?"

"Rosedal."

When Nicolás saw the formation of roses within the flower bed, he was filled with a sense of *déjà vu*. I've seen this before, Nicolás told himself. He could not yet bring himself to tell Tania about his dream. His first thought was that she would be disappointed. Her face was proud and excited.

"I wanted to show you myself. This was my last job. Don't you think it's wonderful nobody has reported it yet? Can you read it, Nicolás?" she asked excitedly.

"Of course, *Viva El Ché!*"

She was delighted with herself, vivacious. "People from all over the city must have seen this, but nobody has reported it. Doesn't that mean something Nicolás? Doesn't that give you reason for hope?"

"How can you explain it?" asked Nicolás.

"Perhaps fascists don't see flowers," she laughed. "Oh, it's wonderful to have fun while you work. "Do you know I've done this in flower beds in public gardens all over the city."

But then Nicolás thought that she should know.

"Tania, I dreamed about this exact flower arrangement the evening before I met you."

"The same evening? That's incredible! I don't believe you. You made it up."

"Have it your own way. But don't you see Tania, the fact that I dreamed this exact same floral arrangement is some kind of tribute to the energy, the karma that you put in action when you planted these roses."

Tania would not immediately accept the idea. "I can't believe this. You're always trying to upstage me. No, somebody told you about it, or you walked by and didn't consciously absorb the formation until just now –"

"I haven't been here for two, perhaps three years."

Tania abruptly walked away from him, out of the garden, and into the street to stand by herself on the sidewalk. God! what a moody and difficult woman, Nicolás exclaimed to himself.

As he came up to her on the sidewalk on Avenida del Libertador, she reached out for him, put her hand on his arm. He instantly experienced something beyond the sensation of her fingertips on his arm. He somehow was inside her, travelling through her body, through nerve passages, encountering fragments of different memory systems.

"I'm sorry, Nicolás," she said. "It's just that I'm a little overwhelmed by all these strange parts of your mind. To tell you the truth, I find it scary—"

They simultaneously felt the charge of energy that passed between them. Nicolás suddenly remembered— "Mendoza. That was the name of the cop who stopped you and Jorge on the street in La Paz. This is all coming back to me from the dream I had last night after we danced together."

Tania could only stare at Nicolás in amazement, and let go of his arm. But he caught her by the elbow and with his other hand firmly held onto her hand. When he spoke this time he was conscious.

"Mendoza reads your Argentine passport: Tania Gutierrez Bauer. Then he tells you that you are under arrest. He is very drunk. He grunts and weaves around unsteadily on his feet. 'What for?' you ask. 'For possession of drugs. What else?' He laughs at you. Is all this right, Tania?"

Tania could only nod in assent.

"Even right now you can see his face. His mouth is full of grey rotting teeth."

"Then what happened after Mendoza stopped us on the street?" she asked.

Nicolás was strangely elated. "You told him that it's no problem. That not only did you not have drugs but that you never use them—"

"Forget about Mendoza, he's not important. But do you remember the rest of the dream, Los Altos and—"

"Yes!" replied Nicolás excitedly. "All of that, Jorge, Puentes, and the cab driver, Ruiz, and the sergeant. But I have to clear this thing about Mendoza out of my head."

Tania was impatient. But she allowed herself to be led by Nicolás back into Rosedal where they sat down on a bench together, like any other loving couple in the flower garden.

"It's like a film unwinding in my head. I'll give it to you just as it appears behind my eyes. And you can stop me anywhere you think I've made a mistake. Okay?"

Tania reluctantly nodded. Nicolás took both her hands in his, closed his eyes, and spoke rapidly but softly:

"Mendoza says, 'It doesn't matter, Señorita Argentina. You're under arrest, anyway.' You whisper to Jorge that you have seen this movie before, several times. Then you ask Mendoza, 'How much is this going to cost?' He wants fifty dollars, American. Jorge wants to know if you can all sit down and discuss the problem over a beer?"

"What did Mendoza say?" asked Tania, who had decided that she would try to move from a passive stance and aggressively test Nicolás.

" 'Of course, señor,' he says, 'I am a civilized and intelligent man.' And he wraps his arm warmly around Jorge. But unable to reach your friend's shoulders, he ends up clumsily hugging Jorge around the elbows."

"Go on!" Tania urged Nicolás.

"Jorge, you, and the cop step into a filthy nearby street bar and–"

"Describe it!" demanded Tania.

"Not a bar really, it's the vestibule of an apartment hallway. A primitive counter is nailed across an alcove. On the other side is a battered refrigerator full of beer. The bartender is only a kid, a little girl of about twelve or so. The three of you drink straight from the bottles. Mendoza is so drunk he has to lean against Jorge for–"

Tania interrupted him again, this time more insistent, "Can't we forget about Mendoza. He's just a cop we paid off. The rest of the dream is important. Do you remember the rest of the dream, Los Altos and–"

"Yes!" said Nicolás excitedly. "All of that, Jorge, Puentes, and the cab driver, Ruiz, and the sergeant."

"Then go to the end of the dream and tell me what happened."

"The rain is now a drizzle. You are all standing around the sergeant. The smell is very bad. This is the village garbage dump. Beside it a creek, swollen by the heavy rains, rushes through a corrugated metal culvert. The smell is worse because the sergeant has shit himself. He babbles away to himself. Jorge says, 'If you're going to do it, please do it now.' You can't move. Your arm cannot lift up the machine pistol. Puentes takes the sergeant's arm. 'Mario Teran,' says Puentes, his voice deep and slow, the rain running down his face, 'the Committee for the Co-ordination of Justice for the Revolution has been ordered to execute you for your responsibility in the murder of Ché Guevara at La Higuera on October 9, 1967.' Puentes lets go of the sergeant's arm. The others step back and look at you. But you still can't move. The sergeant throws himself down in the mud. He whines incoherently. Jorge curses and turns away. Ruiz, the cab driver, still tied to Puentes' wrist, tries to pull free. They begin to struggle together. Jorge goes to help Puentes. In the confusion the sergeant rolls down the bank and throws himself into the creek. The river is fast at full flood. The sergeant is only a darker shadow in the darkness. Before you can shoot, he is carried by the current into the culvert where he disappears. Ruiz begins to laugh. 'God has taken care of the situation,' he says. The sergeant will drown in the creek. It is too dark to follow along the bank. Nobody says anything to you. But you believe they all think you've bungled the operation. You start the long walk back to the car."

Nicolás opened his eyes to find Tania staring at him in shock.

"That's exactly how it all happened, Nicolás," she answered mechanically, her face anxious and tense.

144

Nicolás felt excited, restless. He knew that he had made some incredible breakthrough since the earlier experience with Guido. He needed to walk and think. They left Rosedal, crossed Libertador, and began to walk south. He suddenly had residual images, random afterthoughts. He related one to Tania: "Remember Puentes? I know why you liked him. It's because he had a connection to El Ché. Puentes was related to one of the three guerrillas who survived the ambush on Ché in the Nancahuasú and walked out of the Bolivian jungle to Peru."

Tania silently nodded. They strolled on for several minutes, each lost in their own thoughts, until the reverie was broken by Tania:

"Nicolás, there's something I need to know. It's very important to me. After he threw himself in the river, can you tell me if Sergeant Teran drowned?"

Nicolás shook his head. "The way it works, so far as I can tell, is that it seems I can only give you back what you already know, that is, whatever is inside your own experience."

Tania shook her head, incredulous. "I feel as if I've lost the privacy of my mind."

"Don't be alarmed, I would never abuse you," Nicolás reassured her.

"Have you ever considered that this could make you a very dangerous person, Nicolás?"

"No," Nicolás answered softly. "How could I threaten anyone if I only give back to them what they already know?"

"When you relay that information to a third party."

"Who would ever believe me?"

"I do," said Tania in a matter-of-fact tone. "And that makes you dangerous to me." Before Nicolás could respond, she grasped his sleeve. "Look, *una pintada*."

A few yards ahead five young people burst out of a small van parked by the sidewalk, ran up the steps of a government administrative building – a sign indicated offices of the Minister of the Interior – and with brushes and spray cans frantically painted a variety of political slogans, mostly in support of the Montoneros, on the entrance and pillars of the building. They took no longer than three minutes. They paused momentarily in a group on the stairs to take a heroic stance, fists in the air, and shout more slogans at the surprised pedestrians who had paused somewhat nervously to watch this lightning-strike of a demonstration.

Nicolás glanced over his shoulder and saw the armed men run up. Two more slipped out of the front doors of the building. Nicolás only had time to pull Tania down between two parked cars. The three armed men on the sidewalk all carried automatic weapons. Trapped in the cross-fire on the steps, the students had no chance to escape. The murderous burst of automatic weapons' fire lasted only thirty seconds. But the steps were instantly awash in blood and torn-apart bodies. The futile whine of a flooded engine drew the attention of the armed men. The driver had stalled the van as he tried to get away. He emerged slowly from the passenger door of the van with his hands up in the air in surrender. He looked no more than fifteen years of age. One of the armed men – they were all, Nicolás noticed, dressed in civilian clothes, but wore army combat boots – walked straight toward the boy, unslung an Itaka from his shoulder and fired as he approached. The blast from the shotgun at point-blank range hurled the boy back against the van, tearing a huge hole in his chest.

Vehicles full of police and uniformed soldiers screamed up to the building. Nicolás and Tania slipped silently away through the crowd of frightened but curious pedestrians who milled around fearfully but were being held back from getting closer to the bodies by a cordon of policemen.

"It was a trap," said Nicolás. "They had been tipped off. They were just waiting to murder those kids."

Tania and Nicolás walked in stunned silence, shocked by the murders they had just witnessed. Nicolás felt deeply oppressed. There seemed nowhere to go in Buenos Aires to escape the violence and horror that hung like a shroud over the city. They walked in silence for a long time, an unspoken agreement not to discuss what they had just witnessed.

Finally Tania turned to him. "There is a woman in your life, isn't there Nicolás?" Tania asked.

Nicolás was in such a profoundly depressed state, Tania had to ask him again before he heard her.

"Yes."

"Where is she?"

"She was disappeared eighteen months ago."

Tania wrapped her arms around Nicolás in a hug that he did not have the emotional energy at that moment to return.

"Do you have any evidence that she is alive."

"None."

"Are you still in love with her?"

"Yes."

"Nicolás, I have to be on my own for a while. I'll see you back at the hotel later."

Nicolás nodded. "I understand." He flagged down a taxi and put money into her hand as she climbed in. The taxi pulled away and left Nicolás standing on the sidewalk. In that last contact with Tania he had received an image: Tania at a phone booth, making a telephone call.

Nicolás woke up to Big Man leaning over him. He was dressed in what seemed to be exactly the same clothes in which Nicolás had first seen him: yellow T-shirt, baggy jeans. Big Man knelt beside the bed and pushed the cut-down Itaka against Nicolás's cheek.

Behind Big Man, Nicolás could see The Toad pawing through his books and papers. He picked books up at random and held the covers close to his terrible eyes, examined the titles briefly then, cursing in his cracked high-pitched voice, he threw the books and papers on the floor. Guido hovered nervously in front of the closed door. His eyes avoided Nicolás' gaze.

Big Man pressed the gun against Nicolás' neck, took a handful of Nicolás' hair, and slowly raised him to the sitting position. Then he carefully stood back.

"Good evening, Señor Quintana," squeaked The Toad over his shoulder, his hands busy with the papers on the table.

"What is all this Gypsy shit that you read? I can't believe a grown man like you, with your background – What the fuck is this?" He held up a book and peered at the cover, *Karma and Reincarnation,* and casually tossed the book on the floor.

Nicolás sat naked on the bed. He looked around for Tania, half-expecting to find her unconscious on the floor. But she was nowhere to be seen. Then he remembered she had not returned to the hotel the night before. He felt a surge of joy. At least she had avoided certain arrest.

Big Man emptied Nicolás' pants pockets and threw the trousers in his face. Nicolás quickly slipped them on and hoped that the men didn't see his hands tremble as he fumbled for the zipper. Next his shoes were thrown in his face. As he tied the laces, he felt some of his dignity and courage come back to him. He found his voice.

"Guido," he addressed the night clerk, "I hold you responsible for contacting General Quintana."

148

Even as he said it, Nicolás realized it was a mistake. The wrong opening gambit. Big Man and The Toad laughed scornfully to each other. Guido took his cue from them and smiled uneasily. Big Man took Nicolás' right wrist and handcuffed it to the metal frame at the end of the bed.

"We did better than that," said The Toad, as he turned to face Nicolás for the first time. In his hands he held *The Wisdom of the Planets*.

"Will you just look at this crap," he whined as he tossed the book to Big Man, who caught it with one huge hand.

"You see," he addressed Nicolás, "we talked to the man you pretended to be, your cousin. And he was very unhappy that you have been going around Buenos Aires claiming the general as your father."

Oh, so they had spoken to that slime, José Maria. The knowledge made Nicolás' heart sink, but he was determined not to show it.

"That was *your* mistake, not mine. I showed you my documents and you made the wrong assumption."

"Perhaps," said Big Man, "but you also made a mistake. I talked to my nephew, Moreno, and he told me that the general's son only made twelve jumps. But it was his crazy cousin, Nicolás, who made twenty-five."

"So that's why we went and talked to your cousin," chimed in The Toad. "A very different man from yourself, an officer and a gentleman. He informed us that the irresponsible Nicolás had disowned his own parents because –"

"The truth is my cousin has always been jealous of the affection the general has for me."

" – his father was a patriotic citizen, a judge who endorsed the junta's powers and the plan for national reconstruction."

"And the only visible result of that plan has been to provide men like you with a living," responded Nicolás.

The Toad didn't like that. He approached the bed. Nicolás gagged on the overwhelming smell of stale cologne that exuded from The Toad's body.

"You know what I think we have here, señores? I think we have a fag. A guy with a great build, who spends half his life in the gym and the other half hanging around bars, and then in-between he lies in bed reading" – he took *The Wisdom of the Planets* back from Big Man, his voice rising to a high-pitched scream – "this trash!" And he smashed Nicolás across the face with the book.

Before The Toad had finished his swing, Nicolás had driven his free left fist with all his might into The Toad's scrotum. The Toad flopped on the floor and vomited on the carpet. Nicolás waited for Big Man to come at him. But instead, Big Man shook with laughter. In that moment Nicolás understood how much Big Man hated his partner. These men, thought Nicolás, not only hate everybody, but hate each other more.

They took Nicolás from the Cruz del Sur. Big Man held the gun on Nicolás. Guido went first. He carefully helped The Toad, who shuffled along in a painful half-crouch. Under The Toad's arm, Nicolás saw the envelope of Tania's newspaper clippings. Why had she left them behind? Her research, she had called them.

Big Man held Nicolás back as The Toad and Guido edged down the stairs, and whispered in his ear, "Quintana, I know you know who I am – that business with my nephew – but if you get out of this alive, remember I treated you well."

Nicolás nodded. What did this mean? At the very least that there were some soldiers who saw that morale was so low the military could not last forever.

"Who betrayed me?" Nicolás asked.

"The woman," whispered Big Man.

"Can you get word to my uncle. He will pay – "

"Your uncle can't help you. He's not in favour. We've heard rumours." Big Man paused to listen and heard only The Toad still groaning, as he made his way down the stairs, urged along by Guido who made encouraging noises. "The guys at the top think the general is soft on the Commies. I heard they're gonna retire him. Anyway, he's in Europe, France. On some military weapons' buying mission."

"How do you know all this?" Nicolás asked.

"I make it my business."

Then aloud, so that his voice and actions echoed in the stairwell for the benefit of the others, Big Man whacked Nicolás twice across the back with the flat of his hand, and said, "They're going to make you pay for this, *boludo*. They have specialists for guys just like you. Your tango has just begun."

The men stepped back from Nicolás. The intense agony suddenly stopped. His whole body fell to a low tide of dull pain. In the moments of lucidity that followed, Nicolás heard all his favourite sounds of a Buenos Aires evening. A woman's voice floated sweet and clear across the rooftops, the refrain from *"Zamba De Mi Esperanza," "Sueño, sueño del alma que a veces muere sin florecer,"* hung plaintively in the steamy air.

Nicolás imagined the singer; she had to be under thirty to still sing with that purity of tone in her voice. He pictured her out on a flat roof: plump, good-natured, her hair let down, a collection of silver bracelets jingled on her bare arms as she hung out the family wash. Her youngest child played quietly beside the huge basket of damp clothes. Every few minutes the singer would turn her head to peer down on the older children as they screamed and chased each other in the courtyard below.

From the Calle Salta, Nicolás could hear the soft squeal of car tires on the hot pavement as the drivers manoeuvred their vehicles around the turn. And downstairs, beneath the metal table on which he was strapped, police detectives in the San Justo squad room listened to a soccer game.

" . . . *Zamba a ti te canto porque tu canto derrama amor . . .* "

In the beginning the steel table had been cool against his naked body. But now, when he squinted under the lower edge of the blindfold, the metal didn't even fog when he breathed against the surface. He wasn't sure, the volume of the radio was not turned up quite high enough, and the background roar of the crowd rose and fell, drowning the commentators' frantic spill of words, but Nicolás thought the game was between River Plate and Racing Club. Every few minutes one of the detectives, his mouth half-full with his lunch, would yell: "Go Monze! Go!" Nicolás had never heard of a player called Monze and assumed it was probably a nickname, bestowed perhaps by the cop himself on the athlete who seemed to control a large part of the game.

"My patients have told me," Ramón had said, "there is no formula for resistance to the pain."

"But some people never break. Why is that?" Lara had wanted to know.

Ramón had shaken his head in puzzlement. "Nobody really knows why one individual refuses to give in and another surrenders. My own personal conclusion is that those who do not break are somehow given a brief interval of time to prepare themselves. Many of them have told me: 'When I was first arrested, if they had tortured me right there I was so terrified that I would have told them anything.' But for some reason the torture was not started until the next day. Or if there was a long ride, forty-five minutes to an hour, in which the victims had an opportunity to prepare themselves, once they had that time to be psychologically prepared, it was a question of will. One woman said to me: 'I thought they had already done everything that was possible to violate me physically. But they were despicable sadists. They hung me upside down with my legs over a steel bar. And they put the electric probe in my vagina, in my anus, and then in my mouth. "Eat your own shit!" they said. I no longer felt human. I saw myself as a piece of meat hanging on a hook in one of those abattoirs in La

Matanza. But then I had this thought, yes, I am more human than these monsters who are doing this to me. And I will prove my humanity by not giving them what they want. I decided I would die before I would give in to this last violation to my mind.'"

"Go! Monze, go!" yelled the detective in the San Justo squad room.

Nicolás strained to hear the commentator call out the indistinguishable names of the players; he knew how important it was to make these fixes of time and place. These moments of mental navigation would give him a handle to hold on to, when later in his cell, in total darkness and in moments of terrible need, when he felt himself to be wandering off the edge of his sanity, he would be able to remind himself: I know there's still a real world out there. Because on the evening of November 18, 1977, I heard and understood that women still sang as they hung up their washing, young men played professional football, and others drove their trucks and cars past the No. 1 police station on Calle Salta, where inside, I, Nicolás Quintana, at the age of twenty-nine, was spread-eagled on a metal table in one of the torture cells on the second floor of the detective squad headquarters in the Buenos Aires district known as La Matanza. And –

Nicolás' memorizing of these details was interrupted when the men silently surrounded the metal table again. The pain came back, more terrible than ever. All Nicolás wanted was for them to kill him. Why not? He no longer understood why they continued to work on him. His mind couldn't find its way along the edges of their words, let alone comprehend their demands. Their questions were full of bizarre revolutionary jargon they had clumsily acquired, and evidently assumed he would immediately recognize:

"Give us your *nom de guerre*."

"Who is your *responsable*?

"Tell us your rank in the *orga?*"

Even though from the very first session Nicolás had not understood this double-talk, they continued to use it on him. He had, however, quickly come to interpret the lingo of the torture cell and what to expect.

"Fats, show Superman how to take a long-distance call on the telephone."

That was the one they called Snake.

"Not only are the prisoners kept hooded all the time," said Ramón, "but the torturers also keep their military ranks and identities hidden. They always address each other by phoney street-gang nicknames."

Nicolás had come to match their personalities with their pseudonyms. When Fats turned on the switch, it was Snake who always giggled when the electric current twisted Nicolás' body this way and that on the metal table.

"Blondie, we should have a mirror for Superman."

"Frequently," said Ramón, "an officer from the officer corp will only use paramilitary individuals, or retired personnel to carry out the actual torture. All part of the process of maintaining secrecy."

Blondie was in charge, no doubt about that. The other two, Fats and Snake, always deferred to him.

"A mirror?" Blondie asked, boredom and condescension in his voice. "Why?"

"So then he could see those big muscles of his tremble just like a woman's."

Blondie only grunted.

Nicolás believed that Fats and Snake thought their superior officer had no sense of humour, because Blondie never made jokes or taunted Nicolás. There had been nothing, Nicolás reflected, in his contact with Guido that had prepared him for the monster called Blondie. He asked questions, and spoke to the other two only when he wanted them to increase the intensity of the torture. Nicolás recognized in Blondie's detachment that paradoxical mixture of inhumanity and correctness that was the madness that drove so many Argentine military men.

"... *Estrella, tú que miraste, tú que escuchaste mi padecer* ... " The singer's sweet voice penetrated the cell.

Only once had Blondie entered into a human exchange with Nicolás. At the first interrogation Nicolás had told them to go to hell. Blondie had leaned over the table and shouted in his ear, "This is hell!"

"Then you can't escape either," Nicolás had calmly replied.

"Escape?" Blondie was amused. "We don't have to escape."

"You cannot do wrong without suffering wrong." Nicolás had spoken with such quiet authority and conviction that for a long two or three minutes there was only a tense heavy silence in the torture chamber.

Nicolás squinted out from under his blindfold and saw Blondie nod and gesture with his chin.

"Get on with it." Blondie coldly commanded his men.

They had not liked Nicolás' moral assertion. The torture that followed in that first session had been particularly savage.

Fats and Snake could have been cops, enlisted soldiers, out-of-work salesmen, anyone, but Nicolás recognized Blondie as an officer, an Argentine military officer.

"*Estrella deja que cante, deja que quiera como yo sé* ... "

Nicolás could still track time. This was the fourth night in a row that they had brought Nicolás into this evil room.

"*El tiempo que va pasando como la vida no vuelve más* ... "

Even though blindfolded, he felt the torture chamber was a sepulchre, high-ceilinged, full of hollow echoes. Could the singer of zambas, he wondered, ever hear his screams across the rooftops. And yet the room was strangely and intensely claustrophobic. His body felt bloated, huge. He saw his flesh spilled over the table, it left no space in the cramped room, with barely enough space for the metal table and the three men.

"... *El tiempo me va matando y tu cariño será* ..."

Nicolás sensed the three men silently surround the table. From under his blindfold he saw that Fats and Snake had taken off their sweat-soaked shirts. Blondie would never take off his shirt. He heard the now familiar but always terrifying low hum, the sound of the electrical generator switched on. Then the background sounds of the soccer game from the radio in the squad room abruptly receded. He could no longer hear the singer from across the rooftops. The one called Fats began to amuse himself with the electrical scalpel against Nicolás' penis. The pain was too much. Nicolás felt that they were pulling his insides out through his genitals. He began to hallucinate again. The top of his skull lifted off. His legs stretched out. His feet, it seemed to him, actually pushed through the wall. Everything inside his body turned white with the heat of pain. What had happened to that rule of karma? No one is burdened in any one lifetime with more of his past karma than he is able to bear.

"Kill me," Nicolás pleaded.

"It's not our job to kill you," Fats told him, pausing momentarily from his work, a serious and irritated tone to his voice; a civil servant mildly annoyed at being told to perform a task outside his area of responsibility.

Then if they would not kill him, he would will himself to be nothing, to escape into anything or anybody else but Nicolás Quintana.

At that precise moment, just when he felt himself to have been walled forever into a place of great pain and terrible suffering, Nicolás suddenly passed through this space into an interval without boundaries. And for reasons unknown to him and which he was never able to explain, heard himself say in an angry voice that was his, but with thoughts driven by another: "All right, enough of that!" And then he heard himself give a name and a telephone number in Mexico City. Then just before he lost consciousness, he felt a terrible sense of shame and betrayal that seemed to come from this other strange part of himself, from a part of himself that he had never experienced before.

Nicolás recovered consciousness slumped on a hardwood chair. But even before they took the blindfold off his head, he sensed he was in another place. There was a level of tension but it was different. He could not feel, as he always did in the other place, the evil sadistic energies of Snake and Fats as a palpable presence close to him. In this new location the ambience was not charged with the stench of putrefied human blood and faeces. The smell of this new room was very different, astringent to his nostrils and vaguely recognizable.

How had they brought him here? he wondered. He had no sense of time any more. He was disturbed to think that he might have been drugged, kept in limbo for several days. As his mind cleared he concentrated; attempted to find any immediate recollection he might have of being transported, but could find no image or sensation to focus on.

He felt very different. His body still hurt all over but the pain was dulled. Then he absorbed a new sensation – he was clean. For the first time in days his body felt clean. Somebody had bathed him. Incredible! And against his clean skin he could feel a new pair of pants and a soft cotton shirt. They had dressed him in fresh clothes. How remarkable!

When Nicolás adjusted his position in the hard chair he could feel the dull pain in his groin, but the outer edges of his body felt numbed.

"There are a few butchers who call themselves army medical doctors and who work in the army hospital out at Campo del Mayo," Ramón had told him.

"You know them?" Lara had asked in a shocked whisper.

The three of them had been sitting under a huge red-and-white beach umbrella in front of the Mirador at Mar del Plata. A Tuesday afternoon in late October, the late-spring sun had been pleasantly warm, and only a scattering of families and couples had lain on the beach. Lara had been breathtakingly beautiful in the merest suggestion of a black bikini. The angle of the late-afternoon sun caught the tiny blonde hairs on her body and turned them golden against her tanned skin.

"Oh yes," Ramón had answered drily, "I know them all right. They're some of the same guys I went through medical school with, for Christ's sake!"

Ramón had been bitter, staring into the green-blue waves rolling up the sand.

"How can you be sure?" asked Lara.

"We know they're in on the torture. Some nurses have told me about it. There are just too many people, thousands, being systematically tortured for the military to be able to keep it a secret any longer."

Lara was still absorbing her disillusionment at the involvement of the physicians.

"But what do these doctors do?"

Ramón had grimaced, "These medical officers tell the torturers when to ease up, when to go on. They pump Pentothal, Demerol, or other painkillers, into the people the interrogators have worked on. Anything that will work, just so they can keep the victims together enough for another round of torture."

Lara shuddered. "Our family doctor has a military background. Come to think of it, I know he has some medical connection at the Campo del Mayo hospital –"

"Perhaps you could pump him for some information," suggested Ramón.

"No. I'll never go to him again. I know I have no proof, but just the thought of his hands on my body –" Lara broke off with another shiver of revulsion.

His body felt like a sack of desensitized flesh. But brittle. He remembered the bags of charcoal sold in the marketplace in Santa Rosa where his grandmother used to take him as a child. That's how his body felt: dry, lumpy bruises pushed against his skin. And yet he was irrationally elated. Was this another effect of the drug? He sensed several men in the room. But they talked quietly, some distance away. He could not hear any actual words, only murmured voices, weirdly distorted, as if the sounds were being piped to him underwater.

Yes, that was it. He remembered the smell now, a military barracks smell from his days as a cadet. How could he have ever forgotten? They had woken up to the eye-watering fumes every morning. A few miserable first-year cadets, continually on punishment duty and nicknamed *los desinfectados*, had gone around the academy reeking from the chemical. The harsh sensation in his nostrils came from the disinfectant always used by the military to wash floors. Come to think of it, Big Man's nephew, Moreno, had been a *desinfectado*. From outside the room, Nicolás could dimly hear all the sounds of military camp activity: the faraway voice of a drill sergeant; the unmistakable grinding noises of military trucks starting up. So, Nicolás, he told himself, then they must have finally brought you, drugged and in secret, to a military base.

Ramón had been knowledgeable. "The disappeared live in fear of transfers. Many of the executions are carried out then. They invoke the escape law. The decree of the junta allows a prisoner detained under order of the National Executive to be shot if he attempts to escape."

Then if you have survived the transfer, concluded Nicolás, it means they want to keep you alive a little while longer.

"Perhaps we could begin?"

That was a peevish old man's voice, vaguely familiar, again somehow connected to his cadet days. Nicolás heard feet stir, papers shuffled, men coughed and cleared their throats.

Then everything in Nicolás recoiled as some familiar footsteps approached. His dulled nerves jangled alive again. He steeled himself. He could tell by the rhythm of the walk, the energy he felt, then the identification was confirmed by the smell of the man's body, that not even the cologne he now wore could ever disguise. Blondie was back.

Blondie leaned against Nicolás' shoulder. In that thoughtless and familiar contact Blondie expressed all the casual intimacy and contempt the torturer has for his victim. Nicolás felt nauseated to feel the weight of the man's stomach against his arm. Blondie's hands fumbled with the black hood that had been pulled over Nicolás' head, then wrapped tightly in place with additional cloth around his eyes.

"Perhaps we should leave the prisoner blindfolded."

That was the nervous older man's voice again. Brittle. Worried. But essentially the voice carried no real weight of authority.

Nevertheless Blondie paused in unwrapping the blindfold, his hands rested momentarily on Nicolás' head.

"No. I want to see the son of a bitch's face. Here, take these glasses, let him get used to the light slowly," said a new voice.

Nicolás had been surprised. A slangy Cuban voice: all the *s* sounds at the end of words completely swallowed; unmodulated, with a macho braggadocio of confidence in its tone. What was a Cuban doing here? Anxiety stirred in Nicolás, reached down beyond the drug that had been pumped into his veins to anaesthetize his body.

"As far as we know," Ramón had told him that day on the beach with Lara, "those who have been released have never seen their torturers. They always wore a hood or were blindfolded. Some of the disappeared have spent months like that. The saying is that if they ever let you see their faces, it's only because your ticket has been punched – they have decided that they're going to kill you."

Nicolás' hidden audience must have reached a silent consensus, because the vexed older man's voice did not protest again.

"Put these dark glasses on when I take off the hood," Blondie said.

He pushed into Nicolás' handcuffed hands a pair of dark glasses. At the same time Blondie slipped the wrappings and hood off Nicolás' head.

Light flooded his skull in a blinding explosion that seemed to pierce to the centre of his brain. He forgot about the glasses. They fell to the floor as he clapped his hands to cover his eyes.

"*Qué te parió!*" Blondie cursed.

Blondie bent down, fished around awkwardly under the chair, and scooped up the sunglasses.

162

"Co-operate, Quintana," he whispered in Nicolás' ear as he bent forward, his back to the assembly, and roughly pushed the glasses in position over Nicolás' nose.

"I have to admit you're a tough son of a bitch," Blondie continued in his whisper, as he busied himself with unlocking the handcuffs and then locking them again so that Nicolás' hands were behind him, fastened to the metal frame of the chair.

"Normally we would have shot you a long time ago, just to get rid of the problems you have created for us. But now, just maybe, you've got a chance to stay alive. So take it." Blondie left his side.

The Wheel of Becoming turns again, reflected Nicolás. What could he possibly have that they could want? Nicolás wondered. He sensed a subtle shift in power. Blondie needed something from him. He knew that for Blondie to talk to him that way there had to be something in it for him. For any Argentine officer these days that always meant two gambits: bribery or professional advantage. With this many people involved it had to mean the latter. A promotion? That meant Blondie had found some way to implicate him in something larger, some impossible scenario they could use to feed their paranoid fantasies and rationalize the brutality of their policies.

Nicolás kept his head bowed as he continued to try and protect himself from the light, then felt a wetness against the underside of his thigh. When he looked down under the rim of the dark glasses, he saw a stain of blood seeping through the blue jeans they had put on him. Blondie casually tossed into his lap the black cotton wrapping cloth that had been used to keep his hood in place and went to sit down. In that moment Nicolás caught a quick glimpse of the man who had administered such hideous pain and indignity on his body.

Astonishing! Nicolás could not believe how ordinary the man appeared. He was not prepared for this – Blondie was of regular height, ordinary build, anonymous forty-year-old features, thinning hair. How could such monstrous evil appear in the guise of such a banal human being?

As his eyes adjusted to the light, Nicolás slowly made out the seated shapes of several other men in front of him. He was on show. Nicolás forced himself with a determined act of will, that almost completely drained his immediate reserves of energy, to lift his head up and sit erect. Show them that they can break your body but they haven't broken your spirit. After all, Nicolás told himself, you're still a Quintana.

Nicolás carefully absorbed his surroundings. Impossibly, his first thought was how to escape. He recognized that they were in a small military briefing theatre. He had been in many such lecture theatres as a military cadet. Perhaps in this same one. He was seated in a chair on a slightly raised platform. To one side of him was a blackboard supported on an easel, on the other side a desk on which there was a phone and some electronic equipment. His audience sat in chairs bolted into a series of rising levels that led to the back of the room and the exit doors.

Nicolás pondered the peculiar tension in the room that he had perceived when he was still blindfolded. He identified the uneasiness as an expectation of sorts that came from the men in front of him. He couldn't see them clearly because the lights above the platform shone on him. The audience sat outside the circle of light, in the half shadows, where he had to strain his eyes to make them out.

Some men were in military uniforms he could not quite make out in the dimness. Then there was Blondie in the front row and beside him a tall older man in an

Argentine army brigade general's uniform. Nicolás recognized his face but could not quite place him.

A small copper-complexioned man of about forty sat dressed in a dark suit and tie. Nicolás sensed that this was not the way the small man usually dressed. He looked quite uncomfortable. This was the kind of man, Nicolás surmised, who usually dressed in jeans and a T-shirt with a peaked cap. Why is he here in a suit? He must be the Cuban he had heard speak, thought Nicolás, the one with the slangy street language, and who had offered the sunglasses. Beside the Cuban was a large heavy-boned man who, just from the way he sat in his chair, had to be an American. He was dressed the way most American policemen are attired in Latin America – expensive North American casual clothes that never seemed to fit quite well enough for the money spent on them.

"None of the military intelligence units of Uruguay, Brazil, Bolivia, Chile, least of all Argentina, trust each other, so the CIA has set up some sort of intelligence co-ordination program." That had been part of Lara's contribution at the Mar del Plata meeting.

He had never loved her more than on that day. He could hardly speak he had found her so achingly beautiful as she had lolled back in her beach chair.

They had made love through noon and the earlier part of that afternoon in the Hotel Mirador, before they had met Ramón on the beach; long slow sessions of sensuality in a sunlit hotel room with the sea breeze blowing in through the open balcony door. They had given much and deeply explored each other's emotions. For Nicolás it had been an afternoon of bittersweet passions, feelings, he had realized, that had focused and intensified their lovemaking. Nicolás had anticipated that Lara and Ramón were about to ask him to work with their clandestine group. He was too close to them not to know they were heavily involved in activities against the military. Nicolás had known, too, that if he turned them down it would probably be the end of his love affair with Lara. Because Nicolás knew and understood that Lara had become seized by her political involvement.

"We have to infiltrate the military," Lara had finally said. "More specifically, military intelligence."

She had lifted up her sunglasses and looked straight at him, her incredible blue eyes stared directly into Nicolás' face.

He had held Lara's gaze and heard her words. But all he had in his head had been what he could still feel from that magic of the afternoon, the silky touch of her long blonde hair as it brushed back and forth across his abdomen. He remembered also the forceful awareness of his own obsidian flesh. As he listened to Lara that afternoon on the beach the sensation of her body had still been all over him, overwhelming him. Not even the bitter tang of the Caballo Blanco beer had washed the taste of her flesh from his mouth.

The Cuban spoke, "What are we waiting for?"

The Gringo leaned forward and whispered in the Cuban's ear. The Cuban shrugged and sat back in his chair, where he remained quiet–for the moment. Nicolás intuitively understood that most of the tension in the room came from this man. He foresaw the Cuban would create most of the problems.

Nicolás sensed a momentary psychological vacuum. His uncle, the general, had always told him, "Nicolás, *carpe diem!* If you ever want to be an officer, there's only one really important characteristic you must grasp about the military mind: If you don't define yourself, others will do it for you."

His uncle had always understood him better than his own parents. When Nicolás had gone to tell his uncle he was going to resign from a military career, the general had said to him, "Nicolás, you are the son I wish that I'd had. The army desperately needs young men like you. Sadly much more than you need the army. But I understand your position completely. Come, give me an *abrazo!* And go live your life! If you ever need me, I'll be here for you – as long as I'm alive."

Nicolás cleared his voice. He had a shock when he heard himself speak. The torture, the hours of screaming had altered his vocal cords. His voice sounded guttural, foreign:

"My name is Nicolás Quintana. My permanent address is in Palermo Chico. I have no doubt that you know my family."

The brigade general moved uneasily in his seat.

"I have been kidnapped, tortured, and held in the most barbaric circumstances for more than a week. I demand my release. I also insist that you inform my family, and my uncle, General – "

"You are being detained at the disposition of the National Executive," Blondie shouted him down.

"On whose orders? And why have no charges been made against me?"

Nicolás was relieved to find his voice becoming stronger. But paradoxically his body grew weaker. Blood from the wounds, made by Fats and his electric scalpel, oozed along his thigh to his knee, and had begun to trickle down his calf.

The general spoke in his dry vexed voice; he could just as easily have been giving a lecture to a dozen officers in a military college: "There are judicial norms and standards which do not apply in this instance. The right of habeas corpus for example. In the type of struggle we find ourselves in, the secrecy with which our special operations must be conducted, means that we

167

cannot divulge whom we have captured and whom we want to capture; everything has to be enveloped in a cloud of silence."

As soon as he spoke Nicolás recognized the officer, General Tomás Rossi. The crazy old man had lectured once or twice at the academy when he was of much lower rank. The general was a pretentious fool, but that he was there made Nicolás even more puzzled. What did they have in mind for him that required the presence of a brigade general. Nicolás knew exactly how to play him. But before he could reply the Gringo spoke for the first time.

"I thought that you had made an arrangement with this guy and he was prepared to co-operate?"

The Gringo spoke good Spanish, but with a heavy accent. He stirred his huge body restlessly in his chair.

"We," he said, somehow taking in the Cuban in that verbal gesture, "are too busy to sit around and listen to this shit."

Lara had smiled and leaned forward in her deck chair, ostensibly to reach her iced lemon soda, but really so as to lower her voice as a group of suntanned bathers strolled lazily by on their way into the sea, "We know that the CIA chief of station in Buenos Aires recruits among the Argentine military for contract officers to work for the Americans in El Salvador and in Nicaragua in Central America."

Nicolás had nodded, but looking down into her breasts as she still leaned forward, one hand affectionately on his knee, he could only think of how she had reacted two hours earlier, when he had taken her nipples in his mouth.

"You could do it, Nicolás," Lara had concluded. "I know you. And I know you would be very good at it."

Ramón had only added, "We could set things up so that you only have to deal with Lara and me."

It was time, Nicolás decided, to go to work on the general.

"General Rossi, you have eaten at the same table with me in my uncle's house. I remember you spoke of the unbreakable and holy pact that existed between the traditional families of Argentina. When I attended your lectures you told us the most important loyalties we could aspire to hold were country, family, and home. I charge you with my protection and the responsibility of contacting my uncle, General—"

Rossi thrust himself angrily out of his chair.

These are the forces that keep turning the Wheel of Becoming, thought Nicolás: ignorance, desire, and malice. The general was beside himself with fear and rage.

"You forfeited all of those privileges when you entered into an association and conspiracy with Lara de la Cruz. She betrayed her class and her family, and we will deal with you as we dealt with her."

Lara and Ramón had fallen silent, waited God knows how many minutes for his reply. Nicolás had known that he would never forget that moment. His life would turn and change on the decision he was about make. He had stood up, and walked by himself across the sand to the water's edge, and gazed the length of the beach. Groups of late-afternoon swimmers had emerged from the hotel and begun to crowd the sand now that the heat of the day had passed.

Their excited cries filled the air as they splashed into the sea. Youthful, tanned, almost naked bodies ran gracefully along the sea's edge. The huge expanse of the South Atlantic stretched out before him. In the clear afternoon sky, the silver edge of a new moon moved gracefully over the sea. Water is your element, Nicolás, and the Moon is in your sign, Cancer. Reflect, he had told himself, on what is your greatest fear and move toward it with courage. You believe that in Lara you have met the love of your life, and that if you turn down her request you will lose her. Nicolás waded out and plunged into the sea. When he finally turned on his back to look back at the beach, the red-and-white umbrella was a tiny speck on the shore. He floated, gave himself up to Iemanja, who held him in her arms and through salty lips whispered advice in his ears.

Nicolás slowly returned to the umbrella under which Lara and Ramón patiently waited for him.

"I just cannot work against my family," Nicolás had quietly told them.

Ramón and Lara hadn't argued with him. They had just exchanged discouraged glances and then stared silently out at the sea, where the swimmers shouted and thrashed about in the soft blue-green waves that rolled up onto the rich yellow sand. Nicolás had understood they were deeply disappointed with his decision. He had tried to explain.

"I broke with my parents when my father accepted to stay on in the courts as a judge, endorsed by the military. That break was painful. But I still cannot bring myself to work against them," he had repeated. "And to collaborate with you would mean that I would have to do exactly that."

Then Lara had gently taken his hand in hers. "It's all right, Nicolás. We understand," she had said.

Ramón had found an excuse to leave – "an appointment at the clinic." He had said, "No grudges," and had given Nicolás a bear-like *abrazo* in goodbye, which was very unlike the psychiatrist who usually and impatiently dismissed "all that stickiness," as he often described emotional affectations among his fellow citizens in Buenos Aires.

After Ramón had left, Lara and Nicolás had walked along the margin of the beach, where the lapping waves had packed the sand wet and firm. Lara had waited for a few minutes for them to adjust to being alone together again. "Nicolás Quintana," she had started seriously but tentatively, carefully selecting the words.

He had waited tensely, in expectation of the very worst. Because he could not even bear to look at her while she spoke, he fixed his eyes on a naked, carefree child of two who toddled ahead of them, splashing playfully in the ebbing wavelets.

"I want you to marry me. Not now, at a better time. But I want you to have me as your wife. I know this is right and that I love you, because I want you to be the father of my children."

Ah, Lara. Nicolás couldn't speak, he had been so deeply moved. He could only nod and take her tenderly in his arms.

"And how did you deal with Lara de la Cruz?" asked Nicolás, his heart pounding as he heard himself ask the question. He had waited so long for this answer. Perhaps he'd had to go through all of this just to get to ask the question.

The general ignored his demand. "You are detained on orders of the National Executive," repeated Rossi, "and that is all there is to it."

But Nicolás could hear the general's voice still held an anxious tone as he sat down again beside Blondie. The general was a stupid man. But not so stupid not to be afraid of what consequences this episode might have for him personally. That's why he wanted the blindfold kept on me, thought Nicolás. He knew that I would remember and identify him.

"Play the tape," Rossi ordered Blondie.

Blondie came forward to the platform and inserted a tape cassette into the machine on the desk beside Nicolás. The volume was up very loud. For one brief moment the horrible tail end of a scream, that Nicolás recognized as his and the memory of which instantly filled

171

him with deep humiliation, echoed through the room. Then there was a long sequence of commonplace background noises that Nicolás at once identified: Fats' heavy and wheezy breathing, the taps that constantly trickled in the torture chamber above the San Justo detective squad room. Even deeper in the background, the sounds of cars and trucks making their turn on Salta. Then unexpectedly over the top of these familiar and banal sounds that represented so much evil to Nicolás, the eerie sound of his own voice giving the name and the telephone number in Mexico City. Silence. And then the singer, the pure voice floating over the rooftops: " . . . *Zamba ya no me dejes, yo sin tu canto no vivo más . . .* "

Blondie snapped off the machine. The Cuban stepped forward and took away Nicolás' sunglasses. The light hurt his eyes, but not with the same piercing intensity as when Blondie had first taken off the blindfold.

"What does this name and phone number mean to you?"

The Cuban asked his question in a genial tone; his manner was pleasant. But Nicolás knew this pose masked the personality of a scorpion.

"I don't really know," said Nicolás truthfully.

The Cuban casually put one foot up on the stage and put his hand on the metal armrest of Nicolás' chair. He leaned closer. Heavy garlic breath. He held his face too close to Nicolás, breaking a subtle barrier. Only lovers and torturers break these restraints of privacy, thought Nicolás.

"Someone must have given it to you?"

"Yes. I was being tortured. I had willed myself to be nothing. I think now that I had reached a higher level of meditation when I received this information."

"All right," said the Cuban with amused tolerance. "Then in this state . . . of meditation, who gave you the name and phone number in Mexico City."

172

"Impossible to describe, really. A higher power, another form of intelligence."

The Cuban was already losing his patience. "Oh, so you now have special powers, I see," he responded sarcastically.

Nicolás looked down at the Cuban's left hand, clutched tensely around the metal arm of the chair. On the thin coppery hairless wrist that extended from the suit sleeve was a rugged combat watch with sophisticated secondary dial faces and compass calibrations. The instrument was worn and weathered, an accessory that certainly did not go with the man's suit.

"Why are you wearing Ché Guevara's watch?" asked Nicolás.

The sudden tension that electrified the men in the briefing room was palpable. The unidentified military officers in the room stirred excitedly.

The Cuban was astounded. His right hand involuntarily covered the watch. Nicolás tried to keep focus. Something very strange was happening in his head. Images whipped through his brain like a film out of control. Is this what it feels like to become psychotic? he asked himself.

He felt faint. He didn't want to pass out in front of these men. To restore his mental alertness he pulled hard against the handcuffs that locked his hands behind him to the chair. The bracelets dug painfully into his wrists. The movement pressed his shoulders and chest against the front of his shirt. And under the pressure of the contraction and flexing of his muscles the myriad unhealed cuts and wounds on the surface his skin, left by the hours of torture to his body, opened slightly and began to suppurate into the blue shirt.

The Cuban was excited. The American sensed the quarry had been flushed. He agitatedly hauled himself out of his chair to tower behind the Cuban.

"What the fuck's going down?" he asked in English.

The Cuban shook his head, perplexed.

"When did you last see this watch?" the Cuban asked Nicolás.

"Just a few days after the ambush in the Iripitó zone where El Rubio was killed. Joaquin had been using the watch, and he gave it back to Ché."

"This doesn't make sense. That was ten years ago. This kid's just—"the Gringo interrupted.

The Cuban waved the American quiet.

"Who was El Rubio?" he asked.

"Captain Suarez of the Cuban Army."

"And what was his first name?"

"Jesús."

"Tell me what you remember of that day?"

"The day Rubio was killed?"

The Cuban nodded. "Suarez, Rubio, it doesn't matter. Use his *nom de guerre*."

Nicolás was quiet, watching and listening to the images in his head.

Tania was thankful that the rain had finally stopped for a little while. She felt quite ill. A fever, but she hid it from Ché. She did not want to be left behind with a couple of guerrillas from the rearguard group. Tania wanted to be with Ché, to be part of that invincibility he always projected. They had been for several days beside an arroyo, the Cañadón of the Río Nancahuasú, and Ché had given orders that they were to move out. There had been a lot of troop movements the day before, Bolivian soldiers hunting down the guerrillas.

Nicolás finally spoke to the waiting men in the briefing room, "Ché had already sent out the advance party. We were—"

"We?"

"The centre group."

"Led by Guevara?"

"Yes. He ordered us to pull out next and Negro—"

"That was his *nom de guerre*, what was his real name?"

Nicolás paused for a second. "He was the Peruvian doctor who joined the guerrillas late. His real name was José Cabrera."

"Go on!"

"Negro rushed into the camp to report to Ché that he had seen fifteen soldiers coming down the river."

Tania had been surprised at the amount of gunfire and how close the shooting had sounded. This was her first actual firefight. After the firing had stopped Tuma reported the news to Ché that they had taken several soldiers prisoner in the ambush, but that Rubio had been seriously injured.

Nicolás continued aloud: "They carried Rubio into the arroyo where Ché had previously established the camp for the centre party. Rubio was already dead. He had been shot in the head."

"How did Ché take it?"

"He was thoughtful. Rubio was the first guerrilla to be killed in combat."

Tania remembered two others, Bolivians, who had drowned in accidents crossing the rivers. And also Rubio was a Cuban. There had been a lot of tension between the Bolivians and the Cubans. The other Cubans had all gotten along well with Rubio; they liked him.

Nicolás spoke, "When Ché spoke privately he had said that he had not thought much of Rubio. The captain was a fresh recruit from Cuba. He was young and seemed to have very little combat experience. Ché had thought Rubio would have difficulty with the guerrilla life."

General Rossi stirred agitatedly in his seat. "How is it possible he knows this level of detail. I find this outlandish."

"When you say Ché spoke privately, who did he speak privately to?" This was the American who now wanted to get in on the chess game.

Nicolás seemed baffled. "I don't know. I don't understand that part."

To himself Nicolás thought: Don't give them so much. Even if you don't understand what is happening here, keep the details to yourself, keep them in your own head. Keep the answers brief.

"Did anything else strange happen that day?"

"Yes. Sometime in the afternoon a Bolivian major led a company of soldiers into exactly the same ambush."

Tania had seen that Ché and the guerrillas had found it unbelievable. The army's intelligence and communication must be awful, they had concluded, because the major had led over a hundred men into the same trap. The guerrillas killed ten soldiers, and captured another two dozen soldiers with their commanding officer, a major. Ché had been ecstatic about the large number of automatic weapons they had seized. And also a Browning machine gun, and a 60 millimetre mortar.

"What happened to the major?"

"Oh, he was released with the other prisoners."

"Can you actually tell us his name?" asked General Rossi, incredulous.

Nicolás smiled at the general. "Yes, a Bolivian, Sanchez. He was courageous, unlike most of the Bolivian officers when they were captured."

"What did the major do that was so brave?" asked General Rossi, who despite himself could not resist the fascination for the story that was unfolding.

"Pombo put –"

"Which one was Pombo?" asked the general.

"Pombo was Ché's bodyguard," interjected the Cuban. "He was one of the most experienced Cuban guerrillas. He had come out of the Sierra Maestra with Ché."

Pombo, lean, black, so efficient, so experienced. Usually also so silent. But he had admired Major Sanchez's bravery and Tania saw that he wanted to share the experience with Ché.

"He didn't have a chance, Ché," Pombo explained as he drew a map of the ambush in the dirt. "Benigno and Urbano had the major's patrol in a cross-fire, from here and here. The soldiers threw down their weapons, went down on their knees, and put up their hands. The major never took cover, just stood there with his hands on his hips. He was disgusted. Most of his men were crying. They were just kids. Then we came under fire from another section of his company. I had the major down on the ground beside me. I put the barrel of my gun in his ear. 'Order your men to surrender!' I told him. The major just shook his head, his eyes stayed hard. He said to me, 'So kill me black man.'"

Pombo shook his head in wonder and true respect. Urbano chimed in: "Not with you, Ché, in the Sierra Maestra or even later when we were in the Congo with the Kinshasa rebels did I ever come across a man who behaved like that."

Pombo looked at Ché with the funny little smile he reserved for Ché. Tania recognized this and was once again jealous of the love Ché and Pombo had for each other. It was a place she could not follow Ché to or share with him, and the realization that that place existed without her filled her with irrational hatred for Pombo. The two men had a real bond, a method of communication none of the others shared, not even Rolando who was like a son to Ché. And as for Tania, Pombo ignored her and watched over her at the same time. It drove her crazy.

"Pombo said the major had refused to surrender his men," explained Nicolás.

"What did you do with Rubio?" the Cuban persisted.

"Rubio? The next day we buried Rubio."

They looked for a hiding place in the black-green depths of the forest. They didn't want the Bolivian army to find Rubio's body.

Camba, always the whiner, complained, "Why are we doing this? Rubio is dead. Why don't we do something for the living and just leave him."

Loro reinforced Camba's fears. "Yes. The soldiers are coming, we should get out the hell out of here."

Tania could see the other Cubans were angry at the two Bolivians. They said nothing, contemptuous of their panic. But Ché had overheard them and was furious. He exploded in anger.

"We always bury our dead and carry away our wounded comrades. Always!"

This was a maxim from his rules of guerrilla warfare: Keep all guerrilla casualties hidden from the enemy.

They found it difficult to dig Rubio's grave, because the day before the ambush all the digging implements had been hidden in a cave a day's walk away. So the Cubans took turns. They dug a shallow grave with machetes. Then they carefully camouflaged the ground to make it look untouched.

Tania listened as Ché began to interrogate two of the captured soldiers. Ché adopted a stern but patient tone with them. At first he told everyone else except Tania to stay out of hearing distance. The soldiers were obviously in awe of this strange guerrilla leader, dirty and wild looking with a beard and long hair. And all his men around him, loaded down with the most modern automatic weapons. Any one of them looked as if they had enough firepower to take on a squad of soldiers by himself.

The younger prisoner was dumb with fright. Then Ché called over Camba and Loro to hear what the eldest of the two captured soldiers had to say. He could not read or write. He thought he was "perhaps twenty years of age." He was no more than five feet tall. Tania thought he was no larger than a twelve- or thirteen-year-old child back in Eastern Europe.

Ché changed his tone. He asked the soldier in a kindly, almost fatherly way, what had scared them most in this campaign. What had they found the most difficult?

The captured soldier spoke simply and eloquently, "Our orders were to bring back the bodies of our companions you killed two days ago in ambush. But when we came to the place where our comrades had fallen we were frightened to find that in two days birds of prey had already picked their skeletons clean. It was very difficult for us to pick up these bones of soldiers who had marched beside us three or four days earlier. These bones were much worse than when we have to carry a dead soldier's body back to the camp. Death is one thing. But to be brought home and be buried already as a skeleton, we could not deal with that. Also we never see your dead. This makes us think that you guerrillas cannot be killed."

But Tania saw that this powerful little speech had been lost on Camba and Loro. They were too young and inexperienced. Ché looked at her after he had ordered Camba and Loro to escort the prisoners back to the group of captured soldiers, and saw that she, too, understood.

"They are contemptuous," Ché said. "They have dismissed the idea that they could be that afraid themselves. If they don't learn this quickly, they will soon be dead."

But to herself Tania had thought, Ché doesn't want to understand. Their psychological self-defence mechanism is at work. They don't want to accept that the peasant soldiers are like them. The same age, with less education, less development. No wonder Ché can't recruit anyone from the local peasants. This is a peasant army. They don't want to kill their brothers.

And where we had thought to slay another, we shall slay ourselves. The guerrillas, Camba and Loro, had expected to find the soldiers to be monsters, Nicolás thought. Instead they found themselves.

At six the next morning Ché had called the guerrillas together to hold a memorial. Tania watched and listened. The light was dim under the forest canopy. The men restlessly slapped at the insects and mosquitoes that constantly attacked their flesh. The heat was already oppressive. In the distance they could hear the cool rush of river water. High up in the trees Tania saw the bright brief flashes of parrots in flight, their harsh calls hung in the torpid air. And from the undergrowth came the strange clucking sounds of the urina pheasant. Everyone's face carried a sheen of sweat. Everyone except Pombo. He seemed cool, alert, and somehow neat. Even the insects didn't seem to distract Pombo.

Ché began by complimenting the men, "This has been our first major contact with the enemy, who wants to hunt us down and kill us. Our victory has been decisive. We killed seven of them, wounded five. Twenty-two prisoners captured. We have also captured many weapons and much ammunition. But we have also paid in blood."

Tania marvelled at the way Ché used Rubio's death to point out that this, their first casualty in combat, had been the result of a mistake and lack of communication between the men holding the positions on the ambush. Rubio had placed himself badly in the ambush, and had been easily detected by the first soldiers of the patrol.

"These are the most tragic errors for us as guerrillas to suffer, because they are avoidable," said Ché.

He also pointed out to them that the first blood to be given in combat was Cuban. And he tried to show the men that they should stop squabbling with each other, the Cubans against the Peruvians, the Bolivians against the Cubans, and so on.

"We have to work together more energetically," pleaded Ché. "United is the only possible way we can develop our small army."

As Ché talked to the men, Tania silently and discreetly counted the guerrillas: forty-three; twenty-three Bolivians, sixteen Cubans, three Peruvians, and one East German – herself. She was filled with despair. All the men were already gaunt. Ché himself had lost twenty pounds. Finding food and drinkable water was a continual daily problem.

Ché ended the memorial and they set out on the day's march. The advance group led by Miguel left first. Then thirty minutes later, the centre and headquarters party led by Ché started out. In another thirty minutes the rearguard, led by Joaquin, would follow. Tania had glanced up at an opening in the trees. A great number of vultures hovered in the sky, watching and waiting for the men below to kill each other. Ché followed her gaze.

"That means," Ché said, "the army has not yet buried their dead."

"Hey! Concentrate, Quintana. Let's go back to the watch."

The Cuban took off Ché's watch and dangled it in front of Nicolás' face.

"When did you last see this watch?" the Cuban repeated like a stuck record.

"I told you, it was a couple of days after El Rubio was killed. Joaquin had been using the watch; he gave it back to Ché."

181

"Can you remember the date?"

"I like the way this watch gives you the date," said Joaquin to Ché. "This little window reminded me that today, April 15, I am forty years old."

"Next thing you're going to be telling me that you are too old to be running around playing the international revolutionary," laughed Ché.

"Time to retire to Miami," joked Joaquin.

"Ché is right behind you," said Tania. "On June 18, he will be forty, too."

Ché had frowned and looked down at the ground. Tania could have bitten her tongue. She remembered, too late, Ché didn't like to be publicly reminded of his age.

Nicolás answered the Cuban, "April 15."

"The year?"

"1967."

"Why are we spending all this time on events of ten years ago?" General Rossi grumbled aloud. Did he really want to know? Nicolás wondered. Or was his ego so fragile he had to continually remind everyone he was the ranking officer present? Everybody in the room chose to ignore him.

"Go on," the Cuban urged.

"Nothing, that's it. Joaquin made some joke about needing a watch more suitable for a commander of the rearguard group."

"What was the joke?"

"It wasn't really a joke. That's all Joaquin said."

Ché laughed when Joaquin handed him back the watch with thanks.

"You'll have to buy a rearguard watch, one that always runs thirty minutes slower," Ché had said.

And they both laughed in a way that made it sound like some long-standing private joke they had shared for many years. Or perhaps the humour turned on the knowledge that those closest to Ché – Braulio, Tuma, Pombo – all had identical watches.

"Why do you remember the date so precisely?" asked the Cuban.

Ché came in to the cave out of the light rain, nodded to the Frenchman, and reached out and put his hand on Tania's arm in his familiar way, just above her elbow.

"Let's talk," he said, glancing at his watch. "We've got a few minutes."

She struggled to her feet. Her leg hurt a lot that day. Ché helped her to stand.

"Why are you limping?" he asked.

"It's nothing," she lied. "My foot went to sleep because of the way I was sitting."

He smelled really bad. His body odour almost made her gag. She hoped he didn't want to make love, even though it had been weeks since they last did. There was never enough time or privacy. Why did he make such a big thing out of not taking baths? As if this guerrilla life wasn't difficult enough, did he have to abandon basic hygiene? He often joked about how on the night watch he could identify the guerrilla who occupied a certain sleeping area by the body smell hanging above the hammock.

Nicolás tried desperately to hold onto consciousness. He could feel the blood filling his shoe. He rolled his head around on his neck and shrugged his shoulders violently. The Cuban peered into his eyes.

"He's going out. He's too full of dope."

The Cuban slapped him, two quick stings across the face. Despite his semiconscious state, and the multitude of images and newly found memories that kept rising spontaneously and cinematically in his mind, Nicolás felt the rage rise in his gut. He wanted to kill this Cuban. The little man put his right hand on Nicolás' knee, gripping the flesh of his thigh, and pressed

183

painfully with his finger and thumb into the group of tendons and nerves just above the knee.

"Answer me! Why do you remember the date so well?" insisted the Cuban.

Ché turned, still chuckling, from Joaquin and crossed over to her hammock with Miguel, the young Cuban doctor, whom Tania had first met when he was still a surgeon at the Calixto Garcia Hospital in Havana.

"She has a fever," said Miguel.

Ché nodded absentmindedly, and without a word to Tania, went off to talk with the Frenchman. Tania was furious at the lack of attention Ché had paid her, and was even more determined to show that she needed nothing from him in the way of special treatment.

They marched through the bush to the Ikira River. Four guerrillas were assigned as *macheteros* to take turns cutting the path through the forest. At first the *macheteros* had a hard time of it; the pace was slow and Tania, despite the fever she felt burning within her, could keep up. But then the terrain changed. They climbed up and down boulder-strewn slopes, the bush thinned; the going was a lot harder. Tania had struggled to keep up with Ché's group, the headquarters'company to which she had been assigned. Alejandro fell behind first; then after an hour Tania could not keep up the gruelling pace. The fever seemed to focus all the pain in her body in her left leg. The sciatic nerve had become a hot wire that burned more intensely with every step. But Tania gritted her teeth and absolutely forbade herself to fall as far back on the trail as Alejandro. For two hours she made herself stay at least one hundred metres ahead of him. Finally Negro, the Peruvian doctor, dropped back to check on them. He made Tania sit and rest until Alejandro caught up. The tall thin Cuban was in macho despair. He held the rank of commandante in the Cuban army, and at one time had been the military

184

chief of Matanzas City. Tania could see that it pained him to be ill and barely able to keep up with a sick woman.

Alejandro cut an incongruous figure for a guerrilla. He was in his thirties, with a very long beard and hair that he had let grow down his back. His skin was a dead white that illness had turned to parchment. He was extremely thin and had suffered severe bowel problems since the beginning of the campaign. As he had gotten sicker over the last days, he had withdrawn more and more into himself. Negro saw how ill they were: "It's a good thing Ché sent me back to check on you two." He took their packs, and diplomatically suggested that the three of them take it easy and walk slowly together.

Finally at midday Ché halted the headquarters' group. When Tania and Alejandro caught up, Negro immediately set up a hammock for Tania in the shade, and took her temperature. Alejandro crashed to the ground.

Negro told Ché, "Tania really can't walk any more. Her fever is thirty-nine degrees. Alejandro is in a bad way, too. His temperature is just one degree lower."

When Tania overheard Negro's words, panic seized her. She had to stay with Ché! She tried to stand but got twisted up in the netting and tumbled ignominiously out of the hammock onto the muddy ground. Ché and Miguel, the other doctor, lifted her back into the hammock; the dirt, leaves, and twigs from the forest floor all stuck to her hair. An ant, which in Tania's delirium, seemed as large as a crab, ran across her cheek and painfully bit her lip. Ché brushed off the ant.

"You're sick, Tamarita," said Ché. She felt touched that Ché would use the diminutive of her real name, the name he had first got to know her by. All the clandestine aliases fell away. No more Tania, no more Laura. There was no need for them any more, her cover

185

had been broken. She was simply once again the Tamara of her childhood.

Ché knelt down beside her. "I order you to stay here and rest. Negro here will take care of you and Alejandro. Serapio will be here to stand watch until the rearguard comes along. Commandante Joaquin will be in charge."

"I am not afraid to die, Ernesto."

"Tamarita, I promise you that you're not going to die from this fever. We have medicines. Remember, I am a doctor. Negro is a doctor. Miguel is a doctor. You couldn't be in better hands. Ninety-nine per cent of the Bolivian population doesn't have this kind of access to medical care. You're going to be fine. You just need to rest for two or three days."

"You don't understand," Tamara whispered fervently in Ché's ear. "You've denied me everything else, Ernesto – recognition, marriage – please don't deny me the right to die beside you!"

"Enough of this melodrama. We're just going for a little walk to put the Frenchman, Debray, on the road to Camiri so that he can get out of the Nancahuasú. We'll be back in three or four days at the most. By that time you'll be fit again and probably making a nuisance of yourself, demanding to be one of the *macheteros* to cut a path through the bush."

"Don't patronize me, Ernesto."

Tania clung to Ché's sleeve. Her lips were dry and blistered. Her face and eyes burned from the fever. She could feel that she was seriously dehydrated from the fever and the heat. Water was scarce and she had already drunk her ration on the march. Ché put his arm around Tania to sit her up and gave her his water ration.

"You believe I betrayed you, don't you," she whispered to Ché.

He regarded her curiously.

"Many inexplicable problems have arisen," he said. "But I have never doubted your loyalty."

"My orders are to stay with you," she insisted plaintively.

"Well, I am in command here. And you will do what I say." Ché laid her down gently in the hammock. "You're delirious from the fever," he said, and delicately picked the leaves and other forest debris from her braids.

"The business at Camiri was not my fault," Tamara insisted. Her voice and manner suddenly lucid again.

Ché said nothing. She held onto his hand for a moment, placed her lips to his wrist. She stared at his wristwatch with its impressive assortment of calibrated dials. In her fever the watch was enhanced, a surreal symbol of a technological world that existed outside this primitive landscape in which she now knew she was trapped. Only Ché, Tania believed, could lead her out of this terrible despair she felt. They could never kill Ché; it was inconceivable. If she could stay close to Ché then she knew she would survive.

"Give me something to hold on to, Ché? Just until I see you again," Tamara asked, timidly, because she was worried that her obvious desperation would make him angry.

Ché dug around in his pack for a few seconds. "A present I've been saving for you." And Ché gave her a cassette tape wrapped in plastic.

"You'll have to tell me what it is because my tape recorder won't work. No power."

Ché had grinned: "Something different from all your Latin-American folklore. Oriental music. I'll bring you back some batteries. We're sure to fish some up in the next ambush between here and Muyupampa." He had laid his hand gently against her forehead for a moment, brushed her cheek with his lips, then was gone.

187

Tamara felt as if something had broken inside her. She knew she would never see Ché again. She tried to get up to follow him, but the pain in her leg was too much.

Nicolás felt the pain of the Cuban applying pressure on his leg and replied: "Because the next day we became separated from Ché's group and we never saw them again."

The Cuban relaxed his grip on Nicolás' knee.

"Who was Joaquin?"

"Joaquin is Commandante Acuña."

"Why do you say *is*?"

Nicolás shrugged.

"And he was the commander of the rearguard group?"

"Yes."

"When did you last see him?"

"Just before the group crossed the river. A campesino from the Poblado de Masicurí, Honorato Rojas, led us to a crossing. But I think we were betrayed by Rojas because there were soldiers waiting for us.

"You were there?"

"No."

"No, of course not. Because nobody survived that ambush. You've read Ché's diaries?"

"No, but I think that I will now."

"Then how do you know all the these details."

Nicolás fell silent, giving the question genuine consideration.

"I can't explain it," he said.

"I don't believe you!"

Nicolás shrugged wearily.

"Why should you expect us to believe you?"

"I expect nothing from you."

"What's your game?"

"No game," answered Nicolás faintly.

"You're lying," said the Cuban. "You could have learned these few pieces of information you have given us from the Bolivian diaries that were published after Ché's death."

"I'm not a leftist. I'm not even intrested in politics."

"About that, Quintana is telling the truth. There is nothing in his background. And when he was first seized, his apartment contained no leftist literature. Mostly books on the occult and readings on Oriental religions."

That was Blondie. And Nicolás could tell there was an ancient enmity between these two men. Blondie deeply resented the way this aggressive Cuban with his gringo CIA friend had taken over the interrogation of his prisoner.

Blondie came up to the platform and unlocked the handcuffs, and allowed Nicolás more freedom of movement by just locking one wrist to the arm of the chair. The hated fingers of Blondie around his wrist gave Nicolás a flash image: Blondie and the Cuban jumped out of a helicopter hovering a foot above the ground. They ran, crouched over to avoid the circling chopper blades, for the tree line where they were greeted by a Bolivian Ranger company commander who stuck his hand out and introduced himself: "Captain Andrés Selich. Welcome to the Red Zone!"

"What about the file found in his room?" asked the Gringo. The Cuban paced back and forth on the platform behind Nicolás.

Blondie picked up the file that Nicolás had first seen when he turned out the contents of Tania's woven Bolivian bag on to the sidewalk of Dias Goncalves, the night she had blown up the police launch with the grenades.

"Yes, what about the file, Quintana?" asked Blondie, taking the worn package from a briefcase beside him.

"That's my research," Tania had said as she rested against the brick wall of a factory on Dias Goncalves, her lungs gasping for air. "Be careful how you handle it."

"I've never seen or read the contents of this file," replied Nicolás truthfully.

"We have determined," said Blondie, "that the handwriting in these documents is not Quintana's."

"Summarize the contents," ordered General Rossi, who had the appearance more and more of a man who had completely lost his grasp on the manner in which his world was unfolding around him.

"There are several files, each related to the assassination of an officer–"

"Argentine officers?"

"No. These files are all on members of the Bolivian armed forces."

General Rossi breathed an audible sigh of relief. His dislike for Bolivians was no secret.

"The other common theme, as the author of these documents repeatedly points out, is that all these individuals were in some way connected to the execution of Ché Guevara on October 9, 1967."

" 'File Number One,' " began Blondie, reading from the documents, " 'concerns Colonel Quintanilla, the officer who announced Ché Guevara's death to the world. On October 9, 1967, Quintanilla personally led news photographers from all the leading international news agencies into the laundry shed of the Señor de Malta Hospital in the village of Vallegrande.

" 'The laundry shed had been turned into a temporary morgue. In the shed, Quintanilla, at the request of the photographers, arrogantly'–I am quoting from the document–" Blondie said with an apologetic shrug, " 'postured with the dead body of Ché Guevara; the corpse was naked to the waist.' "

Tania tenderly watched Ché take off his clothes. He came to the bed, still with his shirt on. He was inordinately shy, very modest about his body when he was with her, a trait that had always appealed to her. He seldom appeared naked in front of her, even when they were alone in her room. Ché's self-consciousness, Tania believed, stemmed from his childhood when he was so puny and other boys made fun of him and teased him mercilessly about his lack of upper-body development.

Nicolás listened intently as Blondie continued: " 'In these photographs of the dead and naked Ché, and which were distributed worldwide, the Bolivian officer, Quintanilla, a graduate of the U.S. Army School of Counter Insurgency in Panama, can be seen posing, proudly pointing out the bullet wounds that the colonel claimed had killed Ché in his final battle in the Quebrada del Yuro. However, subsequent investigation has revealed that Guevara was captured alive around 3:30 in the afternoon the day before, October 8, 1967. He was wounded, and his automatic rifle had been hit with a bullet fragment, making it inoperable. The Bolivian military took Ché Guevara and two other captured guerrillas from his band to the two-room school house at the tiny settlement of La Higuera, some twenty-five miles southwest. There, after interrogation and torture, the military executed Ché Guevara at about 1:30 P.M. on October 9.' "

Blondie cleared his throat and paused for effect. "This is where we get to the heart of what this briefing is all about"—then returned to the documents—" 'On March 28, 1971, Quintanilla died from three gunshot wounds fired into him by a woman assassin on a Hamburg Street in West Germany.' "

"Perhaps you could speed this up," said General Rossi in his exasperated voice.

" 'In April of the following year, Colonel Zenteno Anaya was shot to death on a Paris street, also by a woman assassin, or a person dressed as a woman. Again,

191

as in the first case, the killer was seen to flee in a car driven by a man.' "

"Who the hell was Zenteno Anaya?" growled General Rossi.

"The officer commanding the Eighth Division which circled and trapped Ché Guevara in the Nancahuasú," replied the little Cuban, with forced politeness.

Blondie, with a circumspect eye on the general – he apparently didn't want him to take too much abuse – continued, "I'll extrapolate from these documents," he gestured with Tania's research file in his hand, "and fill in the details from our own intelligence sources. Major Andrés Selich was the commander of the Ranger company that captured and organized the execution of Ché Guevara. In September of 1972, Selich was found mysteriously beaten to death in La Paz.

"In August of 1974, there was an unsuccessful attempt by a group of men, reportedly led by an Argentine woman, to kill Sergeant Mario Teran, the soldier who actually carried out the order to machine-gun Guevara to death. Teran had subsequently suffered a mental collapse and had been assigned to an insane asylum."

"And who was the woman?" asked the general.

"We don't know exactly, sir. The description that we have fits the woman who was involved in the Hamburg and Paris assassinations. But Bolivian intelligence informs us that a woman with an Argentine passport in the name of Tania Gutierrez Bauer had been in the area at the time."

"So what? I don't get the connection."

"Tania Gutierrez Bauer was also the *nom de guerre* of Ché Guevara's compañera."

"You mean she's still alive?"

The Cuban spoke: "She was killed in an ambush about five weeks before Ché Guevara was killed."

"You see, sir," Blondie said with stoic patience, "the age difference makes it impossible. Besides" – Blondie broke off for a moment – "the woman simply took the same name as a *nom de guerre* for herself."

Blondie closed up the files. "Apparently the operation to execute Sergeant Teran failed because the group fell to arguing. It seems they never believed that he was really insane. They thought this was a story put out to protect the sergeant from reprisal. It wasn't until they actually came face-to-face with the man that they discovered for themselves he was really mad. Teran was able to take advantage of their confusion. He threw himself into a nearby drainage culvert and escaped in the dark."

The general asked, "And has anybody else besides this woman in that case been arrested?"

"No, General. I finish with the observation that no criminal has been arrested or charged in any of these incidents. Quintana is our first break in this – "

"You've forgotten General Barrientos?"

"No, General Rossi. I imagined everybody – "

"Perhaps, but it's not every day that a general who is also the president of Bolivia gets blown up in his own helicopter."

"Yes, sir," replied Blondie respectfully.

"And we can assume it was President Barrientos who gave the order to execute Ché Guevara."

"We will never know for certain, General. But I believe we can assume that it was also at the suggestion of the CIA, who had made the hunt for Ché Guevara their top priority in Latin America."

"Yes," mused the general, with a dig at the Gringo, "and the CIA had also given Barrientos $600,000 the year before to run his election campaign. And Gulf Oil another $400,000, also at the suggestion of the CIA.

When you think about it, a million dollars is a lot of money to pay for one revolutionary born in Argentina."

The massive Gringo stirred impatiently in his chair. He and the Cuban exchanged glances. To Nicolás it was obvious they considered all of this small talk. But Nicolás could tell that the Gringo was curious, intrigued by Nicolás.

Incongruously, the general giggled. "In the end, it just goes to show those Bolivians that you can't get away with killing an Argentine that easily."

The military men in the room all stared at Rossi in stunned surprise.

"Well, after all," spluttered Rossi, dimly aware that he might have said something inappropriate, "Ché might have been misled, mistaken, but in the end we have to remember he was one of us, a son of Argentina, against the Bolivians."

The little Cuban groaned openly. The CIA Gringo remained impassive. But Nicolás thought that it was not difficult to observe from his body language what the Gringo thought of General Rossi.

Blondie began from what he must have known by now was a position of pure hopelessness: "General Rossi, on the basis of the information presented, I ask permission to detain the prisoner and broaden the investigation?"

"On what grounds?" asked the General.

"That we believe the prisoner, Quintana, is part of a support group to an international conspiracy of communist assassins operating internationally –"

Rossi stared in disbelief at Blondie. "Remember," he warned Blondie. "I'm from La Pampa. There we ride a horse before we buy it."

" – and nationally. They call themselves by various names, the Army of Justice for the People, the Committee for the Co-ordination of Revolutionary Justice, and so on. But we know they are a group made up of individuals drawn from different revolutionary organizations. We believe they are part of the same group that planned and carried out the assassination of Admiral Cardozo."

"But the Montoneros have claimed responsibility for Cardozo," protested Rossi.

The Gringo spoke, "What about the connection to the de la Cruz woman?"

With an apologetic nod to Rossi, Blondie replied, "We are confident that we have established there was no working connection, only an emotional one. They had intended to marry."

"You mean de la Cruz and Quintana did not work together to infiltrate military intelligence?" asked Rossi.

"Yes sir."

"You have established that without a doubt?"

"Yes sir. We have some tape recordings of phone calls in which the de la Cruz woman discussed the disappointment she and a fellow subversive, a psychiatrist by the name of Ramón Ochoa, felt because Quintana would not work with them. Apparently they had tried to recruit Quintana—"

"Why wasn't I informed of this before?" whined Rossi. "It was my understanding that you wanted to arrest Quintana because de la Cruz had confessed that Quintana was part of her operational group."

"We thought so at the time, sir. But subsequent information has revealed that Quintana is really part of a support group to the assassination team – " Blondie broke off. "I think there must have been a breakdown in communication, sir. A file was sent to your office and – but perhaps this isn't the time to discuss it."

General Rossi turned to his aide, seated behind him. The room was silent while the aide whispered in the general's ear. The general waved curtly at Blondie.

"Continue, Major Delgado," he coldly ordered.

Blondie winced spontaneously. Oh, thought Nicolás, so no more Blondie. From now on it's Major Delgado. Nicolás understood the general's action. Rossi had sent Nicolás a message. He had identified his torturer to him. The general was also buying insurance for himself. If Nicolás ever survived all of this, Rossi wanted to make sure that he wasn't the only officer Nicolás would later be able to identify.

Major Delgado reluctantly continued: "I wish to hold the prisoner for further interrogation" – Nicolás could see Rossi shake his head and heard Delgado change gears in mid-stride – "I feel he may well be useful in your attempts to engage in a dialogue with some of the Montoneros in exile, or at least," Delgado ended up lamely, "in some of our operations over there."

"How can you guarantee this guy's co-operation?" the Gringo wanted to know. "Europe's not Argentina. Over there you can't keep a bag on his head all the time."

Delgado responded coolly, as if Nicolás was not present, but no doubt fully aware that Nicolás would understand the second move that was being made in this elaborate chess game. If the general was going to implicate Delgado, then the major would outflank his superior officer: "Señor Quintana will, I'm sure, want to act in the best interests and continued good health and safety of Lara de la Cruz."

Lara was alive! Was it really possible after all this time? Nicolás wanted to test the idea slowly and carefully. What had Ramón said about that sort of manipulation? "The military send people abroad as informers and infiltrators. To make sure they carry out these assignments they keep their family and lovers as hostages. Unfortunately, it works very well for them." Don't over-react, Nicolás told himself, let them make the offer first. In the meantime, keep them off stride. Don't let them think Lara is the only preoccupation of your life.

"I'll think about this, and let you know," said Rossi. The general nodded, a gesture of irritation, to the silent aide behind him. This was perceived by all as the signal that the briefing was over and it was time to depart.

Nicolás halted all movement in the room with his question, which he delivered in the best ringing tones of an upper-class Argentine officer.

"The señor from Cuba still has not told me why he wears Ché Guevara's watch."

Nicolás could see that General Rossi allowed himself a smile of amusement. There was a side to the general that Nicolás was beginning to appreciate.

The little Cuban was easily provoked; he was instantly in an uncontrollable and psychotic rage. He pushed his face in front of Nicolás, nose-to-nose.

"Do you know who I am? Do you know what my name is?" he screamed.

Nicolás remained cool. "No. But I'm sure I could tell you something about yourself that you would prefer to have forgotten."

"So tell me?"

"I must have a definite contact with you. If you unlock the handcuffs –"

Rossi nodded assent, but Blondie had already stepped forward and released Nicolás' right hand.

"Hold my hand," Nicolás asked. But the Cuban refused with a contemptuous shake of his head. "Then put Ché's watch around my wrist."

The Cuban still hesitated. In English the Gringo urged him on: "What the hell, he's not going to blow you away with the goddamn watch."

When the Cuban had slipped the tarnished metal bracelet over his wrist, Nicolás suddenly grabbed the Cuban's left wrist tightly in his free right hand.

The Cuban's rage was immediate. *"Hijo de puta!"* he swore. And with his own right hand smoothly drew a 9-millimetre automatic from a shoulder holster under his suit jacket. He held the heavy gun point-blank to Nicolás' forehead. But Nicolás didn't move. He held the Cuban's hand tightly, then calmly closed his eyes. Everyone in the briefing theatre waited in a frozen silence.

In the few seconds that the two men held this position, a dozen quick fragmented images zipped through Nicolás' mind. All of them showed the Cuban dressed in jeans and a windbreaker, a baseball cap on his head. A house in La Paz, in the basement the Cuban applies electrodes to the breasts of a small peasant woman. Her husband slumped in a chair, already badly beaten, has his head pulled up and is forced to watch. Always the Cuban is with heavily armed regular soldiers; sometimes also with gringos, soldiers in civilian clothes, to whom the Cuban pays much deference. Then a final image, which stays longer than the others: the Cuban, a small calibre handgun in his fist, shoots a naked bearded man, already unconscious, in the back of the head. The body jerks spasmodically, then falls off a row of primitive school desks. The Cuban reaches down and in the easy motion of a practised street criminal, strips a watch from the wrist of the corpse.

Nicolás contemptuously tossed aside the Cuban's arm: a man throwing away a used match. The Cuban kept the barrel of his gun pressed against Nicolás' forehead.

"So tell me what I might have forgotten about myself?" he asked in a tense husky voice.

"You follow orders. You do all the dirty work."

The Cuban didn't like that. He slowly began to squeeze the trigger.

"Don't kill him here, now," said the American, quietly but urgently.

But the Cuban refused to put the gun down. "What else?" he demanded of Nicolás.

Nicolás, his eyes still closed, spoke boldly, with hard contempt in his voice, "You were there at the Nancahuasú, the day Rubio was killed. You had flown in that day in a helicopter with two other American military advisers. You urged the major to go in with his company, but you refused to accompany them into combat. Said it was against your orders. You were also there when the soldiers brought in the skeletons of the soldiers killed earlier."

As the Gringo moved toward the platform, the Cuban pulled the trigger. A heavy click echoed through the room as the firing mechanism struck the empty breech.

The Gringo was angry but kept his composure. He put a massive arm around the little Cuban's shoulders.

"Colonel Sunderland told me you're crazier than a bag of hammers," he muttered in English, as he pulled him away. The Cuban put away the gun, then reached back and with a whip-like movement stripped Ché's watch from Nicolás' wrist.

General Rossi let out his pent-up breath in a heavy sigh. One of the other military men giggled nervously. Nicolás had not been shaken. The hand contact with the Cuban had reassured him; from the moment the Cuban had put the gun to his head, Nicolás had sensed that there had been no magazine loaded into the grip of the automatic.

"They were right about you at Langley," the Gringo continued in English to the Cuban. "They told me you had to be kept on a leash."

So, thought Nicolás, the images were right. It was the American who held the power and had control over the Cuban, but only barely.

Nicolás pondered for a brief moment the mysterious images and memories that had suddenly been imposed upon his mind since that dreadful moment in the torture room over the detectives bureau in Barrio La Matanza. He did not altogether understand what had happened. Perhaps if Ramón was still alive he could have offered one of his sardonic comments; an analysis that would have put it all in perspective for Nicolás: "Visions? Voices? A multiple personality disorder it would seem, my dear Nicolás. I would guess, at the very least, a technical diagnosis of schizophrenia." But then it was Ramón who had introduced Nicolás to the Candomblé sect in Minas.

Nicolás shrugged, whatever was happening had brought him closer to Lara, of that he was certain. If this was the gift of Iemanja, then he would take it to wherever the journey led. He was lightheaded. Only his foot felt uncomfortable, sticky. He looked down at his feet. The lights on the platform had cast heavy shadows, so that the blood that had overflowed Nicolás' shoe had formed unseen a spreading stain under his chair. But now the blood seeped out from under the shadow and into the light.

"Jesus Christ!"

The American had also looked down and seen the puddle of blood. The Cuban poked at Nicolás' thigh and then examined his own fingers. Expressionless he wiped his hand on Nicolás' other dry pant leg.

"What the fuck's wrong with you people?" growled the Gringo. "Can't you see that you're going to get a lot more out of this guy if you get him some medical attention? He's going to die on you from loss of blood."

Nicolás felt oddly embarrassed. General Rossi eyed Blondie coldly.

"Release the prisoner to a civilian hospital. I hold you responsible, Major Delgado, for his safe conduct."

With little enthusiasm the major dialled the phone on the table.

"You didn't answer my question," said Nicolás, as he stared at the Cuban.

200

There was an amazed silence in the room, finally broken by the American's chuckle.

"You gotta admit, Colón, the guy's got balls."

Nicolás snapped up the name; suddenly, oblique introductions abounded. Nicolás persisted: "Why, Señor Colón, are you wearing Ché Guevara's watch?"

Colón tried to ignore Nicolás and turned away as if to begin the walk up the stairs of the small amphitheatre to the door. But the intensity Nicolás projected transfixed all the other men in the briefing room. Each man stopped in the middle of what he was doing in preparing to leave: gathering papers together, closing a briefcase, turning up the stairs. They all sensed they were about to share in or witness some extraordinary event. Even the Gringo, who had started to leave with Colón, sat back in his chair, expectant. The Cuban realized he could not walk away and turned to face the question.

Nicolás paused for greater effect.

"You took the watch from Ché's body after you gave him the *coup de grâce* in the village of La Higuera in Bolivia. You shot him in the back of the head."

"No, that's not true." The Cuban was agitated.

"Yes. You were there." Nicolás spoke sombrely, a judge weighing the evidence.

"I was in La Higuera," the Cuban admitted. "I tried to talk the Bolivians out of the execution. My position was always that it was wrong to kill Ché and make a martyr out of him."

Nicolás shook his head in disbelief. "No, Colón, you wanted to go down in history as the Cuban who put the final bullet in Ché's brain."

The Cuban continued to defend himself, and strove to keep the edge out of his voice. "I spoke with Ché. I told him I admired him as a man but disagreed with his politics. We embraced. He wished me good luck and gave me his watch—"

"And it was you who suggested they cut off Ché's hands and keep them in formaldehyde so that they would have his fingerprints on file forever, and nobody could claim that it was not Ché Guevara who had been killed."

The Cuban began to walk toward the door.

Nicolás was relentless: "And now you live in fear because you are the only one left of all those directly involved in Ché's death who is still alive."

Colón's psychotic personality could not be restrained for long. At Nicolás' words he turned and sprinted down the ramp, intent on silencing Nicolás. But the American CIA officer caught him and wrapped his arms around Colón in a bear hug just as the little Cuban was about to throw himself on Nicolás.

"No! I'm not the only one left," Colón screamed, as he was dragged aside by the Gringo. "He was there, too." Colón pointed at Major Delgado.

The frozen tableau of General Rossi and his entourage abruptly moved into motion again. They filed out of the briefing room behind Rossi with expressions of amusement and barely concealed contempt on their faces. Colón and the Gringo talked in undertones. The American held a restraining hand on Colón's shoulder, physically and psychologically trying to bring the Cuban back under control.

Nicolás turned to his torturer. "So, you were there, too, Delgado?"

"Don't push your luck, Quintana. You won," Delgado muttered in disbelief. Then he added, "For the moment."

"No," said Nicolás, shaking his head. "You just don't get it, do you, Delgado?" And then answered his own question: "The general won."

Delgado waited until the Gringo and the enraged Cuban had left, then he offered Nicolás a cigarette.

"The ambulance will be here in a minute," said the major. Nicolás had to laugh. The humanity of the torturer revealed. Nicolás politely declined the cigarette. He would give Delgado nothing, absolutely nothing of himself. Besides, he had never smoked; he saw no reason to start. Nicolás could hear the clatter of men in army boots rush along the corridor toward the briefing room.

"Comrade Tamara Bunke Bider? Follow me, please."
The uniformed Stazi escort marched ahead of her down
the long empty corridor, his boots clonking heavily and
ominously on the hardwood floor. She had felt so much
fear before that first meeting. Strange to feel so nervous
when she had spent months politicking for this exact
appointment. She had spoken quietly to all the right
people in the Pioneers, the Free German Youth Party,
the Socialist Unity Party, the Democratic Federation of
Women. Her really big chance had come when she had
been allowed to address the executive committee of the
Humboldt University section of the Socialist Unity
Party. She had ended her speech with pledges of loyalty,
"I have learned to think and act as a Marxist-Leninist,"
and self-serving requests, "My greatest desire is to
return to Argentina, where I was born, and do everything possible to help the Party there. Of course I would
only return there with the consent of the Party."

Strohm, the grossly fat Party boss responsible for the
organization and control of East Berlin students, had
been the chairman for the group discussion. Tamara
was introduced to him at an informal gathering in a
student bar after the meeting. Strohm had asked her
some questions about her romance language studies at
Humboldt. When he had invited her to ditch her boyfriend and come home with him, she had immediately

agreed. In his apartment near Weisenssee, he had urged her to perform weird and painful things to his body. Tamara hadn't cared. She had given Strohm what he wanted and in return had extracted from him a promise to set up this meeting.

A lone middle-aged woman in high heels, papers in one hand, clip-clopped awkwardly toward them along the otherwise empty corridor. She was surprised at the atmosphere of total silence, almost abandonment, in this building of secrets. Her military escort rapped on a pale blue glass-panelled door. Tamara remembered there was no sign on the door, except her lucky number, thirty-three.

Gerhardt Mann exuded calm and competence.

"Good afternoon, Comrade Bunke Bider. I am your control officer. From now on you will deal only with me. And this is the last time we will meet in this office."

Mann was well prepared. He had her file in front of him. They sat quietly, studying each other across the uncluttered desk, as the loud footsteps of her escort receded down the corridor. Mann was about thirty, slim, blond. He knew everything about her.

"The work is quite simple," said Mann softly. "We want you to do everything that is necessary to get close to the Latin-American student leaders who are studying here in East Berlin. I will give you a list of the specific individuals we are most interested in knowing more about."

"And then?"

"You will file detailed reports once a week. Don't make any editorial judgements, leave that to us. We want to know what these students think. What they talk about among themselves. Their personal habits, and that includes all their weaknesses."

"Why are we doing this?" she asked.

"If they are going to be the future leaders of the Party in Latin America, then we have to know if they have all the qualities vital for our continued support."

Mann was cold, official. Tamara didn't pay attention. She was elated. She already felt her escape plan from East Germany was in motion. Ah, she had been so naive.

After one of their regular weekly meetings, Mann suddenly showed her another side. He was tense, drawn, his pale blue eyes red-rimmed from lack of sleep.

"I'm moving up the ladder," he revealed to her over a glass of wine in an out-of-the-way bar near Bernau.

Tamara's heart sank; she was just getting used to the extra money for her work with the Stasi. And how was she going to stay in touch with all the contacts she had built up as part of her escape plan? But she instantly felt better when he continued, "But I'm keeping you with me."

"Why?" she sincerely wanted to know.

"Because your work is excellent and you and I will have bigger fish to fry."

Tamara smiled eagerly. Mann brought her up cold with a warning, "Be careful, Comrade Bunke. Don't look so obviously desperate to get out of the German Democratic Republic."

"And who says I'm desperate?" asked Tamara.

"It has come to my attention that you'll fuck anyone in order to get interpreter jobs with visiting foreign trade and cultural missions."

Tamara froze. "Why are you warning me?"

Mann smiled. His pale blue eyes for a moment lost their customary enigmatic expression. "Because I understand your need to get out of the German Democratic Republic. And also because I'm not interested in women and so I will never want to fuck you."

Tamara felt chagrin and embarrassment. How could she have been so guileless in her actions? And exactly

206

how much could she now trust Mann? Well, why not find out? She certainly had nothing to lose.

"Surely it's not just me. I thought that everybody except the Strohms of this country wanted to leave. I mean, isn't that why they built that wall?"

Mann grunted mirthlessly. "Talking about Strohm, did he ever ask you back to his apartment for a second visit?"

"No. Besides, if you knew about the first time, then you already know the answer to your question."

Mann ignored her sarcasm. "Not necessarily. Anyway, it means you didn't please him. You're fortunate. This means he won't try and hang on to you."

Then Mann had tried to make her feel better. She was surprised; he had always seemed so cold, beyond sentiment.

"Perhaps," Mann smiled gently, "Strohm didn't like you because you blush so easily. It reveals you as ingenuous. Men like Strohm are not turned on by innocence."

"We have to put this back on now," Delgado said, as he pulled the hood once again over Nicolás' head.

"I know where I am," Nicolás protested. "Campo de Mayo."

"Imagine that," responded Delgado drily, as he finally secured the hood with the black bandages, "and you didn't even have to call upon your special powers to figure that out."

"Major Delgado, I think you had another purpose for this briefing," Nicolás charged, his voice muffled by the blindfold.

Nicolás felt the officer's hands pause in their work.

"You have a personal agenda in all of this, don't you, Delgado?" Nicolás persisted.

The major was about to reply, but fell silent when Nicolás heard other military personnel enter the room. Orders were quietly given. Different hands guided him firmly but gently onto a stretcher. He was carried through concrete halls and then outside. Nicolás felt the touch of a breeze against his bare arms; it was the most delicious sensation he had experienced in a long time. His intense reaction to this mundane everyday event made him realize how total and brutal his imprisonment had been.

Nicolás tried to inhale what he could of the fresh air through his hood. In the distance he heard a company of men being drilled on a parade ground. Then he heard the heavy rhythmic crunch of a squad of soldiers in full battle gear, equipment jingling, their boots striking the gravel path simultaneously, as they double-timed past the stretcher bearers who carried Nicolás. Perhaps the squad leader saw Nicolás' blindfolded head and knew what it meant, because he immediately lead the squad of soldiers in a patriotic chant that began with his line, called out in a deep singsong bass: "We are the army!" In unison the men bellowed back with the deep-throated response: "We are the fatherland."

Nicolás felt himself being loaded into the ambulance. He heard the doors close and then the side door open, and he sensed a new personality sit down beside him. Skilful fingers felt for a pulse in his neck. Then the medic slit open his pant leg in search of the source for all the blood. When he finally found the wounds, he expressed shock. "God! They really made a mess of you, my friend." He expertly applied a pressure bandage and rapidly taped it in place. "Looks like they got in the camp shoemaker to sew you up."

Nicolás felt the end of a stethoscope against his ribs. The medic moved closer. Nicolás could feel the medic's breath on his neck.

"I'm going to give you an injection to make you feel better. It's not authorized, so don't say anything." A calm, educated, and controlled voice. This was a man who was underemployed if he really was just a paramedic.

"If you want, you can tell me your name and I'll pass on any messages for you to the outside."

Nicolás hesitated. He remembered Ramón saying, "There's a cardinal rule among the disappeared: Never give information to a sympathetic stranger who is in any way part of their apparatus of repression. Nobody can be trusted."

Then Nicolás felt the man's fingers swab the crook of his elbow with alcohol and feel for the vein as he prepared for an intravenous injection. Right away Nicolás saw a smiling young medical student in a white lab coat. He held one end of an enormous street-wide banner that proclaimed the medical students' support for the Montonero Movement. Behind the medical students in lab coats, thousands of men and women marched, singing, shouting, waving placards. It was not an angry demonstration but a political celebration.

"What is it?"

"Adrenalin, and a little something else. You've had a difficult time of it, I'm afraid."

"Go to the Bar Paraíso in Barrio Barracas. Tell the bartender, Máximo, that you have a message for Tania: Nicolás is at the–where are you taking me?"

"Don't know yet. They never tell us until we're moving."

"Well, wherever I end–"

The door opened and closed again, and Nicolás sensed the malevolent presence once more of Delgado as the major seated himself inside the ambulance. Delgado rapped on the glass partition to signal the driver, and the ambulance began to move. The man with his fingers against Nicolás' carotid artery spoke deferentially to the major.

"Sir, the patient's pulse is weak and erratic. I request permission to carry out emergency procedures."

Delgado's bored cynical voice echoed coldly inside the metallic shell of the ambulance. "Do what you have to do."

The movement of the vehicle temporarily lulled Nicolás, and he comforted himself with the knowledge that Lara was still alive. When Delgado had casually revealed that information, Nicolás had used all the self-control he had not to pursue Delgado's oblique offer. He had recognized that he had to wait for Delgado to play his card. Despite his condition Nicolás felt he had a new lease on life. Lara was alive, and he was about to be released. He recalled a memory of Lara from the week they spent at Mar del Plata. She had gone to stand on the balcony of their luxurious suite at the Miramar to look out at the night. Lara was nude. Her back, bathed in the soft reflected light from the room, stood white against the blackness of the sea and sky. Then Lara turned to face Nicolás where he sat inside the room. Behind her was the heavy moving of the ocean, broken only by iridescent waves that crested as they rolled in toward the deserted beach. "You are Iemanja, risen from the sea," he told her. But she couldn't hear him above the noise of the surf on the beach.

The medic's fingers came back and probed for a vein in Nicolás' other arm. Nicolás struggled to pull his arm away, but once again was frustrated to find his wrist was manacled to the stretcher.

"I must free the patient's hands, sir."

"No," said the laconic Delgado, "he has a particularly violent history, and as you can see he is a powerful man."

"No injections," demanded Nicolás, for the sake of the friendly medic.

"This is an intravenous feed." The medic replied in a now matter-of-fact voice. "You've lost a lot of blood. You need plasma or you will go into shock."

"No injections," Nicolás repeated.

"Give it to him. We need to keep him alive, at least for a little while longer." That was Delgado's cold calculating voice. "And take this vial here and give him a shot from it."

"I don't have the medical authority to do that, sir. And—"

"And what?"

"Frankly I don't think it's compatible with his physical condition."

"That's an order, son. And if you don't stop giving me a difficult time, I'll have you arrested as a leftist sympathizer. Is that clear?"

"Yes sir!"

Nicolás felt the prick as the needles pierced his skin, then a reassuring squeeze to his upper arm told him that this capable young man had found a way to substitute the drug without Delgado observing his medical sleight of hand.

Ramón: "Sodium Amytal is the favourite drug of the military torturer. Psychotropic, it tends to block paranoid feelings in normally stressful situations. The victim becomes confident, expansive—"

Nicolás assumed Delgado had an offer to make. It just didn't make sense for a major to escort a prisoner to hospital. Nicolás tried to prepare himself mentally, find some high ground he could psychologically hold. Then it came to him. He had the upper hand. Despite his condition, suddenly he believed that he would prevail. No. He knew he was going to win. The idea made him chuckle. What had the *orixá* told him? "When the

211

monster threatens you, swallow the monster! This gives you its power. Then you can defeat the monster and its demons."

He heard Delgado come in on cue.

"That's excellent, Quintana. You just relax, and we'll take you to a nice clean hospital."

"No more injections," Nicolás repeated, pretending wooziness.

"Of course not, *hijo*. So be quiet now, you sound like a broken record."

The ambulance swept smoothly through the streets of Buenos Aires. Nicolás saw himself move in and out of the different periods and memories that now layered his mind.

"No injections," implored Tamara as she stood in line behind her mother and father. The huge immigration building, more like a concrete warehouse, was unheated. Her feet were cold in a way that she had never known them to be cold. This wasn't just the cold of the bright sun and snow in the mountains she had seen when she was twelve and her mother, Nadja, had taken her as a special treat to Bariloche in the Nahuel Huapi National Park. In all the years she had lived in Argentina she had never felt this penetrating cold, which seemed to come through the concrete floor, seep into the bones of her legs and then into her stomach and heart.

How could her mother and father have brought her from Argentina to this bleak and terrible place? They hadn't been rich. But they had been warm there. And happy. Especially during vacations when Mama had taken her to the sea at Colonia Quequén. What delusions they must have had about this place. When they had talked about returning to Germany, they had made it sound like a paradise. But this was awful. What did they call this port where their ship had finally docked? Rostock. Ugh! What an ugly name. Everything was so ugly. The German language was loathsome. Where were all the fashionable Berlin clothes that Mama used to talk about? These Germans went around all bundled up in what looked like used clothing. And what's more, their breath reeked of sour cabbage and garlic sausage. Ugly, ugly, ugly.

Now Tamara could see that they were close to the head of the line, a group of doctors and nurses laboriously processed the passengers who had just got off the boat.

"Be brave, Ita," encouraged her mother.

"Mama, I want to go back home to Argentina," Tamara demanded.

"Shush, Tamara," scolded her father, "we've only just got here. Don't embarrass us now."

"Don't be irritated with Tamarita, Erich," her mother defended her. "She's just cold and tired and can't understand what people say to her."

"Then she should have paid more attention when we tried to teach her German."

"You promised if I didn't like it here we would all go back home to Argentina," Tamara nagged.

"Please, Tamara. Act your age. You're fourteen and you're behaving like a five year old. This is our home now. This is what Nadja and I have wanted for so many years."

"Then you lied to me! You brought me to this horrible place and you knew all the time you were going to stay. You never meant to give me a choice. You betrayed me!"

"Ah, Tamarita, darling. Please be good. I'll–"

A sour-faced young woman in a Pioneer's uniform came up to Tamara and said something in German that Tamara could not understand. Her mother began to translate.

"She wants to welcome you to the German Democratic Republic and–"

Tamara replied in Spanish. "Don't bother. I don't like her, and she smells bad. I don't want to hear what she has to say."

213

Silently Tamara vowed to herself that she would find a way to get back to Latin America as soon as she could. Even then she knew that she would have to do it by herself. She would not be able to count on her parents. No matter. Tamara promised herself that she would do whatever it took to get out of East Germany and back to South America. She would shrink from nothing. She would come to think of this moment as her first truly adult thought and decision. She stuck to it. Her mother scolded her: "This is your greatest strength and at the same time your weakness, Tamara. Once you decide to do something, you never let go of the idea, even if it turns out to a be a mistake and an idea that in the end might kill you."

"And whose stupid idea was it to return to this stupid country?" Tamara angrily responded. The quarrel never ended. Tamara was so self-centred she could not see at the time how bitterly disappointed her mother was about the way life had turned out.

"You can take off that hood now," Nicolás heard Delgado say. The hands of the paramedic removed the cloth from Nicolás' head. Even though it was dim in the ambulance, he kept his eyelids half closed. Through the rear window of the ambulance he could see trees and buildings flash past. He couldn't be sure, but maybe the ambulance was in the Barrio Palermo. He turned to the medic, positioned beside him. He looked exactly as he had seen him when he had led the parade and carried the banner in demonstration for the Montoneros.

"Which hospital are you taking me to?"

"Fiorito," answered Delgado.

"Why there?"

"Oh, because it has a nice name. And it's run by the Sisters of the Bleeding Heart."

"Tamara," Ché rolled the syllables lazily around in his mouth. "That's a nice name."

214

Ché leaned back in the limousine to look directly at her for the first time. From the heat around her throat Tamara knew that she had blushed, and she felt stupid and girlish.

"Tamara is not German though?"

"My grandmother's name. She was a Russian Jew."

"What's the rest of your name, Camarada Intérprete?"

"Tamara Heidi Bunke Bider," she had laughed.

"So, German, and do you speak Russian, too?"

"Oh yes."

"What else?"

"Oh, I can deal with most of the Latin languages. Some English, too."

"What are your dreams?"

"I never dream; sleep like a log."

Ché laughed, "No, I meant your unrealized ambitions."

She joined in his laughter. "That's one of my problems, I am too literal minded. I'm always being told that I give too much attention to detail."

"You have no idea how many campaigns have been lost because the revolutionaries forgot to concentrate on the details."

"Oh yes, I remember some anecdotes from my reading courses. Wasn't it the first French revolutionaries who forgot to take over the banks?"

"You see, what a detail! They should have had you along with them. But you still haven't told me about your personal agenda."

"To go to Latin America."

"And do what?"

"Travel the continent, record the native music of all the different cultures."

"A music ethnologist?"

"Yes."

Tamara could see how much Ché liked that answer. He regarded her pensively:

"I don't see that as being so difficult to arrange. But tell me, how is that you speak Spanish with an Argentine accent?"

"Because I was born in Buenos Aires and lived there until I was fourteen."

"And how old is Compañera Tamara now?"

"Twenty-two on November nineteen."

Ché smiled. Tamara was fascinated by him but not overwhelmed. He looked tired. His face was white and drawn. She knew that he had travelled constantly for the past two months: Africa, the Middle East, the Eastern bloc countries. He looked so young and vulnerable. Tamara wanted to reach out and touch his long hair, to stroke his scruffy adolescent-like beard, and put her arms around him. To comfort him. She knew that the tour as Fidel's spokesman abroad had been a disaster for Ché. Mann had briefed her.

"Ché's been a bad boy. Moscow is upset with him, Fidel is mad at him. We have to watch him carefully."

"What has he done that's so awful?" Tamara wanted to know.

"When he toured the African countries Ché denounced U.S. imperialism, which was okay in Moscow, but not in Havana."

"But I thought that was Fidel's position, too?"

"Right now Fidel doesn't really want Ché to make a fuss because Cuba secretly wants a rapprochement with the Americans. So of course Washington was unhappy with the speeches, but it was okay with the Russians."

"So why is Moscow upset now?"

"Because Ché next came to Eastern Europe and made speeches in which he denounced Soviet imperialism. Not a diplomatic coup, especially just after the Soviets

216

have guaranteed to pay considerably above the world price for Cuba's next sugar crop. In Washington they liked the speech, but it was certainly not okay with Moscow. Our communications department intercepted a message from Fidel. The tone was very cool. He informed Ché that he has been replaced as chairman of the Bank of Cuba and minister of industrial development. No more of those unconventional Cuban bank notes signed Ché with the trademark accent on the *e*. The announcement won't be made until a month or two after Ché has returned to Cuba. But I'm sure the CIA will have intercepted the message, too, and will find a way to feed it to the media."

Tamara wondered what Ché must be thinking. Did he have regrets? Was he disheartened?

Ché gazed out of the window as the East German countryside slid by.

"What terrible things are they doing to the landscape out there?"

"Lignite. That's open-cast mining for East Germany's most profitable export."

"Where does it go?" asked Ché.

"Mostly to the Soviet Union."

"Ah," he murmured enigmatically.

Mann had told her, "They don't want him to stay around any longer in the Eastern bloc countries. No more forums for him to make pronouncements about revolution and independence in Eastern Europe. No press. Just small controlled conferences with Latin American students. Moscow doesn't want any more speeches that denounce Soviet imperialism. I've arranged for you to travel in the limousine to Leipzig with him as his official interpreter. You'll be alone. His group will follow in a second car."

Ché fidgeted listlessly with the papers on his lap. He seemed depressed. She wondered, was he bitter that

217

Fidel had fired him? It was so ironic. For months he had been the darling of the western press. It was impossible to escape his image. This week his Christ-like face was on the cover of no less than four international news magazines. Wherever he went, before he even spoke, or as soon as he appeared, dressed in his guerrilla's combat uniform, the audience would stand and applaud for at least five minutes. In airports, other passengers spontaneously started to clap as Ché made his way to catch a plane.

She had asked Mann, "The Third World is full of revolutionaries. Why Ché? Why is the world so fascinated by this thirty-four-year-old Argentine?"

Mann had replied in Spanish, *"La angustia de la pequeña burguesía.* The middle class live in a state of guilt and fear about the Third World. To them it is all darkness and chaos. They can do nothing to control their corporations' greedy exploitation of those countries. Then along comes Ché, a warrior and intellectual, down from the mountains. He makes it easy for them. The good guys against the bad guys. It is as simple as that."

"I read that in a poll taken in the United States Ché is more popular with young Americans than President Kennedy."

"That's because Ché doesn't have it within him to talk like a politician. Makes him even more attractive. Gives him that moral presence that is the prerequisite of all martyrs."

"You think he will be martyred?"

"Oh yes. There's too much self-delusion there. Now off to work, my little Argentine agent." And Mann had rushed away to another meeting. Tamara found Mann complicated to deal with. His cynicism was never overt, but ran as an ironic undertone to all his statements. And yet, unlike so many members of the East German

218

bureaucracy, he was a driven, obsessed man. Tamara knew from experience that she could contact Mann any hour of the day or night without fear of recrimination.

"Are your parents Argentine?" Ché asked.

"No. They were members of the German Communist Party who were ordered by the Party to stay and work against the Fascists in Berlin –"

"This was Hitler in the thirties, yes?"

"Yes, but then the Fascists discovered my mother's Jewish background, and so my parents fled to Argentina as political refugees."

"And they brought you back to this, when?"

"In 1951."

"They must have been dedicated Communists."

"Yes, life was very hard in East Germany in 1951. I don't think my parents had any idea how difficult it was going to be. As soon as we arrived we were sent to an industrial city that wasn't even built."

"Where?" Ché wanted to know.

"Stalingrad. Just this side of the Polish border. But after Kruschev came to power Stalingrad was renamed Eisenhuttenstadt."

"What did your parents do there?"

"They were teachers, but there was no school. In the first year they shared a one-room apartment with two other couples. Nothing worked. There was no plumbing, no electricity. The streets were a sea of mud. The priority above everything was the construction of a huge steel mill."

"What did you do?"

"Ah, there was no room for me. I was sent away to live with a family in Furstenburg, a small town on the Havel River."

"Did you like it there?"

"No," Tamara laughed bitterly. "I hated it. There were three older boys in the family. They were after me all the time. And they teased me constantly when I tried to speak German with my Spanish accent. The only time I got any peace was when I went to do the shopping with the mother of the family, who absolutely refused to hear any complaints about her three little pigs. I made a different plan every day to run away to Argentina. But how does a fourteen-year-old girl get to Buenos Aires from East Germany by herself?" Tamara paused to wipe a genuine tear from her eye. "I'm sorry to go on like this, but even when I talk about it after all this time has passed, I still get sad and angry."

Tamara pulled the curtain across the window that separated them from the driver of the limousine.

"We have another hour's drive to Leipzig, and your speech to the conference of Latin American students is not until three, so you can sleep if you wish."

Ché seemed suddenly shy. And that's when Tamara knew everything would be all right. She took a French language textbook out of her briefcase and prepared to study, but it was more a polite attempt to show Ché that he could have privacy if he wished.

He stared out of the window. Tamara's initial attraction to this man had now turned to fascination. He had an international reputation as a ruthless man of action, and yet she had found him gentle, brooding, perhaps even tormented. They both stared unseeing at the bleak industrial zone outside the windows.

Ché spoke softly, almost as if to himself, "Spanish speaking, Buenos-Aires born, the child of dedicated Party members, a brilliant student of languages, and also beautiful. It's all too exact. Only the Germans would overdo perfection in that way."

Tamara was instantly defensive: "You are dissatisfied with my competence, Comrade Guevara?"

"No. But you have to admit this looks, Tamara, as if you were handpicked to spy on me."

Tamara laughed naturally. "No, I blush too easily," she said. She held her finger to her lips, then pointed upward with her index finger in the universally recognized gesture that indicated electronic surveillance.

Ché smiled in delight. At that moment Tamara perceived with a great thrill of excitement that the adventure between them had started, and instinctively knew that it would be a conspiracy that once begun would not end, until it had taken them to their graves.

Tamara also knew for certain that she had fallen in love; she had never felt these powerful emotions before. Impatient for them to become lovers, and somewhat surprised at her own desire, Tamara pulled down the shades on the limousine windows, then took Ché into her arms. When Ché showed a brief moment of hesitation, Tamara smiled innocently.

"*Por qué no! Después de todo, somos argentinos,*" she whispered.

And for the first time in her life she made love to a man because she wanted to. Afterwards, when Ché had fallen asleep, she held him close, tenderly. She felt deep and profound satisfaction. The years of uncomfortable tension, endured since she had arrived eight years earlier in East Germany, all slipped away. This moment would would stay with her forever; one that Tamara would continually return to, rework and polish, until every romantic facet of this beginning with Ché glowed like a brilliant diamond in her memory. She told herself that she had begun the journey toward her true destiny. As wonderful as this moment was for Tamara to always take out and examine, she never could let go of an attendant poignance. On that first occasion Ché never gave her any evidence that he shared her assumptions or was sensitive to what she secretly thought of as what would inevitably be their shared fate. But that awareness came later. As the limousine floated toward Leipzig,

Tamara held Ché in her arms, ecstatically happy. He was thirty-four, she was twenty-two, and for Tamara everything and anything was possible.

Nicolás felt the ambulance slow down and then swing into an entrance.

"We've arrived," said the paramedic, as he started to prepare the stretcher for unloading. Nicolás took a closer look at his sympathetic medical attendant. The blue-eyed young man with golden curls, who had so triumphantly led the parade, had a face that looked curiously worn for a man so young. A fallen angel, thought Nicolás, this is a relevant sign. He heard Delgado order the driver to park away from the entrance doors. And when the paramedic and the driver began to remove the stretcher, Delgado halted them.

"You two, go and smoke a cigarette for a few minutes."

"He's on the edge. He's lost a lot of blood – " The Fallen Angel protested.

Delgado was impatient: "Not again! I warn you for the last time. Remember! In our eyes not all terrorists carry guns. I repeat, this man will not die. Besides, don't you know that near-death builds character. Now get out of my sight. Wait for me outside until I give you the signal," the major ordered.

The driver quickly retreated, The Fallen Angel only reluctantly. Delgado half closed the door of the ambulance. Once again Nicolás luxuriated in the sensual feel of fresh air on his face and a glimpse of the sky. Delgado leisurely lit up a cigarette.

"Listen to me, Quintana. You're no *brujo*. I don't believe in all this psychic business or special powers. That stuff is for the campesinos, the Guaraní, and neurotic women. Lopez Rega could pull that shit with Perón's dim second wife. We're military, Quintana" – Wherever there are hunters, thought Nicolás, there are

222

killers. And whenever there are killers you have men making myths of their own lives – "you and I. And as soldiers we don't believe in magic bullets. I think you're just very smart. Brilliant, really. The edge you have so far is that you're very well informed or some group has done an excellent job in briefing you. But that's not new, is it? I've always said if we had just twenty per cent of the Montonero brainpower in our own intelligence units, this dirty war we have been forced to fight would have been over a long time ago." – The hunter, Nicolás thought, always gives his quarry phenomenal qualities, and so creates a covenant between them. With the inevitable death of the prey begins the myth of the killer – "And that, my friend, is why we're going to end up working together."

"Well, I would say we got off to a bad start, wouldn't you agree, Delgado?" Nicolás found that he could speak only with difficulty. But his mind continued to work clearly through these overlapping states of memory. Even though he had to struggle to express his own thoughts.

Delgado chuckled coldly. "Perhaps, but we have, let's say, a very good understanding of each other. After all, in the end, we are Argentines. And you and I, we more or less come from the same background. I must admit you have had some advantages of wealth and power that I didn't. But so what? I mean where have those advantages got you today? But my point is that no matter how badly we treat each other, when we have to deal with the outside world, we're still family. You agree?"

"You're wasting your time, Delgado. And you know I am not a Montonero."

"Ah, but I'm going to turn you into a soldier of Perón."

Listen carefully, Nicolás told himself, the beast wants you to walk into his belly.

"Add to this noble sense of patriotism, the knowledge that every individual has their vulnerability, and we have an interesting situation. Because now I know, finally, what your weakness is, Quintana."

"Delgado, we have nothing in common. You're a cruel and cynical butcher. And one day you will get the hell that you deserve."

"More in common than you think my impetuous young friend," Delgado continued calmly.

"For example, we both know quite well a young lady called Lara de la Cruz" – Nicolás groaned in deep pain, for himself and for Lara – "I had the pleasure of interviewing her some time ago when our Brazilian colleagues detained her at our request in Rio. There is no doubt that de la Cruz is a beautiful and interesting woman. I have to admit I have become quite fascinated by her – as a woman, you understand."

Nicolás regrouped all his remaining strength and concentration. This was the information he had been waiting to hear for eighteen months, so this was no time to waste energy in anger and contempt for this torturer.

"Where is she now?"

"Oh, in good hands."

"I have to see her –"

"That depends entirely on you."

" – before we make any arrangements, you understand that don't you, Delgado?"

"It might be possible for us to arrange a visit. It would take a bit of juggling, of course, but you're in no hurry. Anyway, the main objective now, *hijo*, is for you to rest, not worry about anything, and just get better."

"What is the arrangement you're looking for, Delgado?"

The officer chuckled without warmth, a cynical and indifferent expression from a man arrogantly confident of the final outcome.

"Well, you're a very perceptive young man," he mocked Nicolás. "You're right, I do have a personal agenda. And from the beginning of our acquaintance I decided to make you an important part of my plans. But we'll talk about all that next time."

He pushed open the ambulance door and tossed out his cigarette. Warm sunlight flooded over Nicolás' body.

"I'm sure you'll want to reflect on our conversation, Quintana. So I'll come back and see you when you've had time to recover. When you feel a bit better, you will be able to see things more clearly."

"Don't count on my being here when you get back, Delgado."

"Oh yes. You'll be here." The major sounded bored. "Because you see, as long as you know that I have Lara de la Cruz, I know you're not going to run away."

Through the open ambulance door Nicolás could see The Fallen Angel hurry across the clean-swept cobbled courtyard of the hospital toward the vehicle, a doctor and two nurses scurrying behind him.

"Tell me one thing, Delgado."

The officer turned and held the medical staff at bay with one upraised hand. He waited for Nicolás to speak.

"While I'm thinking about all this, what was behind the name and phone number in Mexico City that I gave you?"

"You don't know?"

Nicolás weakly shook his head, he had almost reached the end of his strength.

"Well I suppose there's no harm in giving you something back that you gave to us. The name Víctor is the code name for the Soviet control officer for Tania, Ché Guevara's compañera in Bolivia. The phone number was a special line rented by Soviet Intelligence in Mexico City."

●   ●   ●

The warm spring Mexican sun melted Tamara's body. She felt as if she could sit on this balcony forever. But only if she could block out Mann, who lounged in a rattan chair on the other side of the table, absentmindedly toying with the bougainvillaea blooms in the earthenware pot as he tried to reassure her.

"You've been out here for a while, several years now, Cuba, Guatemala, Argentina. And I've always been there for you, Tamara. Remember when we first took on this assignment? I told you we would see it through together. I'm still moving up. I'm now stationed here in Mexico City. They've given me the Latin American desk."

Tamara looked over her shoulder into the cool shadows of the exquisitely furnished apartment, and ruefully thought about the series of mean rooms and flats in which she had so far spent her life. Even in a Communist intelligence apparatus, she reflected, it's the *jefes* who live well, and the workers like herself have to live in all the shit.

Mann had installed himself in a huge and luxurious apartment on Calle Presidente Mazarick in the now fading Barrio Polanco, once one of the most wealthy barrios of Mexico City. He had chosen well, thought Tamara. Mann had stayed away from the diplomatic and wealthy enclaves, such as the Lomas of Chapultepec, where his activities might have drawn attention. In the more worldly Barrio Polanco, there were enough seedy pockets and strata of bohemia to let Mann's behaviour go unnoticed.

Tamara pulled herself out of her dream state and decided she had better listen more attentively and observe with more care what was happening on Mann's balcony. She took and sipped the guava juice brought to them by the slender young houseboy, Ricardo.

"I'm helping the boy through dance school," Mann explained magnanimously.

Tamara could see that the intelligence officer was already exercising his freedom from the constraints of East Berlin. He couldn't take his eyes off the sulky-faced Ricardo when he was in view, even while he talked to Tamara. And in front of her, Mann openly caressed Ricardo's lean brown arm when he brought a tray of fresh fruits. Although Tamara did notice Mann always spoke German when Ricardo was in earshot.

"I have an excellent cover, one to match yours as a music ethnologist. I'm an anthropologist, funded by a liberal West German foundation. My expertise: to study possible ritual connections between North and South American aboriginal tribes. It's also my hobby, so I know what I am talking about. I will be free and have good reason to move around throughout Bolivia, Venezuela, Peru, Argentina, Brazil. We will have lots of opportunity to maintain contact."

"How often?" Tamara wanted to know.

"Your mission to maintain surveillance of Ché Guevara – our joint responsibility – is now a priority operation back in East Berlin and, I must add, Moscow."

Her heart sank. Tamara had always known that working for the Stasi inevitably meant in the end also working for the KGB. But it wasn't the news she had really hoped to hear. Her own self-delusion. And how bizarre! She had been more anonymous as a low-level agent in East Berlin than here in Latin America. Tamara purposefully pushed Mann further.

"What if you're not there when I need you?"

Mann was patronizing. "You must know by now, Tamara, that once you are a member of the Party, especially doing the work we do, there will always be someone there for you. And that means in any city in the world.

"In La Paz? Come off it, Mann."

"From Paris to La Paz."

Damn his snide little memory, Tamara thought. Did he have to bring that Paris craziness up again?

"Remember, my dear, how we kept you out of jail after that bizarre sexual adventure of yours in Paris? I know the Cubans wanted you to establish a cover history for yourself in Europe before you went to Bolivia. But really, was it necessary to take up with petty-criminal elements, a pimp on the Champs Elysée?"

Was it her imagination, she asked herself, or had he started to develop a lisp? His voice had certainly gained an affectation he had always kept reined in before.

"I can see our naughty little Tamara would just as soon we forget. Did you ever tell Ché about that? No? Well, anyway."

"It wasn't quite like that, and perhaps we all act a little strangely, turned loose and alone in the capitalist world for the first time –"

Mann ignored the implication and quickly interrupted her, "But that's precisely it, Tamara. No matter what your situation, wherever you are, you will never be alone. There will always be someone to give you a bed for the night, hide you if it is necessary, feed you, give you money and assistance if you need to move clandestinely across any border to any country and –"

"I'm not talking about emergencies."

"Ah, I see," Mann continued on smoothly. " Well, it's no small thing to break with the Party and lose that kind of security. Very few defectors understand the enormous support system that is always in place for them – until they cross to the other side. And then it's too late. Because there's only one rule, Tamara. If you walk away, you can never come back. That is why the Americans have never penetrated our organizations in any significant –"

Tamara listened carefully. Mann was giddy with his newfound freedom. He had lost his wariness. Back in East Germany he had always first listened thoughtfully, and then questioned carefully and intelligently. Now he babbled on. He didn't listen. He anticipated her questions and intervened with answers before she was finished. Then it came to her what this change in behaviour meant: Mann was planning his own defection. He had probably put as many years into his own escape plan to get out of East Germany as she had in hers.

Tamara had only wanted to escape from East Germany to Latin America. But for Mann there was only one country to run to: the Central Intelligence Agency. Now she knew she had to be extra careful. Intelligence officers like Mann, who worked as controllers over as many as a dozen agents in the field at a time, when they decided to defect, used all their agents as currency. Agents like Tamara simply became the capital defectors used to establish fresh bank accounts in their new lives.

She didn't want to make Mann nervous by indicating she was on to him, nor give him the impression that she was going to break loose as soon as she got to Bolivia. But Tamara was elated. Because she also realized that now Mann needed her more than she needed him. Tamara was Mann's one-way ticket to the U.S.A. He was going to keep her in place for as long as she could. Mann would never let her be recalled to East Germany.

"This is a veiled threat, isn't it? Comrade Mann."

Mann gave his habitual enigmatic smile. "No, just a gentle reminder. Just as I have to remind you that the Cuban groups that have been trained for revolutionary activity in the rest of Latin America have been hopelessly compromised by infiltrators. Their intelligence apparatus is vulnerable because it has been isolated for so long. Have you forgotten already what happened in Guatemala? Another ill-planned Cuban operation. How we got you out of trouble there, and covered up for you?"

Tamara nodded sadly. She remembered the night in Chichicastenango, one-thirty in the morning on the stone steps of the Church of Santo Tomás, crowded with Mayan family groups, as they burned incense and candles to saints and to their ancestors. The cold clear night was filled with the heavy liturgical rhythms of their prayers. In darkness on the other side of the plaza, behind all the crowded market stalls, lit every so often in the exploding glare of fireworks, Tamara could see the white station wagon. Inside the vehicle, Tamara knew, a CIA agent waited with three Guatemalan military intelligence officers, all of them caught in an ominous game of cat and mouse. And then the two French "tourists" arrived to pick her up at the bottom of the stairs of the Santo Tomás church and fold her into the safety of their presence.

Mann continued: "That night, you were the only member of that Cuban-organized group to get out of Chichicastenango alive. If we can protect you like that in a little town in the Guatemalan highlands, we can certainly do the same in La Paz."

Tamara understood she must continue to make Mann feel he was in control, that she was still psychologically dependent on him.

"You still don't understand," she told him. "The real problem is that I'm afraid of being on my own for so long. Ché wants me to take two advance years in Bolivia to organize the lines of communication and support before the guerrillas even get there. What's more, he wants me to stay away from the Party and any known Communist groups. He has told me: 'Tamara, you must do this assignment entirely on your own. We cannot count on any of the local Party organizations, because they're all controlled and manipulated by Moscow.'"

"Excellent!" Mann smiled, reached out, and clinked their glasses of guava juice in mock toast. "This restriction will make our work even easier and more effective. The Party organizations have already been given their line: no co-operation with Ché. You will be in Bolivia entirely clean and independent. This makes it even easier for me to stay in contact with you."

Delgado unlocked Nicolás' right hand from the stretcher and waved forward the medical personnel.

Nicolás was quickly unloaded from the ambulance. The doctor held a stethoscope against his chest.

"That's why I knew you had special information, Quintana. You thought you could fool me with the code name of a guy who defected to the CIA in Mexico City eight years ago." Delgado took Nicolás' hand in mock celebration, "Congratulations!"

Nicolás seized Delgado's hand for only one reason. He concentrated on Lara as soon as he felt Delgado's hand in his. But this time he received no images, no information – nothing. But he refused to let go of Delgado. Even after they had Nicolás on a gurney, he clung with a death grip to Delgado's hand. He could feel himself being rushed along a corridor. Everybody, doctor, nurses, ran beside the stretcher. They attached tubes to his body and held an oxygen mask over his face. Delgado had to also run beside him. Nicolás smiled to himself: *The torturer cannot escape his victim.*

"We're losing him," Nicolás heard the doctor say. Delgado laughed outright in cynical disbelief.

"Let's get into Emergency – fast! Call Father Morán down to give the patient his last rites. Does the patient have a name? Do we have a history?"

Delgado spoke, and Nicolás marvelled that even as he trotted beside the cart, the major could contrive to sound supercilious.

"He is a political delinquent detained under military orders. His injuries were incurred during a desperate attempt to escape from detention. He was fortunate not to have been shot."

The doctor, a stooped and balding man in his sixties, hurried along beside the cart. He barely gave Delgado acknowledgement. He leaned over the gurney and spoke softly in Nicolás' ear.

"I know you want to take the major with you, but leave that business to God, my son. Release the officer's hand," he gently commanded.

Nicolás let go of Delgado's hand, and immediately another hand took his. A gnarled worn hand but one that exuded warmth and sympathy. Nicolás understood immediately that it was the man in the boat, the one he had seen on the small lake. The same man who had yelled a warning to him through the mist just before he was attacked by the three men near the Rosedal flower garden. He held Nicolás in a powerful grip. But because his features were partly obscured by the mist and the darkness, and because the man was hunched over in an attempt to steady the rocking rowboat as it wallowed from side to side in the waves, Nicolás was unable to get a clear look at his face.

The sea lapped around the boat, blue-grey and turbulent; a damp chilly mist swirled around them.

"We haven't got much time," said the man, as he awkwardly held with his other hand onto the rickety wooden dock on which Nicolás stood, "and I've got a lot to tell you."

Nicolás hesitated for a moment. "Can we wait for Lara?" he asked.

"No. She went ahead. We have to pick her up at another place," the boatman replied.

"Where?"

"Everything will be all right. *No te preocupés, che.* Relax. You can sit in the stern and steer, while I row," said the man in a hoarse voice that Nicolás found vaguely familiar. "I can get you out of here without any problems. But we have to leave now because the tide is about to turn, and in another few minutes it will be too late."

Nicolás looked back over his shoulder. The landscape was in total darkness. He could no longer see where the land joined the dock.

"You can't go back," said the boatman. "You won't be able to find your way without a guide."

Nicolás finally overcame his indecision and lowered himself carefully into the rowboat and sat in the stern. The boat looked weathered, the hull and trim needed to be scraped and repainted, but it appeared seaworthy. It was the kind of simple but sturdy craft fishermen have used for hundreds of years to singlehandedly fish the shorelines of the Atlantic. Nicolás took the tiller and in the worn and polished handle discovered a row of God's eyes that had been carved and painted in the hard wood.

"Give me the course?" he asked the boatman.

But the man didn't at first reply. With a surprisingly smooth and powerful thrust, he pushed the boat off, and the rotten dock collapsed behind them into the sea. He took his position in the bow where he started to pull on the oars. Nicolás was mystified at the way the boat moved swiftly and effortlessly through the choppy waves.

The boatman called out repeatedly: "Straight ahead, straight ahead, *che*. Straight ahead." And in a quavery old man's voice the boatman began to sing, and Nicolás couldn't believe his ears:

"El amor es torbellino de pureza original,
hasta el feroz animal susurra su dulce trino."

The ancient voice belied the powerful strokes that pulled the rowboat through the sea. This is completely bizarre, thought Nicolás. If I am dying, why is there no dignity in my death? How is it that I am in this boat with this crazy old man? And why are we singing this popular song about a middle-aged woman who, much to her surprise and ecstasy, has fallen in love with a seventeen-year-old boy? But despite himself Nicolás joined in the song:

> " . . . detiene los peregrinos
> libera a los prisoneros
> el amor con sus esmeros . . . "

The old man's voice became stronger, until he and Nicolás were joined in easy harmony, and they suddenly found laughter and companionship in their voices.

> "Al viejo lo vuelve niño
> y al malo sólo el cariño
> lo vuelve puro y sincero . . . "

The sea began to lose its heavy swell. But the mist still hung in thick patches over the ocean. The boatman abruptly abandoned the Violeta Parra song, leaving Nicolás to trail off alone on the line:

> "De par en par la ventana
> se abrió como por encanto . . . "

In a few powerful strokes the silent rower pulled the boat through an especially thick bank of mist to surge on to an unexpectedly calm deep blue-black sea. A huge full moon hung in a pale sky. *The moon is your planet and water is your element.* Nicolás looked over his shoulder. Behind him lay the huge dark brooding land-mass of South America. Unexpectedly the boatman began to sing the tango "*Cambalache*." Again, the song was hardly appropriate. But his voice was pure now, powerful in its projection across the calm water:

> "Que el mundo fue y será una porquería ya lo sé
> en el quinientos dos
> y en el dos mil también . . . "

The boatman rested on the oars. Because the man's back was to the moon, Nicolás could still not get a clear view of his face. After a careful examination of the horizon that appeared to leave the boatman satisfied, he hung the oars with smooth skilful movements across the gunnels of the boat. And then without disturbing the equilibrium of the craft, he moved with graceful agility from the bow to lower himself into the seat directly opposite Nicolás. The boat drifted and turned until the moonlight shone clearly in the rower's face. Nicolás could see that he was a strikingly handsome young man. His skin was brown, his eyes were deep impenetrable black mirrors that caught and flashed the reflection of the moonlight. He had long black hair that fell in curls to his shoulders. He was dressed in the eclectic put-together combat fatigues of a guerrilla: ankle-high laced-up jungle boots, mismatched combat pants and jacket; a black-and-red bandanna tied around his forehead; belts of ammunition for an automatic weapon draped criss-cross across his chest; a machete slung from his waist; and on his head, a black beret stuck with the metal pins of common fronts and guerrilla forces of Latin America.

"Who are you?" asked Nicolás.

"That's not important right now. Besides, we've met before."

The guerrilla seized Nicolás' hands in his own. Nicolás felt remarkably transformed; a powerful wave of strength and serenity flowed through his body. To Nicolás it seemed they sat and drifted across the dark still sea for long moments of tranquillity; a calm that however did not last long.

"Why are we here and where are we going?" Nicolás finally asked.

"We are here so that I can pass on to you my memory," said the boatman in a quiet and sombre voice.

"No!" Nicolás exclaimed. "No! I don't want it. I don't want this information. I am already burdened with memories that I never sought, a memory which came to me under terrible circumstances. I already carry enough. No. This is too much pain and confusion. Any more and there will not be the smallest part of myself left."

The boatman was stern. "Enough of this self-pity. Don't waste any more of my time. You yearned to explore this world, and now you rail against the responsibility you have been chosen to carry. We are all brothers and sisters in the flesh. Accept. Embrace and enter into the spiritual experience of your fate and you will be in control of the powers that have entered your being. Only then will you be at peace and have the strength to deal with your life."

"Why do I need the memory of a guerrilla? I'm not even interested in politics."

"Politics are for today. Revolution is forever."

"That is only rhetoric, more slogans. If that is what you have to give me, I don't need it. Through violence, revolutions plant the seeds of their own ultimate self-destruction."

"No. The need for revolution will always be here, it transcends all ideologies. People must always have the right to fight against social injustice. *Mirá, che*, don't waste our short time together with political argument. I am here because I'm the other side of the river. I am the connection that will pull you through this tangle of confusion you find yourself in. And because I was there with Ché from the beginning–"

"Where? Which beginning?"

"In the Sierra Maestra, in the Congo, and in the last battle at Vado del Yeso, close to the Río Grande."

"Which one are you?"

"I am Nico, who Ché executed because I raped a peasant girl before the taking of Las Villas in Cuba. I am Serapio, who guarded Tamara when she first became ill near Bella Vista on the march to Muyupampa in Bolivia. Later, by the Río Iquira, I fell wounded in an ambush of Joaquin's group. I was taken to Lagunillas by the soldiers where I was tortured and executed by the Bolivian Rangers of the Fourth Division under Colonel Luis Reque Terán. I am Rolando, who was wounded in an ambush on the road from Ticucha. They carried me to the priest's house at El Meson, where I died on the table as Miguel and Ché operated on me. I am Tuma, Ché's personal bodyguard for eight years. I fought beside him in the Congo with the Kinshasa rebels; I never left his side, until I fell by the Río Seco. The bullets tore out my liver. Ché tried to aid me. But we both knew my time had come. I gave him my watch to wear. This is the watch that the Cuban *gusano* and CIA executioner Colón took from Ché's body and now wears. This is the connection that brought you to me. I am all the ones who fell in combat at Ché's side, and I'm all the ones who were captured and executed by the Bolivian military. I am also all of those betrayed by the weakness, stupidity, yes, and even the cowardice of my comrades. I am also Loyola, the student leader who Ché unwittingly condemned. Selich found my name and address, uncoded, in Ché's journals. Selich raped and tortured me on the top floor of the building the Cuban *gusanos* and the CIA had taken over in La Paz. I refused to talk for three days, to give my compañeras time to escape. On the third day the guard left me alone for a moment in the washroom. I threw myself out of the window."

The moon had become obscured by clouds, and the boat was once again surrounded by heavy banks of mist. The calm sea turned grey and moved in heavy swells that rocked the small uncontrolled boat precariously. Nicolás did his best to put the tiller over as the boat slid sideways down the waves. The young guerrilla held Nicolás' face in both hands.

"Don't you see. I am all the ones who have been forgotten, betrayed, or abandoned. But without us there never could be a revolution. We believe. And we live worse than the animals live in the forests. We sleep in the mud and the rain. In the cities we live with a terror that is our daily bread. We think we kill the enemy, but we slaughter our own brothers and sisters. We believe we can build a new world, but daily we are driven deeper inside ourselves. We make sacrifices of our bodies and demands of each other which if asked of soldiers of any ordinary army would meet with mutiny. We endure all because we believe, right to the bitter end, that without us there could not ever be revolution and the struggle for justice."

"*Demasiado!* I can't take this. This is too much for one man. I will go mad. Take me back to the shore."

"Too late!" said the guerrilla.

He turned to move back to the bow, through the chilly strands of mist that had once again invaded the boat. And as he clambered over the thwarts Nicolás saw the young man lose the suppleness of youth and, transformed, move with the decrepit awkwardness of an old man, as once again he became the boatman who had first met Nicolás by the disintegrating dock. Nicolás was mesmerized. Behind a curtain of mist the old man fumbled with the oars until they finally splashed heavily into the water. He pulled weakly on the oars and groaned loudly in pain. The boat was surrounded by damp white mist that blocked out the moon and stars.

He heard the soft whispered exclamations and felt gentle but inquisitive fingers running over his body before he could force his eyes partly open. Through half-raised eyelids he saw a nun, whom he took to be one of the sisters who ran the hospital, bent over him. With one hand she had lifted up his bed sheets to peer down the length of his naked body. And with the other hand delicately, as if to absorb the injuries, caressed his skin. Then he recognized her voice.

"Oh, what have they done to your beautiful body, my sweet lover? And why is your lovely cock all bandaged like that?"

Then he heard the demanding whisper, "Nicolás! please talk to me!"

Tania gently lowered the sheets over his chest and lovingly put her cheek beside his on the pillow.

"Nicolás," she whispered in his ear. "We have to get you out of here before they come back to take you away again."

To see Tania again, feel her presence, and hear her voice was so emotionally powerful that Nicolás was amazed at his own first reaction. He was truly overwhelmed to see her again, and deeply moved that she had disguised herself to get into the hospital to be with him. But the unanswered questions, and the flood of conflicting information he held in his mind about Tania, blurred his initial feelings for her.

She sat down on the chair and pulled it close to his hospital bed. More alert, he got a better look at her, and for a moment wondered if the drugs and punishment his body had been forced to absorb had damaged his brain and reduced his vision to monotones. Because Tania, dressed in the traditional white nun's habit, her normally suntanned face made pale with makeup, her dark hair covered in a white cowl, looked ethereal, a soft chalk drawing against the white walls of the hospital ward. The only relief in her disguise was a black ribbon on the arm of her habit.

"Why are you in mourning?" he asked in a husky whisper. "I'm not dead yet."

Tania smiled tenderly and gently stroked his hair. She was so happy to hear him speak; love poured out of her eyes. Nicolás, confused, made himself resist the powerful and positive energy that flowed from her body.

"No, my love. I knew you wouldn't die. The sisters told me that when they brought you back to life you were still unconscious, but that you were singing tangos and love songs. They say you've become a medical case study. Personally, I think they're all enchanted by you."

"You make an excellent Sister of Mercy."

Tania couldn't but help appear pleased: "I carry it off well, don't I? But that's because I was a novice for a year."

"What happened?"

Tania laughed. "I went home from the convent for a two-week vacation and discovered men."

"No. I meant why the ribbon of mourning, or is it just another theatrical touch?"

Tania, slightly embarrassed by her inappropriate revelation, caught the flat tone in Nicolás' voice and restrained her outpouring of emotion.

"No. The black ribbon is real. My old friend, Felipe the street singer, you remember him? He died. We've just come from his funeral –"

"We?"

"Máximo took me. There were a lot of people from El Paraíso at the funeral –"

"Where was the funeral?"

"La Recoleta," and Tania held a hand to her mouth but couldn't suppress a laugh.

"Incredible! Was Felipe secretly rich?"

"No, but Máximo was wonderful. He raised this enormous amount of money from the customers at El Paraíso, enough to buy – for a couple of years at least – this tiny little crypt space for Felipe's ashes in La Recoleta. Don't you think that's a wonderful irony, Nicolás? A poor old bum like Felipe goes to his final resting place alongside the rich and renowned in probably the most expensive cemetery in the whole of Latin America."

"Yes, I think Felipe would enjoy that."

"But come on Nicolás. We can't waste any more time, Máximo is outside in his van, waiting for us. We've come to take you away."

Nicolás closed his eyes. "When did Felipe die?"

"Three days ago. He disappeared from the streets, and didn't show up at El Paraíso where he used to come every night. We began to look for him in all his usual haunts. But then we got a phone call from the police. Apparently Felipe had decided his time had come. He took a bus down the coast, and from a tiny fishing village somewhere past San Clemente del Tuyú he took a boat in the middle of the night and rowed out to sea. He must have chosen to die out there on the ocean. Or maybe the exertion killed him. So lonely but so dignified, don't you think, Nicolás?"

Nicolás couldn't speak.

"The next day," Tania continued, "the boat drifted back to shore with the tide. He was dead. He had left letters in his pockets, and that's how the police got in touch with Máximo. He went down to claim poor old Felipe's body. I'll tell you more about it later. But we have to go now. There are people here who will help us. I'll go and get a wheelchair."

Tania stood up to go into the corridor.

"You betrayed me," Nicolás accused Tania coldly. "Just as Tamara betrayed Ché in Camiri. In exactly the same way with the documents she left behind in her Jeep."

Tania halted in mid-motion, one hand on the door. She returned to the chair to peer intently at Nicolás.

"Why do you call her Tamara?"

"That's what Ché called her all the time."

"How do you know this?" Tania demanded.

Nicolás shrugged, "You know. Reasons I can't even understand, let alone explain–" his voice trailed off in puzzlement.

"*Mierda!*" Tania was infuriated. "Why does this have to happen to you? El Místico, a trifler in mysticism. A wealthy self-preoccupied liberal who doesn't have an ounce of political passion or revolutionary discipline in his whole body. Why was this experience wasted on you? Why couldn't it be given to me?"

"Believe me," Nicolás replied fervently, "I wish it had been given to you. But that doesn't answer the question of why you left your file on the *ajusticiamientos* for Ché in my room at the Cruz del Sur. They were incriminating documents to make me appear as part of your group. And I know that your group carries out assassinations in the name of political justice."

"You don't trust me?"

"What's that got to do with it?"

"There's a perfectly logical explanation of why you were disappeared."

"I would like to hear–"

"You're breaking my heart Nicolás. We have become very special lovers. You touched my soul. That was so beautiful, so real. I gave you something no other man ever had from me–"

"No. This is more real." Nicolás pulled back the sheets to show all the wounds on his body.

Tania wept, suddenly tender again.

"Ah, Nicolás," Tania continued so sadly. "These are such awful times. They have done terrible things to all of us. You've lost so much weight."

"The flesh I can replace but not the trust."

"I swear I didn't betray you. I left the documents in your room because I went to pick up the false identity that you had paid the policeman for – remember? I didn't want to have the papers with me when I went to meet him."

"I don't believe you."

She returned the sheets to cover up the cuts and bruises that seemed to cover almost every inch of his skin and sat on the bed close beside him.

"Nicolás, I grieve for what happened to you. Not only did they wound your body, but they also did something terrible to your mind. You weren't like this before. You were so sweet, so generous."

"Yes, that was true then," replied Nicolás. "But now I have only the demons of rage and revenge inside me."

As he spoke, Tania tearfully slipped open the bodice of her habit and took Nicolás' hand inside to place it against her naked breast.

"Here," she said, "if you have special powers, can you try to feel my heart? Can you see my soul? Then you must know that I would never betray you?"

Nicolás felt the unbearable sweetness of her body under his hand. An uncontrollable tremor ran through him as her complete acceptance of him was made all the more powerful after the days of rage and humiliation at the hands of Delgado.

Ché was barely under control, just on the edge of exploding with anger.

"It's always the same," were the first words Tamara heard him say the afternoon he returned to the Nancahuasú base camp, "lack of discipline and organization. This is what will destroy us, not the soldiers of the Bolivian army."

Tamara was shocked to see that Ché already looked so thin and drawn. Like most of his guerrillas, he suffered from malaria and intestinal infections. The preliminary training march for the guerrillas had been planned for twenty-five days but instead had taken an exhausting forty-eight days and had turned into a chaotic nightmare.

Tamara, who had arrived in the base camp earlier from La Paz, had already been briefed by Ché's most trusted aide, Pombo, who had led the advance group in to the base camp earlier and had given her insight into what had happened on the gruelling march.

Serious rifts had broken out among the men, based mostly on Latin chauvinist distrust and narrow historical antagonisms.

Pombo had told Tamara, "The Bolivians are completely inexperienced and undisciplined. They cross roads and open areas without precautions. They set up ambushes that put everybody at risk. They refuse to take instruction. Half a dozen Ché calls *resacas*. These dregs actually believed they would be paid. Ché told them only the CIA pays for revolutionaries by the hour."

"What is Ché going to do with these mercenaries?" Tamara asked.

"Send them back!"

"But what about the security risks? They'll start blabbing to the first military patrol that stops them."

"What else can he do, shoot them? Besides he has bigger problems with the rest of the guerrillas. The Cubans and Bolivians are at each other's throats. The Peruvians won't take orders from anyone – not even their own *jefe*. We're in a worse mess than we went through in the Congo. And yesterday we received a coded message from Monje: All the official Party organizations in Bolivia are to break ties with us. Monje has also forbidden any Party member to join us. This means we have no replacements."

Tamara already knew about the collapse of support from the cities. She felt overwhelmed with guilt. But then could she have singlehandedly changed anything?

"So be careful," Pombo had concluded. "El Ché is in one of his brooding rages; anything can happen."

Tamara knew that the march had been intended to help the guerrillas get to know the "operational zones" around their base camp on the Nancahuasú, and to explore both sides of the Río Nancahuasú, and the upper reaches of the Río Grande.

But according to Pombo, the military maps Tamara had obtained for Ché, pilfered from the Bolivian Department of Defence itself, had been hopelessly inaccurate. Consequently the guerrillas had wasted days and nights, wandering around lost in the canyons and the heavy forest around the Río Nancahuasú and the Río Grande.

The weather had been awful; the rain incessant. Two of the Bolivian guerrillas, Benjamín and Carlos, had been swept away and drowned as the groups had crossed

245

the swollen rivers. Some of the other Bolivians had unfairly, so Pombo thought, blamed these accidents on the incompetence of the Cuban leaders.

Ché had hoped to recruit campesinos but had been bitterly disappointed. Communication with the suspicious peasants they had encountered had been extremely poor.

"Always in broken Spanish," shrugged Pombo ruefully. "Because not even the Bolivians can communicate with the Indians. They speak a Guaraní dialect that these city slickers from La Paz can't understand."

Pombo's ironic complaint was not lost on Tamara. She had seen the intelligence research on the Bolivian interior, prepared by the other members of Ché's advance team who had worked in collaboration with Bolivian sympathizers, and she thought it had been abysmal. Based on information relayed to him in Cuba, Ché had spent months in Havana struggling to learn Quechua, only to find when he arrived in Bolivia that the campesinos in the operational zone around the Río Nancahuasú spoke Guaraní.

The march over the difficult terrain and through the forest – the men had daily taken turns as *macheteros*, cutting paths for themselves through the otherwise impenetrable forest – had imposed severe hardships that had revealed serious psychological and physical weaknesses in some of the Cubans of whom Ché had held the highest expectations. He was also very unhappy with the leadership of some of the units.

Pombo said, "There is a lot of tension among the Cubans, too. Ché has openly criticized Marcos, and obviously thinks he is unfit to command the advance column. Alejandro is without experience. He has quickly become sick and apathetic. Ché thinks he is already too weak physically to withstand the rigours of the guerrilla campaign ahead."

Tamara had waited anxiously for Ché. She knew he was not going to be happy with her news. She was also on edge because Loyola Guzmán, the twenty-five-year-old student leader from La Paz, who had been placed in charge of finances and made official treasurer of Ché's guerrilla operation, was also in the camp with a report for Ché.

The younger woman was transparently excited to see the great man. Loyola had yet to meet Ché and was unabashedly in awe of his reputation. She pestered Tamara for advice on how to present her report, and she had an unquenchable thirst for anecdotes about Ché's past exploits. Even though Loyola was only four years younger, her innocence and enthusiasm made Tamara feel like an old woman.

At one glance, Tamara had known that Loyola was just Ché's type. In fact Loyola reminded Tamara of what she was like just a few years ago: eager, gentle, and heartbreakingly vulnerable in her blind faith to Ché's Latin-American revolution.

At the same time, Tamara could see that Loyola possessed a will of steel. She had already been purged from the official Bolivian Communist Youth Party because of her support and activities for Ché. No small act, something Tamara had never been able to do, break from the Party. Tamara, knowing she was going to be in disfavour, felt insecure and didn't need this added competition. They were, after all, the only two women in the camp.

But when Ché finally led the centre column into the Río Nancahuasú base camp, Tamara's heart went out to him, and she was ashamed of her petty jealousies. Ché already looked so haggard, how was he going to survive the months ahead? Perhaps Fidel had been right.

Mann had told her, "Fidel doesn't really think Ché's going to come back from this alive. We have a transcript of a phone conversation between Fidel and his brother Raúl. We heard Fidel say, 'At forty, Ché's too old for this guerrilla campaign stuff. He's a sick man. He hasn't really had time to recover from the Congo disaster with the Kinshasa rebels. He won't be able to hold up too long in the Bolivian interior.' "

Although it was a long and arduous trip, four days in a Jeep from La Paz, Tamara had always seized any excuse to visit the Nancahuasú camp, especially after Ché had arrived in Bolivia. Often it meant braving his wrath, but she couldn't stay away from Ché for very long, after their long absence from each other. Just to be around him, listen to him talk, share meals with him, was such a luxury. Ché was the only man in Tamara's life who really listened to her. And she felt a deep romantic attachment to the Nancahuasú. She had actually found the property with Coco Peredo, one of the Bolivian guerrillas. They had posed as sweethearts while they had searched southern Bolivia together for an appropriate base camp. Tamara had funnelled the money from Cuba to Coco for the purchase of the three-thousand-acre property a year before Ché arrived.

The camp itself was a wonderful natural fortress. Except for a small area of cleared land, it was surrounded and covered by inpenetrable forest and bordered on one side by the Río Nancahuasú. The river was a great natural barrier, impossible to cross at that point because it roared past the base camp between the walls of a thirty-foot ravine.

The only approach to the camp itself was along a narrow trail that ran beside the ravine cliffs. The track ended at a small piece of cleared land and a tiny tin-roof farmhouse. La Casa Calamina it was called by neighbouring ranchers. But behind the house, in the hillside under the forest, Ché and his men had spent months building a hidden complex network of tunnels and caves to house the guerrilla force and all their equipment. Only Coco was allowed to live in the farmhouse. The rest of the guerrillas had to stay out of sight in a hidden area near the tunnel complex.

Tamara loved to lie in her hammock at night and listen to the jaguars cough in the jungle. Deer, bears, and other game roamed through the area. Whenever the rain approached across the top of the jungle all the monkeys, parrots, and other birds would raise a huge uproar in the forest. Then seconds before a curtain of rain fell, the birds and animals would fall into a dead silence, broken only by the nervous coughs of the jaguars. The Nancahuasú is where she felt she belonged. When Ché and she were there together it gave her a sense of privacy and intimacy that they had never had before in their relationship. Tamara would lie awake in the dark beside Ché and fantasize that the Bear Camp at the Nancahuasú would become their permanent home. It was always with great reluctance that she left the Nancahuasú and returned to her work in La Paz.

As luck would have it, Ché returned to the base camp when she was in a self-indulgent and silly moment. Miguel had given her a combat jacket to wear, ostensibly to keep off the mosquitoes. But Tamara had never been able to resist uniforms. The men had made a great fuss over Tamara and Loyola, who in turn had gotten into the act, happy to pose with automatic rifles on their laps while, despite Pombos's protests – "These photos will get these women killed if they fall into the wrong hands" – everybody snapped pictures of each other. Tamara realized with chagrin that the others were heady with the idea that they were making history. And everybody wanted a little piece of evidence from this time.

Tamara could tell by the look Ché gave her when he came upon this embarrassing photo-taking session that he was unhappy to see her there. And doubly unhappy to see her dressed up as combatant.

"The same old story," he reproached the group. "No discipline and no organization."

But he gave no orders for the photographs to be destroyed. Perhaps he was just too preoccupied with other problems. And he said nothing more directly to Tamara as she introduced the new arrivals and the two guests she had brought in from La Paz, the Frenchman, Régis Debray, and Ciros Bustos, the Argentine.

But shortly afterwards, when Ché insisted that Tamara walk up the hill into the forest with him, he turned on her:

"Despite all orders and instructions to the contrary, again you have arrived without being sent for. Your usefulness to this revolution is on the outside. We have and will in the future have more than enough men to carry guns. When we started to talk about this plan more than four years ago, you accepted from the beginning that you would work in the cities. That you would set up our intelligence-gathering apparatus, independent of the Communist Party organizations. You have done extremely well so far. Better than anybody else in the advance group has performed. But every time you come here you put at risk that invaluable intelligence network we have worked so hard to build and maintain."

How could she ever tell Ché what the Party, through Mann, had ordered her to do:

"We now move to the next phase, Comrade Bunke. You must find ways to withdraw and dismantle the support structures you have put in place for Ché Guevara's guerrilla activities in the Bolivian interior. Abandon your work in the cities. Give up your personal advice column on the Santa Cruz radio program, "*Suspirando de Amor*," which you have used to broadcast coded radio messages to Ché in the jungle."

Mann paused for a moment and added softly, "And then, Tamara, they want the impossible. Your orders are to somehow keep us informed of Ché's activities but break off direct connections with the guerrillas."

"I suppose that means they now want me to become the mistress to the chief of the Bolivian armed forces. And that way monitor the pursuit of Ché from the inside. Any other orders?" Tamara asked sarcastically.

"Yes, and you won't like this," replied Mann. From now on you are too big for me to handle. A KGB officer will be your contact. He will leave instructions of how and where to meet in the drop box at Santa Cruz."

Tamara understood and rattled away nervously, "They're going to abandon Ché, aren't they? And that means I'm of no use any more. So you're going to get rid of me, too. You know it's all over don't you, Mann? Fidel must also know this too. Correct, Comrade Mann? Listen, we all know that the situation is impossible. The only one who refuses to believe it is Ché. But tell me why doesn't Fidel put together a rescue plan to get him out?"

Mann had no immediate answers for her.

"You're upset," he told her. "Naturally, but when you've calmed down –"

"Don't patronize me, Mann. I'm not that naive little bitch you picked out of Humboldt University in East Berlin. No, I've been through too much shit."

"Have it your own way then –"

"I see it all quite clearly," Tamara reflected bitterly. "Moscow puts the lid on revolution in Latin America, and Fidel finds a way to rid himself of the popular and zealous revolutionary leader, Ché Guevara."

"Personally, I think you're wrong about Fidel, although you should know best. But Moscow does not want to take the heat internationally, especially from the United States, for fomenting revolution in Latin America. It's simple geopolitics, Tamara. Europe

251

remains important. But the Third World will always be a pawn, no matter what happens in Europe and the United States."

"But this doesn't explain Fidel's silence and inaction."

Mann shook his head. Tamara could see that Mann just wanted her to shut up and go away. But she couldn't let go. Not yet. For the first time in her life she knew real panic. Mann represented the Party to her, and the Party was abandoning her.

"You knew that I was always caught, didn't you?" she asked him.

Mann raised a cool quizzical eyebrow, but betrayed his nervousness when he chewed absentmindedly on his colourless lower lip.

"In the beginning, when I first met Ché – "

"You forget, Tamara, how desperate you were to get out of East Germany. Ché was your ticket out – "

"But I always loved him. You knew that."

Mann nodded gravely in agreement.

"Tell me, Mann. How long can a system last that demands if you want to be with someone you love, you must betray them first?"

"This is becoming maudlin, Tamara. You wanted to see Ché again after he returned to Cuba."

"He invited me to Cuba."

"But you needed permission to leave the country. It was quite straightforward. If you wanted to be with your lover, you had to work with us, give us the information we needed on the Cubans."

"Which you have passed on to the KGB all these seven years."

"So why didn't you fall in love with any one of those Latin American students who studied in East Berlin and who you spied on?"

"That's not the same thing!" Tamara felt exasperated and tormented by this German.

"Look into yourself, Tamara. If you had fallen in love with anybody else but Ché, you would never have gotten permission to leave East Berlin. And that's the gentle truth."

"I should have escaped over the Wall."

"And then you would never have got in to Cuba. The Party would have branded you as anti-Communist. I doubt whether Ché would have bothered—"

"Yes, he would have," Tamara yelled defiantly. And the other patrons of the Bonanza in downtown Santa Cruz all turned to stare at these two quarrelling foreigners. The owner, a moon-faced Bolivian, smiled at Mann and Tamara, and increased the volume of the radio just as a spate of commercials for Coca-Cola gave way to a bolero.

Mann was angry, but lowered his voice to speak with even more intensity.

"Listen, Tamara! If Ché cared so much about you, why didn't he stop you from secretly marrying that middle-class Bolivian kid?"

"He knew I had to do it to obtain my Bolivian citizenship papers. And so what if a young man fell in love with me?" Nevertheless, Tamara could not hide her hurt at the memory. "Nobody else ever offered to marry me—"

"The first truth is that you manipulated that little boy—"

"No, never—"

"C'mon, Tamara. You told me he was a virgin."

"What's that got to do with anything? He was sweet and he loved me—"

"Did you ever stop to think that maybe it's just possible that he loved you in the same way that you loved Ché? That he went off to Europe only because you wanted him to?"

Tamara shook her head in tears. "What's the second truth?" she demanded.

"The second truth is that if the Cubans had a half-decent document service in their intelligence department they could have made you the documents you needed, and you wouldn't have had to marry that child."

"You owe me, too, Mann. We both know that you got out of East Germany on my back."

Mann refused to reply. He had had enough. Instead, he called for the bill.

Tamara sank into deeper despair. "Ah, what does it all matter anyway. It's all over, isn't it?"

Mann still wouldn't talk. Tamara watched as he discreetly placed an envelope of money for her inside a magazine he left on the table. Then he silently picked up his "anthropologist's" pack, coldly shook her hand in proper Germanic fashion, and with a nod walked out of the Bonanza Restaurant. Tamara watched him stroll across Calle Junín to the Santa Cruz post office. She knew that he was going to defect, and use her and everyone else to buy freedom for himself in the United States. Then it struck her: Of course, Mann had already paved his way in advance. He must have already fed the CIA information on Ché and Fidel, information that she had collected.

When Tamara finally opened the envelope she found a note folded around the wad of U.S money. The note had two words in German: *Rette dich!* Save yourself!

Ché was determined. Tamara could hear the frustration in his voice: "Now, listen to me. No more of these unauthorized visits unless I send for you. This silly fantasy you have of serving in the jungle as a guerrilla has to stop."

While they talked Tamara jumped at the report of a single shot fired in the forest. Ché dismissed it as one of the men hunting for food. Tamara felt mortified. She didn't have the courage to tell him right there that the papers she had purposefully left behind in the Jeep, parked in Camiri, would make it impossible for her to return to her work in La Paz and Santa Cruz. She was sure that the military would have inspected the vehicle by now, found the papers, and seized the vehicle. She was also certain that they were too unsophisticated in counter-intelligence work to put the papers back and leave the vehicle under surveillance. Tamara counted on them to impound the Jeep.

What madness, Tamara asked herself, has driven me to this stage? She was about to blurt out everything to Ché, she was at the point where she didn't care any more, when luckily, the scatterbrained Loro appeared at that moment to report excitedly that he had just killed a lone Bolivian soldier. That had been the single shot they had heard. Loro's story was that he had been surprised while on guard duty on the path to the base camp by a military patrol. Tamara could see that Ché didn't believe him. Somehow the story didn't ring true to even her inexperienced ears; there had been no return fire, which meant the rest of the military patrol didn't attack, an implausible lack of reaction under the circumstances.

Pombo had witnessed what had happened. Three soldiers on foot had made a cursory inspection of the farmhouse. They had not even bothered to enter the gate, and had already begun the return walk to Lagunillas when Loro, for no other reason than he held a weapon in his hands, fired and killed the third soldier who lagged behind. The other two had run for their lives. Pombo had tried to catch up with them to prevent their escape, but they were too far ahead.

Ché could hardly control himself. Loro was the son of one of the most prominent families of Bolivia. And although he had spent a year in Cuba in a guerrilla warfare training base, Loro often acted as if he had never got out of an expensive prep school. Ché was enraged at this stupid and unnecessary killing that would now bring so much unwanted military attention to the base camp.

"You realize now," he told Loro, "they will send a company. We will have to set an ambush and kill many men at a time and place where we do not have a choice but to stand and fight. All of which breaks the first rules of guerrilla warfare: We must always decide when and where we are going to fight."

Just when Ché had calmed down a bit, Rolando came in to report that the Jeep Tamara had left in Camiri had been seized.

Rolando observed, "There is no way out now for Bustos and Debray." The Frenchman became very excited and panicky.

Then Braulio entered the camp to report another disaster. From a hilltop vantage point he had watched an army patrol follow the unit led by Marcos, who had proceeded without any diversionary precautions, straight to the base camp.

Ché was extremely angry. Months of work in establishing the base camp had now been lost. The camp would have to be quickly evacuated so as to draw attention away from the Río Nancahuasú base. Discovery by the military of the mountain equipment that they had collected and hidden in the tunnel complex on the hill behind the farmhouse would be an almost insurmountable disaster. This latest development also meant that before the guerrillas had a chance to rest and recuperate from the arduous training march, they would have to move out and keep the military patrols occupied with diversionary tactics. As well they would have to carry away as much as they could to be cached in other secret places that had yet to be found.

The next morning, in front of the entire guerrilla force, Ché stripped Marcos of his command and replaced him with Miguel. This was a stunning development. Marcos held the rank of commandante in the Cuban army. Miguel was only a captain. Ché followed this ceremony with a lecture in which he criticized Loro and some of the others.

"In the next two days each of you must come and discuss with me, individually, a list you must prepare of your military and psychological weaknesses for self-criticism–"

Ché was interrupted by the roar of an aircraft, followed by a muffled explosion on just the other side of the Río Nancahuasú. The first bomb, of what would become daily bombing runs of their zone, had been dropped.

The Cubans showed no reaction, but the other members of the guerrilla who had no experience with this dimension of combat were visibly shaken.

They began the evacuation of the camp. Ché ordered Loyola and Tamara to leave. But Braulio arrived with a radio report from Santa Cruz that revealed that the military in Camiri had informed the press that papers found in the Jeep disclosed the presence of an international guerrilla force in the area. After Loyola left, Ché immediately took Tamara aside.

"How bad is it?" Ché asked.

"Very," she replied. "They show that I, as Laura Gutierrez, worked as a secretary and interpreter for the Bolivian presidential press secretary."

"What else?" asked Ché, resigned.

"There are photographs of me with ministerial aides attending various social functions, and a few where I am chatting with President Barrientos himself."

"That's it?"

"No. There is also a letter I forged for you in–"

"For me personally?

"To use only in an emergency."

257

Ché, puzzled but scenting something he had not counted on, asked, "What kind of emergency, Tamara?"

"The letter identifies you as Adolfo Mena, citizen of Uruguay and a special envoy of the Organization of American States, assigned by the OAS to study and compile data on economic and social relations in rural Bolivia. The letter calls upon all authorities to aid you in your travels and tasks. The idea was that you could use this letter with the same false passport with which you entered Bolivia."

"But now that the letter has been captured I won't be able to use that passport anyway"

"No, you won't," said Tamara, and her heart again contracted with guilt. Finally she had been the one to close the bolt on the last practical escape hatch for Ché in Bolivia. If he wanted to get out now, the only way he could withdraw would be to walk out 800 kilometres through the mountains to Chile. A march that, given the terrain and the military pursuit, would take a band of men at least three or four months. And Tamara knew Ché was not about to do that.

Ché tried to make light of the loss of the passport.

"Revolutionaries don't really believe in passports. We don't recognize the government we are fighting to overthrow, so why should we recognize their systems of administration and control?"

Tamara did not know what to say.

"Who signed this letter?" he wanted to know.

"I forged the signature of Gonzalo López, the press secretary to President Barrientos."

"Why?"

"I did it for you, Ernesto. I thought if everything collapses, in the worst possible scenario, you might need a cover to slip out of the country."

"But all of what you've described so far doesn't indicate the presence of international guerrillas?"

"No, except that my East German I.D. documents as Tamara Heidi Bunke Bider are in the same briefcase."

"How did this happen?"

"When I brought Bustos and Debray to Camiri, I was only to drop them off for the escort to bring them here. But nobody showed up–"

"Damn that Loro's eyes! He was supposed to take the Jeep to meet them."

"Apparently there was a confusion in the times. Anyway, everything quickly became complicated. A truckload of soldiers arrived and began to do a document check street by street through Camiri," Tamara continued, "and neither Bustos or the Frenchman wanted to hang around, for fear they would be picked up. So I couldn't leave them alone, and I couldn't drive all the way here in the yellow Jeep. It would have given away the location of the base camp–but that's not a problem now."

Ché winced. "But then it was," Ché finished for her. "All right. You made the right decision. And so you began to guide Bustos and Debray in on foot?"

"Yes. We got a ride on a truck to Lagunillas, and then Braulio picked us up in the Jeep. But I was trapped overnight. In retrospect I realize I should have brought the briefcase, but we had to walk past the army post, and it would have been so bizarre, so suspicious, to walk around a miserable little place like Camiri with a briefcase, I might just as well have been leading an elephant. The military would have stopped me for certain and searched the briefcase. And the documents would have been found anyway."

"No," Ché said, "the first mistake lay in that you should never have been driving around with those kinds of documents"–My God, thought Tamara, sometimes the man drives me mad. He just can never resist the opportunity to give a lecture. You would think that a man with all his combat experience would realize that this is a waste of breath. – "You should have driven a kilometre outside of Camiri and burned the papers, returned to Camiri, and only then proceeded to Lagunillas."

"That's hindsight, Ernesto. On reflection, what should you have known about Marcos?" Tamara finally fired back.

"That is another issue. Do not try to deflect the necessity for your own self-criticism."

What a nag! That's all he is, really. And he presents himself to the world as the Revolutionary New Man. Why do I keep doing this to myself? Whenever I am away from him, I forget all these unbearable qualities in him that drive me insane. Why didn't I pay attention to Mann. I should have just got out. *Rette dich!* Mann had written in his note. Save yourself, Comrade Bunke. Take the first plane to Buenos Aires. To Rio. To New York. Back to that pimp in Paris. Anywhere. Tamara felt the rage continue to mount within her. Ungrateful *hijo de puta!* Two years of letting myself be pawed around by all these sleazy little Bolivian Fascists in order to establish an intelligence network. Weekends at stupid nudist parties, so as to curry favour with lecherous ministers of the Bolivian government. Months of nerve-wracking subterfuge. And what do I get? A dumb fucking lecture on how to burn documents.

"Ernesto," Tamara cut Ché short. "I met you in the summer of 1960 when I was twenty-two. For these past seven years I have loved you, followed you, and worked for you. It is now April 1967. I will be thirty years of age on November 19 of this year. Given the way the campaign is going so far, it is highly unlikely that either of us will live to celebrate my thirtieth birthday."

Ché laughed and, in that sudden and magical switch he could so often make, went from a boring pedant to a charming irresistible man full of a deep human warmth and sincerity. It was a kind of mysterious power he had. Perhaps in the end, thought Tamara, it had nothing to do with politics. Why else would people follow this man to their graves? Ché put his arm around her shoulders to take her in his stride and marched her toward the tunnel complex. She, as always, melted when he bestowed his acceptance on her.

"But that's how we have to fight a revolution, Tamara. With no thought that tomorrow it will cost us our lives. Now go to the storeroom and find some boots so you can march in the jungle with us."

That night, as they camped near some caves the guerrillas had found in a canyon off the Río Nancahuasú, Ché surprised Tamara when he called upon her to step forward at the usual evening meeting Ché held to discuss problems and issue instructions for the next day.

Ché was the only one standing. All the others sat or squatted in semi-darkness around two low-burning camp fires.

Ché began, "A brief introduction to a compañera who for the past two years has worked in the cities of La Paz and Santa Cruz where, at great personal danger to herself but with enormous personal courage, she has done the equivalent work of a battalion of revolutionaries."

Then Ché unslung his own combat rifle from his shoulder, and with a little ceremonial flourish presented the weapon to Tamara.

"This," he told everyone, "signifies our acceptance of Tamara as a combatant. Tonight Tamara becomes Compañera Tania, the guerrilla."

Tania took the weapon amid polite applause from the guerrillas. She felt moved by Ché's formal recognition of her in front of the others. And felt that she should find some words to respond. But for Tania there was a certain hollowness to the moment, so she simply took the automatic rifle and thrust it over her head.

"*Venceremos!*" Tania cried out into the black-purple night. From out of the half darkness, the deep guttural voices of some fifty men responded instantly and in unison, "*Victoria o muerte!*"

Tania was engulfed by the powerful masculine energy that rose up in that primitive male war cry from these warriors around a camp fire in the middle of the jungle. And was disconcerted to discover her internal emotional response was immediately sexual. Ché began to speak again and Tania somewhat self-conciously returned to take a place beside the camp-fire. As she passed by the seated guerrillas, some of the men reached out silently to shake her hand in congratulation. She sat down between Coco and Pombo. Coco put his arm around her shoulders in a brief comradely hug and, incongruously, sexual images from a weekend Coco and she had spent together a year ago, when they had searched for land to establish a guerrilla base, flashed through her mind. A weekend she had completely forgotten about. Tania was nonplussed. Was this really what she wanted to feel and remember of this moment, after she had strived all these years to fight by Ché's side?

Pombo read her easily: "Strange isn't it," he said, the flames from the low camp fire gleaming on the mahogany skin of his face. "All your life you strive for something. You get it, and then, surprise! you don't know quite what to do?"

Then Pombo laughed his deep throaty chuckle. Before there had always been communion in that laugh, now Tania heard only mockery. Then Pombo left to take his turn in the night ambush set up to guard the approach to the camp.

Pombo, who had always been businesslike with her, became even more aloof and distant. He knew, Tania realized. He understood all along what she had been about. Tania turned her attention to the discussion led by Ché.

Loro asked, "But why Bolivia, Ché? Frankly, I've thought about it a lot, and I just can't understand why you would choose to begin here."

"Let us begin with the idea of a continental revolution," replied Ché. "We have to make Latin America another Vietnam. Bolivia is simply the heart of the continent. Tonight we stand in the middle of a country that is bordered by five countries: Peru, Brazil, Argentina, Paraguay, and Chile. You can see immediately that with a powerful revolution focused in Bolivia the explosive effect it would have on those neighbours, and how simple it would be to attract and encourage rebellion by revolutionary movements in those neighbouring countries."

But Loro had studied abroad as an engineer in Europe and was not satisfied.

"I dare say you're right, Commandante. But I have not met anyone who believes Bolivia is ripe for revolution. For one thing, the peasants in Bolivia can buy their own land –"

"It is not necessary to wait until all the conditions for revolution exist; the insurrectional forces can create them," Ché interrupted.

Pombo added, "And for the moment, the conditions are better here than anywhere else. Show me a poorer country in Latin America."

The men fell silent, more than half of the group were Bolivians. Tania could understand what they were thinking. How can a band of fifty guerrillas, many of them already tired and ill, hidden away in the jungle of the Bolivian mountains make the huge leap of the imagination required to see themselves as liberators that would set the continent of South America on fire.

Loro spoke slowly, as if he were thinking aloud, "Then if we succeed in this theory of *foquismo*, in which armed struggle creates revolutionary conditions, we will make history not just in Bolivia but for the whole of Latin America."

Ché nodded. "That is our responsibility," he replied gravely.

Debray, the Frenchman, began to lecture the guerrillas on the theoretical development of *foquismo* and immediately lost his audience. Tania's mind jumped impatiently away from the French intellectual's harangue.

Ché actually believes it is possible, she wondered to herself. Do you have to have this level of absurd delusion in order to succeed, or have I become cynical and negative over the years, especially the last two spent so much alone in Bolivia?

She ran over in her mind what sources Ché could count on: the Soviets had given their official Communist Parties and organizations orders to work against Ché, and that included the powerful Mine Workers' Union. Fidel had become invisible and silent at a time when Ché desperately needed assistance. The urban organizations and their potential for insurrection in La Paz and Santa Cruz, Tania knew from firsthand dealings with their leaders, were a bad joke. So in the end this was all there was, these forty-nine men and one woman in these caves beside a godforsaken canyon near the Río Nancahuasú. And of these men, only about a dozen of the Cubans were truly disciplined and toughened by the experience of guerrilla warfare in Cuba and in the Congo. So, thought Tania, when it came right down to it, Ché could probably count on only a dozen men in the whole of Bolivia, or the rest of the world for that matter, to help him start his revolution. Now she recognized the real reason for the mockery in Pombo's laughter, that what she had wanted above all else, to fight beside Ché, was going to be her personal hell.

• • •

Tania tried to control her impatience and anger. She moved closer to the hospital bed so that she could speak more softly, more urgently,

"Nicolás, we've taken a big risk to come here and get you."

Nicolás looked straight at Tania.

"No, I can't leave. I have some unfinished business. If I stay here, I have a chance to find out if Lara–"

"Oh, her again!"

Tania rolled her eyes in exasperation.

"Nicolás, I don't want to appear insensitive, but they've really messed up your head. I think you've fallen for the oldest trick in the book. I bet I can tell you what has happened, and as you know, my sweet friend, I am no psychic." Tania couldn't keep the edge of scorn out of her voice.

"They've offered to let your Lara go if you successfully carry out a mission for them?"

Nicolás nodded and struggled to a sitting position in the bed. He had a momentary sensation of dizziness but otherwise felt a great deal stronger than any time since his interrogation at Campo del Mayo.

"I must have been here four or five days," he wondered aloud, more to himself than to Tania.

He carefully examined the intravenous feed attached to his arm. Already, he could see, his arm musculature had decreased. His muscles were atrophying from lack of food and exercise. Tania was right, his whole body felt diminished.

"Have they told you what they want you to do?" asked Tania.

"Not yet," Nicolás replied.

He could see that Tania was becoming more and more impatient and upset. She paced anxiously around the tiny hospital ward, caught up under a powerful tension.

"Relax," he told her. "I have nothing to lose by finding out what they want me to do for them. And you can be assured that I'm not going to sell out you or anyone else."

He must have pressed against a raw nerve, because Tania suddenly swung on Nicolás with a stricken but determined look.

"It's all right," he reassured her calmly . "I know that your group has sent you to kill me."

Tania recoiled in astonishment.

Nicolás softly continued, "You have told them what has been happening – my dreams, voices, visions – and they fear that I am a threat to your and their security. I knew that this was probably going to happen. But I also know that it is not going to happen today. My time has not yet come."

"How can you be so sure, Nicolás?" asked Tania drily. "I am in awe of these images and telepathic insights that you have, but you know you're still human, subject to all the paranoia and irrational emotions we humans have. Don't forget that."

"Perhaps. But I decided to make it easy for you. That's why I sent the medic with a message where to find me."

"Why?"

"Because I have something that I know your group wants very much for your program of *ajusticiamientos*."

"What?" asked Tania.

"Who is at the top of your list for El Ché and still remains alive?"

Tania began to speak, "Max –"

"– Colón, the Cuban and CIA executioner," Nicolás completed for her.

Tania nodded. "You mean, he's here? In Buenos Aires?"

"Yes. And how about," Nicolás continued, "Major Roberto Delgado of the Argentine Third Army Corp?"

"Him, we know about," said Tania with a certain apprehension in her voice that Nicolás found puzzling.

"Well that's why you're not going to kill me, because I can deliver both these men to your group."

"How?"

"Major Delgado has a deal he wants to make with me if I want to obtain Lara's release."

Tania hesitated, not wanting to leave but torn.

"Listen, Nicolás, I would never have killed you. But I understand your suspicions. After what you've just gone through, you're right to examine every thing that comes up very carefully. But I'm upset. I know if you don't come with me I will probably never see you again."

"But you can see that I have to wait here to find out what Delgado's offer is all about. And only then can I be of use to you."

Tania dug inside the folds of the nun's habit she was wearing and placed a small wallet in front of Nicolás.

"I was going to let you find this out in your own way and in your own time. But we have been overtaken by events. Open the wallet."

Nicolás flipped open the wallet and found himself staring at an I.D. picture of Tania, but made out in the name of Lara de la Cruz. Nicolás felt that horrible empty feeling again inside his chest.

"Where did you get this?" he asked Tania in a shocked whisper.

"You paid for it. Remember the cop in the restaurant behind the Teatro Cólon?"

Nicolás was devastated. He started to move out of the bed.

"I need my clothes. I have to find him and talk to him."

"It's too late, Nicolás. He's dead."

"Why? How am I ever going to find out –"

267

"After I met the cop and gave him the rest of the money, he tried to follow me. Máximo had no alternative, the situation became too complicated. Máximo had to kill him. Unfortunately we only understood later that he wanted to give us a message."

Nicolás continued to stare hopelessly at the I.D.

Tania continued as gently as she could, "But before he died he, uh, talked to us. He told us Lara had talked. She is a *chupado* and now collaborates with Delgado. That's why the cop passed on her I.D. Apparently it was intended as a message from your father."

Nicolás steeled himself to show no reaction.

"Then I will have to wait and see what Delgado has to offer, won't I?" he finally replied.

"No, Nicolás," Tania answered, sad and resigned. "We can take you to see Lara."

Nicolás took only a moment to decide, "Then why don't you go and find that wheelchair."

Tania smiled sadly and opened the door to the young blond ambulance medic, who had arrived simultaneously with a wheelchair.

As they wheeled Nicolás out into the parking lot and toward Máximo's van, Tania reached into a bag and placed in Nicolás' lap Felipe's ancient and battered portrait, the photograph that used to sit propped up in the street singer's guitar box.

"Felipe left a note. He said he wanted you to have this picture of himself as a young man."

Nicolás gazed into the face of the young guerrilla in the rowboat.

Nicolás sat alone at one of the worn wooden tables in El Paraíso. Between his hands he held Lara's identity card superimposed with Tania's photograph. He had been locked in meditation like that for a long time, perhaps two or three hours, he hadn't kept track of the time; he did nothing more than steadfastly keep his eyes fixed on the ID card. Earlier, Máximo had several times ventured past Nicolás' chair, to enquire politely if he needed a *cortado* or a sandwich. But Nicolás had always declined, politely, in a low murmur, but without so much as a glance up at Máximo. The bar owner finally wandered over to Tania, who sat by herself at a window on the other side of El Paraíso. She was immersed in a French book, *Les Religions Africaines en Brazil.*

"What do you think he's up to?" Máximo asked her, unaware that Nicolás was in such a state of heightened awareness that he could hear their voices from the other side of the bar.

"Do you think he's cracked up?"

Tania, her concentration interrupted, put her book down with a show of controlled patience, to take a look at Nicolás.

"Sometimes, you know, there's a delayed reaction for the *desaparecidos* like Nicolás who have been kidnapped and then resurfaced."

Ramón had once told Nicolás, "My patients will never get over the experience of being disappeared and tortured. Not a day will go by for as long as they live when it won't surface, at least momentarily. And certainly it will always be lurking there in the subconscious. Some people are prematurely aged by the experience, others regress to some age in their childhood when everything was taken care of for them. The very best I can ever do for them is just help them to learn to live with it for the rest of their lives."

"No," Tania said, disgruntled. "He's just doing his weird psychic thing."

"Have you told him about La Señora, yet?"

"No," Tania snapped. "And I wish you would relax, you're making me nervous."

"My, my, dear heart, a little irritable today are we? Maybe El Gordo can fix you a little English tea, perhaps laced with a dash of arsenic?" Máximo enquired with good humour.

"Thank you, Máximo, and I'm sorry."

"You know that jealousy is corrosive, I think the French call it the bitterest of our discontents."

Tania laid down her book and chose her words carefully.

"Máximo, I could never feel jealousy for that poor woman, only compassion for the hell she has gone through and now lives. My only concern is how Nicolás will deal with the information. Now please go away, my friend, and let me read my book in peace."

Chastised, Máximo returned to the bar where, as he served the occasional afternoon customer, he continued to cast curious glances at Nicolás.

Nicolás had heard everything in the exchange between Máximo and Tania. But in his mind's eye he had seen Lara as she walked along a beach. She looked exactly as when he last saw her eighteen months ago.

Perhaps even a little younger, but in good health. Her hair was longer, almost to her waist. Even though it was a cool day she only wore a summer dress and went barefoot. She was alone on the beach. She skipped and danced about on the sand, singing to herself; a woman taking innocent pleasure in being alone and outside by the sea on an invigorating and blustery day.

The South Atlantic rolled in on angry grey-green waves. White caps stretched as far as the eye could see. And when the waves hit the beach they hissed and roared. The wind was so strong that it carried the spray across the beach until the salty iridescent flecks caught in Lara's windblown hair. She seemed happy. Lara carried something in her arms that Nicolás could not quite make out, but something he remembered. It was the way she cradled it in her arms, the way a child would a doll, that made him pause and concentrate more deeply. Yes, of course that's it. Not a doll but a worn stuffed zebra from Lara's childhood. What had she called it? Think now, Nicolás told himself, an African name. Yes! That was it – Zulu! Now Lara carefully placed Zulu in the sand, anchored his stuffed legs by packing sand around them, so that her stuffed toy would not blow away.

Lara sat down beside Zulu, chin cupped between her hands, elbows balanced on her knees, and dreamily stared out at the sea. For a few moments Nicolás thought he was going to lose it all because he got lost in the hypnotic action of the waves. But then Lara turned away and began to dig playfully in the sand. There was something quite vulnerable about her body posture. She didn't sit like a woman, but like a child at play, totally unselfconscious, her dress up and her legs wide apart. Then a voice called to Lara. Her name carried and twisted strangely on the wind. At first she didn't hear it. But the voice, a man's, called several times, and finally broke into Lara's absorption with the sand castle she was building. She jumped up and ran happily toward the man who, dressed incongruously in a business suit, stood some way down the beach. Lara had gone maybe fifteen steps, when she suddenly remembered Zulu and darted back to snatch him quickly out of the sand.

"Naughty Zulu, you thought you were going to hide from Lara," Nicolás heard her say.

Then she ran down the beach toward the figure of the man who had already started to walk awkwardly across the sand in his polished dress shoes toward a rambling wooden beach house, weathered by the sea and the wind. The beach was not clean and cosmetic like some of the resort beaches closer to Buenos Aires. Palm fronds, driftwood, and huge piles of algae weed littered the sand. This beach house, Nicolás thought, had to be quite out of the way. Perhaps near a fishing village in the south.

At the bar of El Paraíso, Máximo muttered in exasperation.

"The TV must be on the blink again," he complained irritably to an old pensioner who sat nursing a shot of Tres Plumas brandy. Máximo clicked the channel selector knob back and forth a couple of times, but nothing happened as he tried to recapture the film of great soccer games of the past that had starred Pele. Exasperated, Máximo hit the side of the TV with an angry slap from his huge hand, and it bumped into life again. But instead of the soccer game the screen showed a sepia-toned movie: Lara on the beach in a cotton dress.

Máximo gasped in amazement. "Tania, you must see this!" he quickly beckoned her to the set. She got up reluctantly from her book, irritated at being interrupted one more time. But then she caught and recognized the image of Lara on the TV and ran to the bar. Tania immediately looked over at Nicolás, who was still in a profound state of meditation. Máximo followed her gaze, understood, and let out a deep breath.

The wind and her running motion streamed out Lara's hair and dress as she ran across the sand toward the vague form of the man in the suit. She was a beautiful animal, graceful, bursting with energy. The man turned at the last moment and caught Lara up in his arms. But the motion was so blurred his face could not be distinguished.

"Nobody will ever believe this," Máximo said quietly.

"Turn it off," said Tania nervously.

"Why?"

"I don't know, Máximo. I'm just scared."

But as Lara fell in step with the man in the suit, and they walked down the beach together, hand in hand toward the weathered house, the beach scene quickly faded from the screen and soccer players emerged, running around on the pitch inside the Brasilia Stadium. Reruns of World Soccer Cup matches took over the screen once more. But it was the scene of Lara on the beach that stayed imprinted on the minds of Tania and Máximo.

Tania struggled across the Río Grande. Other guerrillas waited on each shore, to give covering fire if necessary. The current was strong but luckily the river at this point was only as high as her thighs. She poked ahead, feeling her way across the riverbed with a stout branch that had become her everyday walking stick. Her leg had slowly gotten better. But she had learned to keep the stick beside her all the time. Tania had used it to whack that clown Chingolo across the head when he had tried to come after her two days ago when she had stopped to urinate behind some bushes. "El Ché will hear about this," she had warned Chingolo as he lay sprawled on the ground. He had rubbed the side of his head where she had hit him. But even hurt, Chingolo hadn't stopped staring fixedly at her crotch. He was so small and skinny he had looked more like a thirteen-year-old boy lying there instead of a guerrilla. She had pulled up her pants and heard someone snicker behind her. She had turned to see that Chingolo's friend, Eusebio, had watched the whole incident. Enraged, Tania had picked up her rifle, levered a round into the barrel, and fired it over Eusebio's head. Instantly there had been whistles and calls from the rest of the guerrilla group, as they demanded to know who had fired, or if it was incoming fire, and were they under attack.

"You try anything again," Tania had screamed at the two Bolivians as they skulked off, "and I'll kill you."

Joaquín had come over to find out why she had fired her weapon. When Tania complained to him about the attempted sexual attack by Chingolo, Joaquín had just walked away. She heard him mutter bitterly to himself: "*Resacas*. Just the dregs, the very worst." Did he include her in that description, she wondered angrily.

Ché had said he would be back in three days. Starved, often lost, they had gone in circles as they tried to elude the military patrols hunting them down, and still stay in the zone to link up again with Ché and his group. But as the days became weeks, and then months, and there was still no sign of Ché or contact with any of his guerrillas, Comandante Joaquín became more silent and withdrawn from those around him. He was ill and lacked concentration. He had made some dangerous mistakes, lapses in command; at times he even forgot to give the orders to set up ambushes or to send point men ahead on the trail. Joaquín, who had fought alongside the Viet Cong, who was a veteran of the Sierra Maestra and a senior instructor of the guerrilla warfare school in Cuba, knew better, but he was falling apart.

274

Braulio, another veteran from the Cuban revolution and the Congo, and without a doubt the most formidable fighter in their group, took over de facto command. It was Braulio who, after Tania's brush with Chingolo and Eusebio, had assigned Negro, the young Peruvian medic, to stay at Tania's side. And he had punished Chingolo and Eusebio. He took away their weapons and made them little more than porters.

Braulio was an uneducated black man, born in the heights of the Sierra Maestra in Cuba, and only four years older than Tania. He was fighting in Bolivia simply because he was a devoted follower of Ché. But as the days went by and they lost Serapio in an ambush, then Marcos and Victor disappeared while scouting, and finally, when nobody was watching them, Chingolo and Eusebio deserted with the two packs of medical supplies that they had been assigned to carry, Braulio, too, fell silent. But Tania noticed he never lost his fighting spirit.

At dawn that morning, the military had crept up on their camp and killed Pedro, asleep on guard duty.

They had fought off the patrol without further losses, mostly because after the firefight began Braulio had wordlessly tapped Tania on the shoulder and motioned for her to follow him. Together they had run downriver through the shallows, and opened fire on the military patrol from behind. Braulio had been absolutely fearless. While Tania had laid down cover fire for him, Braulio had run from tree to tree firing bursts at the enemy positions. The patrol had panicked and quickly retreated, leaving their screaming wounded behind.

Tania had advanced with Braulio through every move in the fight to give him support fire. When they finally pulled back to the river, he had grinned and given her a huge hug, two veteran comrades. They were covered in dirt and sweat, and their bodies exuded that strange bitter odour only humans in combat produce. But it didn't matter. Their eyes were on fire; they had been triumphant. And Tania could tell that Braulio now truly respected her.

They crossed the Río Grande one more time, and again in flight. On the other side of the river they discovered a huge clearing in the jungle: a strange rock formation of giant slabs and boulders, thrust out of the forest floor to form a natural amphitheatre. The group collapsed on the rocks to rest a few minutes. Tania felt emboldened to speak out. She had shown herself reliable in combat, not for the first time, so she had a right to speak out, she told herself.

"We have been walking and hiding in the area for three months since we lost contact with Ché's group on April 17. We are being worn down through attrition. Our radios don't work. We don't know if Comandante Ché Guevara has left the area. In this jungle we could have passed within two hundred metres of each other and we wouldn't know. We can't go on aimlessly walking around like this."

Then everybody tried to jump in and speak at the same time. After a few minutes Joaquín finally spoke. It was the first time in weeks that he had addressed them as a group: "It's apparent Bolivian army units have set up blocking forces in the valleys of the Río Grande and Río Nancahuasú. They know where we are. And presumably they will continue to squeeze and contract the zone until we have no room to move. Either El Ché is trapped in the same zone or he has broken out."

Mosiés demanded, "Then we have to try and break out, too."

Miguel spoke: "Or we have to make more contact with the peasants to let him know we are here."

Braulio only spoke once: "We have to find El Ché. If he has gone anywhere, he would have gone back to the base on the Río Nancahuasú. That's where we have to go."

276

Then Braulio left to stand guard by the river trail. He returned in a few minutes, two scared and unarmed peasants marched ahead of him at gunpoint. After some discussion the guerrillas agreed that the two peasants would be held hostage until they decided on their plans. In the meantime they were sent down to the river to catch fish for the guerrillas, who hadn't had a real meal in three or four days. Braulio assigned Moisés to stand guard over the two peasants while they fished.

They had been gone half an hour when Tania said to Braulio, "I hope Moisés watches those two carefully because they look like soldiers to me."

"Why do you say that?" Braulio asked.

"They look too well fed to be peasants," Tania told him. "And did you notice their bare feet in their sandals? They are very well kept. Those are feet that spend most of their time inside boots."

Braulio started to run toward the river. But even as he did so, they heard a couple of shots. Braulio returned disgusted, Moisés embarrassed to the point of tears. The peasants had caught one huge fish in the river, given it to Moisés who, lulled into thinking they were sympathetic, sat down and dozed for a few seconds as the peasants went back to fishing. He woke in time to see them disappear into the forest on the far shore.

Braulio blamed himself. "You were right, Tania. Those peasants gave up too easily. I should have been more suspicious. The military are so close to us they are sending us soldiers in disguise to obtain information on our next moves. Quick, everyone, we have to move out of here." Unable to stop and cook the fish, but desperately hungry, they sliced up the fish with a machete and devoured the raw chunks as they marched deeper into the jungle.

•   •   •

"That's the place isn't it?" asked Nicolás, as he walked over to the television set in the Paraíso bar. Máximo and Tania waited for him in an astounded and respectful silence.

"The weathered old beach house. You said you knew the location where Lara is being held. You recognized it, too. When can we go? It's been seven days now and I feel strong enough to travel. Where exactly is the place, Tania? C'mon, tell me! I know you recognized it on the TV.

"Yes," she replied thoughtfully. "We can go tomorrow if Máximo can get away."

"No." Nicolás argued. "Better it should be just you and me."

"I don't know that I can trust you alone, Nicolás. You might lose control of yourself and do something foolish that will get us killed."

"Yes," interceded Máximo. "Why don't we wait until after we've contacted Delgado, and find out what it is that he wants from you."

"I don't really care who goes," said Nicolás calmly, "but I just need to go soon. And I am not prepared to meet Delgado until afterward."

Máximo and Tania exchanged glances. The bar owner shrugged his huge shoulders, and he and Tania nodded in mutual agreement. Máximo led Nicolás to a quiet table in the bar, Tania followed.

"Nicolás," Máximo began when they had all sat down, "it is time to brief you on what we know about Delgado. He is not all what he seems—"

"And neither are you, Máximo."

The jovial bar owner waved a bear-like forearm in silent and modest self-deprecation and continued, but this time Nicolás noticed that Máximo dropped the continual amusing banter that was his usual camouflage. Máximo, behind the mask of comedy, was a very serious man.

"Delgado is much more than a sadistic military torturer. He is a man with a dangerous political agenda." Máximo broke off to let Tania continue, "The major is an ultra-rightist. He knows that the generals and senior members of the junta are seeking ways to open talks with Montonero leaders in exile. Delgado, along with another group of officers of his age, is deeply disturbed and feels betrayed by his senior army commanders."

"Why do I have to know this?" asked Nicolás.

"Because," Máximo answered, "we know that General Rossi ordered your release, because he wants to use you as a messenger or emissary to the Montonero leadership, wherever it lives in exile, Mexico City, Havana, Paris. Excuse me – " Máximo broke off to tend a customer who had walked in off the street. "Fill him in on the rest," he nodded to Tania.

Nicolás shrugged, "And so I'll be a messenger."

Máximo paused as he turned away from table, "But Nicolás, that's just it, Delgado won't let it happen." Then he turned on his customary Falstaffian chuckles to wait on the impatient customer. "*Sí, caballero?*"

"Delgado and his group do not want any reconciliation. Every last piece of resistance against their aim to take us all back to a political feudal state must be crushed. We know already," Tania continued, "that two or three would-be messengers for the junta have been killed by the younger officers, before they even had a chance to get out of the country."

"Delgado could have had me killed me at any time. It would have been much simpler for him – "

"Yes, but given that Rossi has now indicated that he wants to use you . . . we believe that it is the only reason you have been allowed to go free in such an unorthodox way. We know of no other previous release like yours . . . Delgado will kill you, too. But because of your class, your family name, and your uncle, Delgado must set an elaborate trap to kill you and protect himself."

The floorboards creaked behind Nicolás to signal Máximo's return to the discussion.

"Why haven't you and your group moved against Delgado?"

"We have wanted to for a long time. And we've had several opportunities, but we received orders to wait—" Máximo broke off lamely.

"Why don't you tell him the real truth, Máximo?"

The big man shrugged. "We have lost most of our top leadership. The people who remain in command have to live outside the country. There is a lot of internal dissent and confusion."

Nicolás understood: "I see. You believe the top leadership of the Montoneros has been infiltrated by military agents?"

Both Tania and Máximo remained silent. They stared into the middle distance, avoiding Nicolás' question and his eyes.

Finally Máximo spoke again. "It is a possibility and one we find extremely painful to examine. Nevertheless, we must go on. Our own intelligence apparatus, here in Argentina, continues to function extremely well. Don't forget—from the days when we were still a legal organization, we probably have over a million sympathizers."

Tania, seen only by Nicolás, rolled her eyes in scepticism.

"But we do know," Máximo went on in the careful and thoughtful manner Nicolás now realized was the real persona behind the jolly mask, "that Delgado is involved in some criminal activities. He and his special group have taken to kidnapping businessmen and even the odd relative of a high-ranking military officer. Delgado holds the hostages for ransom. It's the easiest thing in the world for them to carry out. They have permission to act secretly, armed men at their disposal, and clandestine heavily guarded prisons."

"And they blame the kidnapping on the Montoneros?" asked Nicolás.

"Yes," replied Tania, "ever since the Montoneros were paid $63 million in 1975 to release the Born brothers, every hostage-taking for money is blamed on us."

"The final piece of irony is that Delgado sets himself up to negotiate and deliver the ransom money. So far this smooth little scheme has worked very well for him."

"Why?" asked Nicolás. "Why would someone with Delgado's political agenda do this?"

"He and his colleagues want to build their own war chest—"

Tania interrupted Máximo. "I think they're just opportunists who are not going to pass up a chance to get rich quickly."

Their attention was caught by an ambulance that quietly pulled up outside El Paraíso. The Fallen Angel climbed out of the passenger seat and casually entered the bar. He greeted the other two quietly and spoke directly to Nicolás:

"I can't stay long. I just dropped by to warn you that Delgado is looking for you."

"How do you know?"

"I walked in on the last line of a conversation he was having with two other officers at Campo del Mayo. He said, 'We have to find him, because we need Quintana to jump out of the plane with the money.' That's all I heard." Then the paramedic turned to Máximo. "Just to make it look good for my new driver, can you give us two sandwiches to go, please?"

• • •

281

Tania lay in the dark undergrowth of the tree line. In front of her was a small cleared field. In the early dawn it was not yet light enough to see much more than the outlines of the primitive farmhouse of Honorato Rojas on the other side of the field.

Behind her, in the forest, most of the guerrillas still dozed. They had marched through most of the night under a full moon. Braulio crawled up close beside her, and gave her a crooked smile. Tania nodded back, unable to smile. Her tongue constantly played with the teeth that were loose in her gums; another sign, she realized, of the malnutrition they all suffered. They surveyed the scene together. A cock crowed inside the farm shed. Eggs! The thought of an omelette, or even just a simple boiled egg, made her head swim. They could hear the lowing of penned cattle.

Braulio hummed to himself. "Tonight we are going to eat," he told Tania, with the force of conviction and enthusiasm his voice always carried. Tania never ceased to be amazed at Braulio's continued strength and health given the privations they suffered. She loved to hear the warmth in Braulio's voice. Some days, Tania realized, it was the only sound that sparked her will to live. A month had passed since the attack by the military by the Río Grande in which Pedro had been killed. In the past month Braulio and Tania had developed a warm but tacit friendship.

"Will he sell to us?" asked Tania.

"Yes. But I don't trust him. Honorato Rojas will tell you whatever he thinks you want to hear: 'Are the military around?' 'No, the soldiers have all left,'" Braulio mimicked the peasants response. "'But wait a minute, we saw some soldiers ten kilometres away.' 'Oh, yes, the soldiers are close.' See what I mean?" asked Braulio.

Tania nodded. Braulio was usually never this talkative; it must be the thought of the calf they intended to buy that had loosened up his tongue.

"But we were here before, during our first sorties with El Ché. And we paid Rojas well for our food."

El Ché! Strange, Tania thought. Here they were slowly dying of hunger, living like animals in the forest, all because they had to wait for El Ché, and she hardly ever even thought about him any more. Tania began to chew on some leaves to stop the hunger pains in her stomach.

Braulio turned and caught the attention of the others with a low whistle. He gave the whispered commands of who should go where; Joaquin stayed out of it, silent, apathetic. He was given the rearguard position. To watch for a patrol that might happen down the trail, and to cover the group as they withdrew from the house. Then they quickly moved out to take up their positions around the small homestead.

Tania's responsibility was the farm shed. As she came around the corner she encountered a dirty-faced little girl of about six, who carried in the lap of her dress a few hen's eggs. The startled child let go of her dress and the eggs splattered on the ground. Tania fell to her knees, and with her fingers desperately scooped the broken yolks and whites up into her mouth before they soaked into the soil. The child watched in silence and fear as this mad white woman, loaded down with weapons, ammunition, and a pack, smiled, and with the sleeve of her stained fatigues wiped the bits of dirt and goo of raw egg from her mouth and chin.

Máximo drove his battered van south on Route 2 which runs along the coast to Bahía Blanca, where it then joins with Route 3 to run all the way to the most southern tip of the continent, Ushuaia.

"Let's drive on forever," Tania said suddenly, a note of desperation lining her playful suggestion.

"Not in this old brute," answered Máximo.

Nicolás remained silent. Seated by the passenger window, he stared across Tania and Máximo at the sea.

"You didn't always used to brood like this before, Quintana," observed Máximo.

"Let him be," sighed Tania. She laid her head on Nicolás' shoulder and closed her eyes.

"Nicolás," she murmured as she moved her head around to get comfortable. "You have to start eating again. Your shoulders are getting bony."

Nicolás listened to the roar of the engine, the vibrations of the old metal body, the whoosh of passing trucks, and the wind as it whistled around the tops of the windows.

"How did you get into this Máximo?" Nicolás wanted to know.

"On May 1, 1967, I was the seminarian leading the altar boys through their paces in the special mass for the military in the Metropolitan Cathedral. All the big shots were there, even General Onganía himself. When these three madmen, led by a former priest and graduate of my own San Isidro Seminary, García Elorrio, broke up the mass. He denounced the institutional church as a defender of the military dictators." Máximo shrugged. "Everything that happened that day in the cathedral, and everything Elorrio said made sense to me."

"How did he reconcile a young would-be Catholic priest to political violence?"

"Elorrio showed me you can't be a phoney. I was going to be a priest. In the seminary I could never understand how I was going to tell people what is good and evil and then retire to my study to read a little more of St. Augustine. Elorrio opened my eyes – I had to stay with the people and fight against true evil."

"Are you prepared to give up your own life in the armed struggle?"

"Of course. That is what makes it legitimate for me. There is no greater proof of Christian love – to give up my life in defence of others."

"And no higher form of redemption," smiled Nicolás.

Máximo stared silently for a few moments through the cracked windshield of the van before he replied: "If I did not know that you had been tortured and gave them nothing, I might think you were mocking me."

"Why did you kill the policeman who was following Tania?"

Máximo looked over at Tania asleep on Nicolás' shoulder. "Oh, that's so like Tania. I'm sure she forgot to tell you that the cop was busy strangling her."

Tania stirred restlessly against Nicolás. But nobody spoke again until they reached Quequén.

Máximo pulled into a truck stop where they filled up with gas. Tania wandered over to a roadside market and bought some fried fish from an open stand. They stood around on the gravel apron of the truck stop, while Máximo and Tania hungrily devoured the fish, held in a sheet of newspaper. Nicolás was not hungry and stared down the highway, patiently waiting for them to finish.

"It's only about a half-hour from here and then you walk in for about another half an hour," said Máximo.

Nicolás nodded. His body felt paralysed with dread.

"I should tell you how I found out about all this," said Máximo. "When I came down to pick up Felipe's body, I asked the cop if I could thank the fisherman whose boat Felipe had taken out to die in that night. The cop was helpful and friendly, so after we got old Felipe into the back of the van, I took the cop out for a beer and a meal. We got talking. He told me that a woman had actually found Felipe's body when the boat drifted ashore. I said I'd like to thank her, but told me to forget it. She lived in a house by the beach, and she was quite strange, a stunning beauty, but perhaps a bit

285

simple in the head. Then he whispered to me that a high-ranking military officer from Buenos Aires, an older man, kept her as his mistress, and that this officer flew down in his own private plane every weekend to be with her."

Nicolás felt such terrible pain seize his whole body that he had to walk away for a few minutes. Tania wanted to follow after him, but Máximo restrained her.

"He'll come back, he reassured her. "In a way, we know that he already is aware of what has happened. It's the affirmation that is so painful."

Nicolás returned to where they stood by the side of the highway. The cars and trucks roared past.

"Go on," he urged Máximo.

"Let's get back in the van. We have to keep moving if we're going to get there on time."

The three of them climbed into the van, and in a few minutes Máximo turned the van off on to a rutted sideroad.

"I found the fisherman," Máximo continued, "and paid him for what had happened to his boat. He confirmed the cop's story. He told me that every afternoon between three and five you can find her on the deserted stretch of the beach. There's no one else around during the week, except a middle-aged housekeeper who lives in the house. It hapened to be just that time, so I went to the beach myself and saw her there."

"How did you know it was Lara?"

"I didn't. But Felipe left a series of short notes. Some of them made sense, others didn't. But this is one of them."

Nicolás smoothed the crumpled note. Felipe had written on a scrap piece of paper, a torn handbill the old street singer must have picked up on some street corner. He read aloud the shaky old man's words.

"The man who holds Nicolás, holds Nicolás' woman.' "

"Don't ask me, how or why he knew," Máximo continued. "Anyway, I checked out some of the union guys at the local airport and found a compañero who told me that it was Major Delgado who flew in every weekend."

Máximo pulled the van over. The sideroad was deserted. Nicolás and Tania climbed into the back of the van to change. Tania, suddenly modest, turned her back to Nicolás as she removed her clothes within the narrow confines of the van. Nicolás examined the priest's suit and collar that Máximo had acquired for him. Tania, in her underwear, knelt down and opened the suitcase that held her nun's habit.

"Oh, I forgot to tell you, Nicolás," she mentioned casually. "After they had taken you away, Guido let me back into the room at the Hotel Cruz del Sur. I picked up most of your stuff. Also the letter from La Señora for your next appointment. Uh, I hope you don't mind? But I filled in for you."

Something happened inside Nicolás. He began to laugh. A control mechanism inside him broke. He could not stop laughing.

"Did you wear your nun's habit?" he managed to ask between bouts of laughter. He fell on the floor of the van, his chest heaving, his eyes weeping from laughter.

Tania laughed uncertainly at first, unsure if this was not some fit of madness Nicolás had fallen into. But then she also got caught up in appreciation of the absurdity of the image. She lay down beside Nicolás, they put their arms around each other, and Tania began to laugh as uncontrollably as Nicolás.

"And you know what, Nicolás," Tania added between gasps, "she wants to give me a television show. She thinks I'm even better at it than you are, 'more empathetic,' she said: Probably because I'm a woman." And they both started laughing all over again.

When the last bout of laughter finally subsided, Tania held Nicolás tenderly in her arms.

"Nicolás, I love you."

"You betrayed me. How could I ever trust you?"

"That was a terrible mistake. We survived. Don't be so romantic. What we have between us is more real now."

"It's as simple as that?"

"Yes. Come and be my lover."

"I can't," Nicolás said sadly, "my cock is broken."

"But not forever. In a while I can help you make it like it was before, even better. The doctor told me it would be all right –"

Máximo hammered on the van door.

"Come on you two, we're running out of time!"

"Here, Nicolás. Something I have being keeping for you. Your *kpoli*. I found it in the bed when I went back to your room at the Cruz del Sur. It must have come off that time we made such wonderful love together." She hung the little cotton bag around his neck. "It doesn't work for me," she said ruefully.

The suit hung loose on Nicolás, but it didn't matter, because he sat in the special wheelchair that Máximo had rented in Quenquén. The chairs were for invalids to be pushed along the beach and enjoy the sea air. The usual narrow wheels had been replaced with wide tires, to move more easily across the sand.

With friendly waves, they left the knot of curious villagers at the outskirts of the tiny fishing village. The people had come out of their shacks to watch this strange trio – a crippled priest, pushed along over the sand in a wheelchair by his huge brother, already hot and sweaty in the afternoon sun, accompanied by their sister, from the order of the Sisters of Eternal Mercy – disappear down the deserted beach.

"For a picnic," they had said, "and to commune with the spirit of our dear departed father, who washed ashore a few days ago in one of the village's rowboats." To Nicolás it seemed an eternity from the moment they saw Lara as a chalky stroke against the sand dunes to the moment she was close enough that he could recognize her features. She slowly approached them with a strange smile of wonder on her face. The three faced her for long seconds. Nobody seemed quite to know what to do.

"Hello," said Tania finally. "What's your name?"

"Lara!" and she held out her hand spontaneously, the way a child who had decided to be friendly would behave.

"Why do you wear such a funny dress," Lara asked.

"I'm a nun. Do you know what a nun is, Lara?"

"No." And uninterested in any explanation, she asked Nicolás, "Can I ride in your cart?"

Nicolás could only bring himself to nod and got out of the cart. Lara jumped with delight into the chair.

"Push me," she demanded of Máximo. "Faster! Faster!" And she squealed with delight as Máximo raced the wheelchair along the hard packed sand of the beach.

Tania sat down beside Nicolás and held his hand.

"Nicolás, do something! Yell! scream! But please don't just sit there and stare at the sea."

Lara came back with Máximo, who was panting heavily from all the pushing he had done. Lara got out of the chair and watched Nicolás draw the formation of the Southern Cross into the damp sand with a stick.

Lara cried out delightedly, "Cruz del Sur!"

Nicolás handed the stick to Lara. She quickly finished the formation and laughed as she elaborated on the design of the stars. Then handed the stick back to Nicolás with no indication that this was a game they had once idly played together.

Lara turned to Tania. "Why is your brother crying?" And then without waiting for a reply, she leaned over and kissed Nicolás on the cheek.

"There, don't cry. You can have your wheelchair back." And she led Nicolás to the chair.

The three of them began their return journey, but Nicolás quickly got out of the chair and began walking by himself.

"Come back tomorrow," Lara called after them and waved goodbye. She began to giggle as she watched Nicolás stride fully clothed into the waves. Then Nicolás ripped off his shoes and clothes, piece by piece, and threw them over his head behind him into the sea, until he was naked as he waded through the surf. He fell often as the waves hit him sideways and knocked him off his feet into the surf. His heart was a desert. Sand and saltwater from the roiling waves filled his mouth and choked in his throat. He called out for Iemanja, but the goddess of the oceans did not answer him. He continued to battle his way along the surf, parallel to the beach, raving incoherently and waving his arms at the sea and the sky. Tania scurried around behind him, her habit hiked up around her hips. She picked up the soaked articles of clothing, as they floated on the waves, and carried them back to pile them in the wheelchair, pushed along by the silent and patient Máximo.

Delgado laid out the colour polaroid photographs of Lara on the rough wooden trestle table in front of Nicolás.

"It wasn't suitable to bring her out to this farm today, but you see in that photo she is holding yesterday's paper. See the date. See how happy and healthy she appears! The moment our little operation is over you will be reunited with her."

"The price, Delgado, has gone up," said Nicolás with quiet determination.

"What now?" was Delgado's bored response.

"Colón, I want to know where to find him."

Delgado laughed, he waved his arm around the courtyard of the *estancia* where they sat.

"You seemed so serious, I thought for a moment you were going to ask for this beautiful *finca*, the labourers, the armed guards, the livestock. But listen, Quintana. My God, Colón! you'll be doing me a favour."

The major took out of his pocket an exquisite silver-tipped pen and searched for something to write on. Nicolás handed Delgado the Tarot card, the Tower.

"How appropriate," smiled Delgado, and quickly wrote on the back of the card addresses in three different cities in Latin America, and handed it back to Nicolás.

"Now we begin?"

Nicolás nodded.

"Here are two packs. One you must recognize, being an expert sky diver. The other pack holds a lot of money. You don't have to know how much, except that it is a ransom payment that has been agreed upon. A group of subversives in Rio are holding a general and his wife hostage."

"Who?"

"You don't have to know because that plane over there in the field, my own private Skyhawk, is never going to land at the agreed upon location in Brazil where the exchange is planned to take place."

"You want me to jump out of the plane with the money."

Delgado smiled in approval, "Quintana, I knew you were the man for this job."

"Who is going to fly this plane?"

"Excellent question. That man over there, seated in the truck between those four guards."

"What happens to him when he arrives without the money?"

"The plane will not arrive. On the craft there is an ingenious little bomb. Once the plane takes off an atmospheric trigger sets a delay mechanism. As soon as the plane descends again below one thousand feet to land the bomb is detonated."

"Does the pilot know this?"

"He knows nothing. Don't waste any pity on him, Quintana. He's not like you. He's a *chupado*. He sang and gave up many people."

"Then why is he doing this?"

"I've told him if he can fly the plane to Brazil he is a free man." Delgado couldn't mask the amusement in his voice. "As far as you are concerned, he thinks you are the military escort to be taken to a destination in Brazil. By the way, he is an excellent pilot."

"How do I stop him from flying the plane anywhere he wants?"

Delgado reached into a briefcase and handed Nicolás a .38-calibre revolver. Nicolás opened the weapon and found it fully loaded. On the landing strip of the *estancia*, a mechanic fired up the plane.

"You're not just in this for the money are you, Delgado?"

"You're such an intelligent young man, Quintana. These operations are out of political necessity," smiled Delgrado. "These are desperate times, and so desperate remedies have become part of our political agenda."

"Then why do you need the money?"

"We have to be able to fund our own operations. Our superiors think the ideological struggle is over. They're wrong. This was just a battle."

"What is the war?"

"Once we have killed all the subversives, then we will kill their collaborators, then their sympathizers, then those who remain indifferent, and finally we will kill the timid."

Nicolás had no reply. He walked over to the pilot, a tall thin young man with a face deeply scarred and inflamed from burns. They regarded each other without speaking. Delgado silently watched the two men. Nicolás saw the pilot had a certain quiet dignity. Nicolás offered him his hand, and when they shook Nicolás knew the pilot understood everything. The pilot was escorted to the plane; Delgado followed with Nicolás. The pilot climbed in, completed his instrument check, and gave a thumbs-up signal.

Delgado threw the money pack into the back seat of the four-seater plane, and indicated to Nicolás he should climb into his parachute harness. He had to shout above the roar of the engine.

"Just in case you think I've forgotten anything, Quintana, there is only one parachute between the two of you, and you have it on your back. Here's the map. Your jump point is clearly marked inside Argentina. Good luck. When you land, stay there until I arrive with the lovely Lara de la Cruz."

"Here!" The major handed Nicolás the revolver with a tight little smile and a slap on the back. Nicolás jammed the revolver in his belt. He had to turn and back awkwardly into the plane, encumbered by the parachute pack. The pilot watched them over his shoulder.

Delgado reached up to give a helpful shove, and Nicolás in one fluid movement drew the revolver and shot Delgado between the eyes. Even as the major fell to the ground, the pilot, who acted as if according to plan, opened the throttle and roared down the runway, as Nicolás scrambled to close the door of the cabin.

Tania's belly was bloated. All of the guerrillas were ill; their bodies, after weeks of semi-starvation, were unable to digest the meat from the *asado* they had cooked the night before. They all knew it was dangerous to stay for another few hours in the same location. But everyone, even Braulio, was too sick to march. And Honorato Rojas, their host of the night before, had urged them to stay and rest. He offered to guide them through the forest on a trail that would take them to an easy place where they could ford the Río Masicuri. Under the circumstances they could do nothing but accept.

The plane flew steadily on automatic pilot; a small white bird above the dark continent of the *selva*. Nicolás, no longer hampered by the parachute, sat alone in the cabin. The pilot was gone and with him the parachute pack and the huge pack of ransom money. Nicolás was at peace. The black-green carpet of the jungle spread below him. Nicolás switched off the automatic pilot and pushed the controls of the plane into a slow climb. He opened the door and waited. The plane stalled and banked.

Nicolás dived out into the abyss, then spread his arms to float. The plane spun past him in a screaming nosedive and exploded below him. Nicolás floated down above the black-green jungle: The Searcher falling for eternity from the Tower.

As they rested for a minute in the forest before attempting to cross the Masicurí, Tania put on her last clean shirt, a black-and-white striped garment she had found in the bottom of her pack, not really fitting for the jungle. Braulio shook his head in disagreement, but had no energy to argue. Somehow she didn't care. They all seemed to suffer today from a collective fatalism.

Honorato Rojas went among them, to shake each by the hand, indicating he had to get back to his farm work.

"Masicurí no fast," he said in his broken Spanish, and indicated the water in the ford came only below the knees.

"What is the name of this crossing?" Tania asked him.

"Vado del Yeso, yes."

"If you betray us to the soldiers," Tania told him, "El Ché and his compañeros will come back and kill you."

"Yes, yes," Honorato Rojas smiled, and nervously drifted away to shake someone else's hand.

"Why did you threaten him like that?" Braulio asked.

"Because I don't trust him. I think he poisoned the meat last night so that we were too sick to leave early. Now the military has time to catch up with us."

Braulio immediately shook off his lethargy and looked at his watch. "Then we have to move quickly," he whispered to her urgently. "It's almost five-thirty. We have to cross now and set up a safe perimeter on the other side of the river before it gets dark."

"What about Rojas?"

"We will make him cross with us. Rojas!" Braulio called out. But their peasant guide had disappeared into the forest.

"Moisés! You were supposed to keep an eye on him."

"My guts are bad. I had to shit."

They all stared nervously at each other, except for Joaquin, who stared down at the ground between his feet. Their small band was down to ten, nine men and a woman. The forest around them was full of the enemy. They could hear the rush of the river, just a hundred metres through the trees. Everyone knew what had to be done. But none of the men volunteered. They all looked to Braulio. Tania threw off her pack, slipped a magazine into her weapon, and released the catch.

"I'll go and bring him back –"

"No," Braulio stopped her. "It's already too late. We have to cross the river before dark."

Then Tania heard Braulio mutter to himself: "If only Pombo, Benigno, and Urbano were here, we might just be able to make it."

Braulio entered first and told the others to wait. The river was about two-hundred metres wide at the El Vado del Yeso. Rojas had lied. The water was chest high in the Río Masicurí and running fast. Braulio had to hold his rifle and pack over his head to keep them dry. A third of the way across he glanced back over his shoulder and yelled. Tania couldn't hear him above the noise of the river but understood that they should follow. She began to wade into the fury of the Río Masicurí. The others followed her into the water.

Tania never heard the shots fired. But saw Braulio as he waded through the shallows of the far shore suddenly flung about and then crumple into the blue dark water, instantly streaked with red. Then came the piercing blow of the bullet through her heart that dragged Tania and her soul down into the cold racing current of the Río Masicuri. *Dónde está El Ché? Por qué me abandonas en este desierto? Yo que te segur hasta al final.*

The Río Masicurí carried the spirit of Tania into the Río Grande as it rushed east through the *quebradas* of the Serranias de San Marcos and then north into Río Mamoré where the travel of her tormented soul was slowed by the lush lowlands of the Beni; past the lonely and awesome ranges of the Codilheira dos Parecis where a soaring condor witnessed Tania's voyage into the Río Madeira; north through the great brooding rain forests of the Amazonas; and finally east out of the mouth of the Amazon and into the Atlantic where Iemanja, black goddess of the ocean, waited to embrace Tania.

Iemanja folded Tania into her arms to give her comfort and peace, to acknowledge the travail of Tania's life; and then finally, after many months of such bliss, Iemanja returned Tania's soul, whole once more, to the world again.

The arena was a circus of noise, lights, music, and jammed with an audience that participated avidly in every moment of the most popular weekly twelve-hour nonstop television show South America had ever seen: *"Sueños Para Todos!"*

At nine in the evening came one of the high points of the spectacular: Tania, Queen of the Tarot, gave a public reading for the nation. The cards pulled from the Tarot deck were illuminated and projected onto a huge screen. A member of the audience was selected by one of the five frenetic hosts roaming through the stands. After Tania had chosen the first card, the Significator, the selected member of the audience was asked to predict the next card that Tania would draw. If correct, he won $10,000. If the individual predicted all ten cards correctly, he won $100,000. Nobody had ever won more than five cards in a row. Then Tania would do a brief five-minute good-news tarot reading for the immediate future of the nation.

A female host, a machine-gun-mouth woman with a mike at her lips and a joke for every moment, called out the six numbers printed on one of the admission tickets the audience had purchased at the box office.

A tall thin young man stepped forward, the winning ticket held aloft in his hand. He was gangly, his face deeply scarred and discoloured by burns. The audience was whipped into hysteria by the hosts when the thin young man, who generated calm and dignity in the midst of all this chaos, guessed the first three cards correctly. When he got to the eighth, the crowd only muttered excitedly, fascinated. Nobody could quite believe what they were witnessing. And when the young man predicted the ninth and tenth cards before Tania drew them from the deck, the arena was totally silent, not even the hosts could speak.

The thin young man with the scarred face walked down the steps to the stage. Tania, enthralled, moved slowly as in a dream, to meet him. She took his hand in hers and immediately felt suffused with incredible warmth and acceptance.

"Who are you?" she asked in a whisper that echoed through the microphone on her lapel and across the arena, now as silent as a cave.

He handed her the Tarot card, the Tower. The card was torn and weathered. On the back, barely legible and handwritten, were addresses in three cities of Latin America. "My name is Nicolás," he said quietly.

298